If Ever I Should Love You

By Cathy Maxwell

The Spinster Heiresses
IF EVER I SHOULD LOVE YOU

Marrying the Duke
A DATE AT THE ALTAR
THE FAIREST OF THEM ALL
THE MATCH OF THE CENTURY

The Brides of Wishmore
THE GROOM SAYS YES
THE BRIDE SAYS MAYBE
THE BRIDE SAYS NO

The Chattan Curse
THE DEVIL'S HEART
THE SCOTTISH WITCH
LYON'S BRIDE

THE SEDUCTION OF SCANDAL
HIS CHRISTMAS PLEASURE
THE MARRIAGE RING
THE EARL CLAIMS HIS WIFE
A SEDUCTION AT CHRISTMAS
IN THE HIGHLANDER'S BED
BEDDING THE HEIRESS
IN THE BED OF A DUKE
THE PRICE OF INDISCRETION
TEMPTATION OF A PROPER GOVERNESS
THE SEDUCTION OF AN ENGLISH LADY
ADVENTURES OF A SCOTTISH HEIRESS
THE LADY IS TEMPTED
THE WEDDING WAGER
THE MARRIAGE CONTRACT
A SCANDALOUS MARRIAGE
MARRIED IN HASTE
BECAUSE OF YOU
WHEN DREAMS COME TRUE
FALLING IN LOVE AGAIN
YOU AND NO OTHER
TREASURED VOWS
ALL THINGS BEAUTIFUL

CATHY MAXWELL

If Ever I Should Love You

A SPINSTER HEIRESSES NOVEL

AVONBOOKS

An Imprint of HarperCollinsPublishers

IF EVER I SHOULD LOVE YOU. Copyright © 2017 by Catherine Maxwell, Inc. All rights reserved. Printed in the United States of America. No part of this book may be used or reproduced in any manner whatsoever without written permission except in the case of brief quotations embodied in critical articles and reviews. For information, address HarperCollins Publishers, 195 Broadway, New York, NY 10007.

First Avon Books mass market printing: January 2018
First Avon Books hardcover printing: December 2017

Print Edition ISBN: 978-0-06-280410-5
Digital Edition ISBN: 978-0-06-265575-2

Avon, Avon & logo, and Avon Books & logo are registered trademarks of HarperCollins Publishers in the United States of America and other countries.

HarperCollins is a registered trademark of HarperCollins Publishers in the United States of America and other countries.

FIRST EDITION

17 18 19 20 LSC 10 9 8 7 6 5 4 3 2 1

This one is for
Linda Brown

I am wealthy in my friends.

Chapter 1

London
March 10, 1813

"*Marry?*" Roman Gilchrist, newly named tenth Earl of Rochdale, stared at his solicitor and godfather, Thaddeus Chalmers, as if the man had just suggested he cut off his own right arm.

They were in Thaddeus's office. Thaddeus, a mild-mannered man of Roman's stepfather's age, sat behind a huge mahogany desk. Roman had not yet taken the chair offered him. Instead, he threw down the pieces of paper with the ninth earl's hastily scribbled signature upon the desk.

Roman continued. "I come to you with a stack of gambling chits that *I do not believe* I should have to pay and your only suggestion is that perhaps it is time for me to marry?"

"What other solution can there be?" Thaddeus asked. He was well respected amongst the loftiest circles of the *ton*. Roman usually valued his opinion. Now, he feared his godfather had gone senile.

"You can tell me that I don't have to honor them," Roman answered. "My uncle owed everyone. But he is dead. If they wanted their money, they should have petitioned him before he croaked—not lay in wait on my first day taking my seat in the House of Lords and then delivering these to me. It was a scene. Everyone was there. They all couldn't help but overhear what

Erzy and Malcolm were saying to me, and then they handed me these. I wanted to wipe the smirks off their faces."

Thaddeus pushed aside the ledger he had been writing in before his godson had stormed into the room. "How much do you owe?" He spread the chits out to read them over the spectacles on his nose.

"Just under ten thousand pounds."

"Their presenting the debts to you publically is bad form."

"Damn right it is."

"You will have to pay it."

Roman slammed his hand down on the desk, hard. *"No.* It is not my debt. A man's debt should die with him."

"They do if they are to his tobacconist or bootmaker and if there is no money in the estate—"

"There is no money in Rochdale's estate. You of all people know that."

"I do, young Roman. I do . . . but those notes there represent something more than a jacket or a pair of boots, or even the bread that graces a table. No, these are debts of *honor.* As the Earl of Rochdale, you are 'honor bound' to pay them."

"They are not mine—"

"They are Rochdale's and you are now Rochdale. See? The name Rochdale is on each slip."

"But that isn't me."

"Yes, you are correct and most men would not have given the debts to you to pay. Unfortunately, Erzy and Malcolm are hardened gamesters who have no thought for anyone but themselves."

"If they are not honorable men, then I see no 'honor' in paying gambling debts that aren't mine." It all made perfect reason to Roman. "Especially since I don't even have the money to repair the leak in Bonhomie's roof let alone buy a pair of boots for myself." Bonhomie was his recently inherited estate in Somerset and the first home he and his family had ever had.

"Exactly," Thaddeus said in triumph, stacking the gambling chits. "Which is why I suggested marriage. I mean, you could sell off a portion of the land. The last earl had not seen to the entail—"

"Absolutely not," Roman interrupted. "The land will not be sold." He'd been overjoyed to discover that Bonhomie boasted six hundred acres of forests and fields waiting for him to turn them into something meaningful.

"Very well, then." Thaddeus reached for a decanter from a tray of them on a table behind his desk. He uncorked what Roman knew was a very fine whisky and poured generous portions in two glasses. "Sit," he told Roman. "Be reasonable and hear me out."

"I have no desire to take on a wife."

"Posh, of course you do," his godfather said. "You will need an heir or what will become of your plans for your estate, eh? Do you want all your fine work to go to a nephew that you didn't know? Just like what happened to the ninth earl with you? Besides, a man needs something to poke at night. If he doesn't have it on a regular basis, his balls shrivel."

"I don't believe that is true."

Thaddeus pointed a finger at him. "How do you know? Have you been going without? Are you saying you don't have any-thing to poke *with* anymore, Roman?"

"I have balls a'plenty." He was no monk, but he was no lo-thario either.

Thaddeus cackled at his own jest. "I knew you did. All your years in the military should have made you a man of the world."

Roman sat and picked up the whisky. "It did. But I have very high standards."

"Then marry a wife who meets them. Because, lad, the way matters are going . . ." He tapped the small stack of gambling debts. "You could lose everything you inherited with the title. Erzy and Malcolm could force you to sell, and then the old earl's tobacconist and bootmaker would be right behind them. It is never wise to stir a pot."

He was right. Except . . .

"What heiress who isn't lame or hideous to look upon would settle for penniless me? Or are you going to tell me, Thaddeus, that it doesn't matter? That I should leg-shackle myself to a woman and then live apart?"

"Well, that is one solution."

"So much for heirs," Roman muttered.

Thaddeus gave a sharp bark of laughter. "And here I thought you were a realist."

"I am," Roman assured him. "And I know that any heiress worth her weight in gold can attract a man with more to offer than empty pockets and a ramshackle estate."

"Ah, but then there are the Spinster Heiresses. They are three young women, all marriageable, very attractive, and wealthy beyond your dreams."

"Then why are they called spinsters? Why hasn't someone snatched them up?"

"Because their fathers are very particular, just like yourself. They wouldn't let a Captain Gilchrist near them, or even a Baron Gilchrist, or a Sir Roman, and very few earls—but Rochdale is one of the oldest titles in England. Before the last three holders of that title, blast their gambling souls, they were respected statesmen, the sort historians praised and the world never forgot. I want you to be that sort of earl, Roman. I want you to do me proud."

"I will try . . . if I'm not in debtors' prison."

"Which is the reason I believe you should shine yourself up and call on one of the Spinsters. Their fathers will not look down their noses at one of their daughters becoming the Countess Rochdale, I can promise you that."

"And how can you make such a promise?"

"Because this is their third year on the Marriage Mart." He

referred to the round of social events, balls, and routs where marriageable young women hunted for suitable husbands. "They are becoming a bit long of tooth. Their fathers will have to lower their standards if the daughters don't make a match soon. One almost claimed a duke but he ran off with an actress instead. Bad bit of business. Delicious gossip though."

Thaddeus poured himself another drink. He offered the bottle to Roman, who with a shake of his head refused it. He needed to keep his wits about him right now and he wasn't one to see a virtue in overimbibing.

However, he was intrigued with Thaddeus's plan. "What is wrong with them?" he asked, settling back in his chair. There must be a hidden cost.

"They are all decent young ladies," Thaddeus assured him, putting the cork back in the decanter.

"Decent?"

His godfather eyed him. "You're not in a position where you can be choosy."

"Granted. However, does one of them limp or the others have pox marks? I'd rather be forewarned."

"First, three Seasons does not a hag make. And they aren't hags," Thaddeus hurried to add. "They are each actually lovely."

"Lovely and rich and unmarried?" Roman made a dismissive sound. "Spill it all, Thaddeus. Spare nothing."

"Well, if there is a drawback they are each just on the border of being unacceptable. Not one could gain vouchers to Almack's. However, most of the concerns are about their families. For example, Cassandra Holwell's grandfather made his money in the mines. He started off as a miner and ended up by dint of hard work owning the mine. Her father is currently in the Commons."

"That is not such a shabby thing."

"Aye, but his manners are atrocious. He eats like a bull who has been starved for days. Throws food all around him."

"And his daughter? Is she covered in food as well?"

"I've never seen her eat but I've not heard a complaint. She has yellow hair, rosy cheeks, and, from what I've heard, is very educated. She is a book lover as yourself."

"A bluestocking?" Roman liked to read, but he did not like to debate.

"She is known for being outspoken, which isn't a terrible thing if one is in your circumstances and needs the Holwell fortune. However, if a man has his choice of ladies to choose from, and perhaps a mother who is a stickler for family blood-lines, Miss Holwell and her mining ancestors will not stand a chance. She is also rather tall. Of course, that is not a problem for you. You're over six feet."

"*Is* she six feet tall?"

"I don't believe she quite is."

"An *Amazon* bluestocking."

"You are putting a bad slant on this. Last I saw her, all I could think about were her breasts, which were just about to my eye level."

Thaddeus was short for a man, short and clever. Roman also knew he liked breasts since that is usually what he commented upon about women.

"So, the powers of Society don't like Miss Holwell because she is a tall miner's daughter who likes to read."

"That is the gist of the matter. The families with sons her father would approve of her marrying believe they can do better than Miss Holwell. Or their sons are my height. So, she languishes on the Marriage Mart."

Roman set his empty glass on the desk. "What of the others?"

"There is Miss Reverly. I believe she is the loveliest of the lot and the wealthiest. However, she is very petite, a mite of a woman."

Roman shrugged. "I like petite women."

"Don't we all. But she is truly tiny. Perfectly formed but just barely five feet, perhaps an inch more, and fine boned. There are whispers amongst the mothers of eligible sons that she might not bear a child, and since for those families an heir is all important—as it is to you, my lord—well, Miss Reverly is not a first choice. Mind you, both of those young ladies would be snatched up by would-be husbands if their fathers would accept an offer from lesser titles or just decent gentlemen. Those like me who are called to the bar do not stand a chance. Reverly has made it clear he will not settle for anything less than a duke or a marquis for his daughter."

"That leaves me out."

"I thought I should at least mention her."

"And you did. What of the third?"

"Ah, now she is the one I believe would interest you. Her father is with the East India Company. He is an officer in the Company, but from what I hear, not as clever and successful as his grandfather and father. His money comes from the family. He wishes his daughter to be married to an old and distinguished title because after generations of service to the Crown, the best his family could earn is a knighthood, and not one that could be passed down. Earl of Rochdale will meet his needs nicely."

Roman shifted his weight. "I am not fond of nabobs."

"You will be extremely fond of the daughter. There is something striking and different about Miss Charnock, whether the rumors are true about her heritage—"

"*Charnock?*" Carefully, Roman said, "What is her first name?"

"Leonie. Leonie Charnock—her great-grandfather was one of the most important men in India."

Roman straightened, stunned to hear spoken aloud the name he'd struggled to eradicate from his conscious for the last six years. Leonie Charnock. Ah, yes, she was beautiful . . . and the person who had destroyed his military career.

"Is something the matter, Rochdale? You have the strangest expression. Have I said something wrong?"

Roman faced his godfather. Should he tell him? Roman had not spoken a word of the incident to anyone. He'd been bound by a code of honor, his *own* code and one that had nothing to do with matters as frivolous as bad gambling debts.

He decided to break a portion of his silence. It could not hurt.

"You have never asked why my military career stalled. Were you not curious?"

Thaddeus sat back in his chair. His gaze shifted away from Roman's. "I would not pry. I knew from your letters you were disappointed."

"Disappointed" was such an understatement; Roman gave a bitter laugh. "Leonie Charnock destroyed my career. If it hadn't been for her, I would have been able to leave service in India. I would have found myself fighting Napoleon on the Peninsula and be a full colonel by now."

Instead, his fellow officers had branded him a disgrace. He'd been ignored for promotions and sent on countless excursions to battle the Marathas and pirates, the most dangerous tasks no one else wanted. Every time they sent him out, Roman knew they did not expect him to return.

"Good heavens." Thaddeus leaned toward him. "I was aware that something had happened. I know you, lad. I believed you were a better officer than the way you were treated."

"If not for Rochdale's death and no other male heir between us . . ." He let his voice drift off. Military service appeared romantic to those who had no idea of how cheap life was in battle, especially when one couldn't trust the men behind him.

"You are damned fortunate."

"I am."

"And, of course, Miss Charnock is *unsuitable* for a wife for you—"

Roman held up a hand to stop him, a new thought striking him. "How rich is she?"

"She's a ripe plum. Charnock has no other children. The houses, the business interests, they will all go to her husband."

Roman pictured Leonie as she'd been when he had first seen her all those years ago—coltish, tawny golden, full of life. But there had been something sensual about her as well. Even at seventeen, she made a man think of rumpled sheets and morning romps. Her dark eyes seemed to have more knowledge than they should. The pout to her full lips begged to be kissed away . . . and her breasts . . . God, her breasts. It was all a man could do to not stare at them.

And because of all her "attributes," he'd been the fool to fall on his own sword.

"What is holding her back from landing a husband?" He could think of one very strong reason, but considering the lengths her parents had taken to protect her, it would be ironic if all of Fashionable Society knew.

"She's different."

"What does that mean?"

"She has an exotic look to her."

Yes, Leonie didn't look like the other English roses.

"Her eyes are so brown, almost to being black," Thaddeus said.

Roman knew they weren't black but had flecks of gold in them.

"And there is a refinement about her," Thaddeus continued. "An air of elegance."

Aye, that was true. But what did Thaddeus mean? "Is that a bad thing?"

"Oh, no, except her father doesn't look a thing like her. He is a blustery sort and the mother is all yellow haired and creamy skin. Charnock dotes on his daughter—or at least claims he does. Her mother is a different story. Apparently, she and her husband are not close and she is not always . . . what to say?"

"Discreet?"

"That is the word. There are rumors she was that way in India."

The rumors were true. Mrs. Charnock had loved to prey on the young officers, especially when they first arrived in Calcutta. She'd chased Roman, but once he'd met the daughter, he had not been interested in the mother's games . . . even though Leonie had still been in the schoolroom, but allowed to attend the dances held amongst what passed for civilized society in the British colony.

"You are suggesting there are those who do not believe Charnock is Leonie's father?" No one had believed it in Calcutta either.

Thaddeus appeared almost relieved to confess. "Yes. There are whispers. I don't give them countenance. Then there is talk of a scandal. I heard a duel was fought over her—" Thaddeus broke off and then said as if putting pieces of information together, "You wouldn't know about that, would you?"

Oh, yes, the duel.

"I shot a fellow lieutenant over Leonie Charnock." The words were bitter in his mouth.

"You dueled, Roman? I thought you had more sense."

"Apparently not."

There was a moment of silence.

Thaddeus uncorked the whisky decanter and poured himself another drink. This time, Roman accepted one.

"Miss Charnock almost married a duke last year," his godfather said. "Baynton apparently had no qualms about her heritage or the rumors. However, the match fell through."

Roman stared down into the amber liquid in his glass. He was disturbed that the thought of Leonie marrying another man bothered him. "What happened?"

"He was the duke I mentioned who ran off with an actress."

That sparked another sharp bark of laughter from Roman.

Poor Leonie, so lovely and yet fate always played her the losing hand. Then again, he had knowledge that she was often a victim of her own schemes.

Still, she had been special, unique . . . and with that memory came a surge of energy he could not countenance save that he had a desire to see her again.

"How do I meet these heiresses?"

Thaddeus sat up as if surprised he had persuaded his godson. "They will be at the Marquis of Devon's rout tonight. I have an invitation and you may come along. Everyone will be there."

"Are you including Erzy and Malcolm in 'everyone'?"

"Indubitably."

"Good, then maybe I shall have the opportunity to smash one of them in the face." At Thaddeus's sound of distress, he said, "I will be all that is proper. I wouldn't want a scandal, would I?"

"Why do I have a feeling you have already been involved in one?" Thaddeus asked, gathering the gambling debts.

Roman merely smiled his answer. He took the chits from his godfather. "I will come round at seven. Is that good?"

"Yes, of course."

Leaving his godfather's office, Roman had more purpose in his step. Leonie Charnock had put it there.

Roman found himself anticipating a long overdue reckoning, and the only thing that would save her was her dowry.

She owed him at least that.

Chapter 2

*A*nything could happen when Everyone of Importance gathered, and they were all here for the Marquis of Devon's ball. The room was a crush. The air was filled with expectation and the gossiping hum of guests waiting for the receiving line to end and the dancing to begin.

Leonie Charnock stood next to one of the giant papier-mâché pots filled with long-handled, gilt fans like those used by the ancient Egyptians. The Marchioness of Devon's theme for the evening was "The Nile," and apparently these pots in the four corners of the room were to give the sparkling company an impression of being on that famed river.

All Leonie felt was boredom. She was here, dressed in muslin and lace, her hair piled high on her head, to face another year of being treated little better than a fishing lure. She understood her role. She was to act a certain way and speak in a certain manner while her person and her substantial dowry were dangled in front of eligible bachelors in hopes of a strike. In truth, with the money involved, she could have been dressed in sackcloth and her head shaved and the men would seek her out. The *poor* men.

Wealthy ones with title and influence felt themselves too good for her, although they didn't seem to mind staring at her breasts.

The ritual of husband hunting was growing tiresome—

especially since, if she had her way, she would never marry. She wanted nothing to do with men and their lust, and yet she was trapped in the expectations of Society.

After all, if she didn't marry, what would become of her? Single women had no power.

Leonie longingly watched a tray of iced wine pass by her to be offered to others. Proper young women avoided anything that could lead to indiscreet behavior. She was free to enjoy all the orgeat, an almond syrup mixed with lemonade, she could consume. She could possibly have *one* glass of iced wine over the supper that would be served later without damaging her reputation. Anything more would make her the subject of gossip and her father would be furious since there were enough rumors about the family already.

She told herself the lack of wine didn't matter. She'd had a good nip of brandy before she'd left home, furtively taken from one of the many decanters in her father's house. She'd learned a wee bit could take the edge off life, especially for events like this one where she was to be anyone other than herself. It also made living with secrets a touch easier—

"Here you are." Her friend Willa came up beside her. Her glossy dark hair was threaded with pearls. Her dress, like Leonie's, was a demure white that was excellent for her skin tone. Because of her petiteness, she had a habit of looking up at the world around her. It gave her an air of perpetual curiosity that was actually quite true. Willa was far more intelligent than anyone credited her.

Leonie had witnessed more than one incident where people, men in particular, seemed to patronize Willa because of her height. Her friend was not afraid to show them the sharp side of her tongue.

She leaned toward Leonie and whispered, "Is it my imagination or does this year's crop of debutantes appear younger and hungrier than ever before?" She nodded to a gaggle of young women and their mothers, excitedly comparing notes and sizing up rivals. There was a burst of nervous giggles over something that had been whispered by another. They sounded as if they were pigeons about to take off.

"We were never that young," Leonie assured her.

"Hopefully we weren't as goose-ish. Is your mother here?"

"She came with us . . . but has probably left. I haven't seen her for the past fifteen minutes." Her mother always arrived with Leonie and her father, but often slipped away from whatever rout they attended to meet a lover. "I believe she is bedding a member of the Horse Guard. He might be younger than I am."

Willa made no comment other than to offer a consoling glance. She knew Leonie hated pity. "Father escorted me. He's in the card room already."

"As is my father."

Willa said, "Oh, look, Cassandra has arrived."

The two of them turned toward the receiving line to see Cassandra finish her last curtsey.

One couldn't miss her. She was the tallest woman in the room and she did not stoop like so many others would have done. Better yet, she piled her gold curls high on her head to be artfully held in place with jeweled pins. The jewels were probably real. Any other reasonable person would have used paste but Thomas Holwell, MP, wanted one and all to see his wealth.

With just a green ribbon woven in her hair, Leonie feared she appeared drab next to her friends, and the thought amused her.

Cassandra spied them. She gave a small wave and began making her way toward them. The three friends took a moment for welcoming kisses on the cheek.

Leonie gave her friends considering looks. "Tonight, the two of you remind me of goddesses. Willa is the moon goddess Selene and, Cassandra, you are like Demeter, queen of the harvest."

"What a flight of fancy you are on tonight," Cassandra declared. "How shall we christen Leonie, Willa? Aphrodite?"

Leonie winced. "Too obvious. And nothing could be further than the truth. I'm far from the most beautiful woman in the world."

"You say that," Cassandra said, "however, I watch men look at you as if you were a spoonful of honey they'd like to drip into their mouths."

"Or a flower they would like to pollinate," Willa agreed.

Heat rushed up to Leonie's cheeks. This sort of talk embarrassed her. "Now you are being silly. Men hardly notice me."

"You captured the interest of a duke last year," Cassandra reminded her.

"One who was so entranced he jilted me for an actress," Leonie answered. It had not been pleasant being the target of spiteful gossip after Baynton had withdrawn his offer. But the truth was, Leonie had been relieved that she didn't have to marry. In fact, if she had her way, she would rather die a spinster. She had no desire to submit to a man. Not ever again—

For the briefest of seconds, the bad memory threatened to overwhelm her. She glanced at the sterling punch bowl on its table across the room. There was quite a crowd in front of it. She knew better than to join them—

"Persephone," Willa declared. "You are like Demeter's daughter, who was stolen to the underworld, Leonie. You appear so at peace and yet there is this sorrow about you."

Dear Willa, too perceptive.

Leonie forced a smile. "What nonsense do you speak?"

"I agree," Cassandra said breezily. "Leonie is the goddess of Love, not the Underworld."

Willa shrugged, unintimidated by their responses. Instead, she asked, "Are we playing the game this year?"

Leonie had forgotten the game and she had devised it.

"Please tell me we are going to play the game again this year," Cassandra agreed. "Father went on all afternoon about my failure to attract a husband and of what would happen if

I don't finally marry. I know Helen put him up to it." Helen was Cassandra's stepmother. "I need something to make all of this"—she waved a gloved hand to include the dazzling company—"more interesting. I'm fatigued of the whole thing and we haven't even started."

Leonie's thoughts exactly. She felt her spirits lift.

The "game" had started as a jest between them, a friendly wager. Each one of them had placed five pounds in a reticle and whoever received the most points by the end of the Season became the winner. The points were easy to earn since they were assigned to different acts of courting. It was a test of flirting prowess but it also helped keep their fathers appeased in the belief their daughters were doing what all eligible young ladies should to catch a husband.

To make the game more interesting, they had decided points could only count for one particular gentleman. They had chosen Lord Stokes because his name had been mentioned most by their fathers.

Willa had won the wager. Stokes had been like wax in her hand until his family informed him they would not support such a match. He'd claimed to be heartbroken but then he quickly offered for Lady Amanda White, a slender blonde with bloodlines better than the king's. She didn't have Willa's fortune but she had dowry enough for Stokes.

Leonie had barely registered a point because of the Duke of Baynton's interest. She'd had to play the demure, shy virgin while he'd been evidently carrying on with his actress.

"The game would make this Season vastly more entertaining," Cassandra predicted.

"And why do you say that?" Leonie asked.

"Why? Because of the Duke of Camberly," Cassandra answered, and Willa quickly nodded.

"Camberly? I've not heard of him," Leonie said.

"You wouldn't have heard of the former duke. He was frightfully old," Willa said.

Cassandra nodded. "Yes, and his sons died before him, leaving a grandson to inherit. A young, reputably *handsome* grandson."

"Have you met him?" Leonie asked.

"Few have," Willa answered. "He is supposed to make his first appearance in Society tonight."

"He is a *poet.*" Cassandra could not keep the excitement from her voice. She was a great fancier of the arts and dreamed of holding an important salon *à la française*. To that end, she'd held a few salons in her father's front room. They had been small gatherings where every destitute poet in London tried to take advantage of her. Willa and Leonie faithfully attended as good friends should and they made up the majority of the crowd attending. Cassandra's salons were not popular.

MP Holwell was there as well. He chaperoned with such disapproval on his face the poets never lingered in his daughter's presence, although Cassandra had given her pin money to more than a few of them.

"Is the duke wealthy?" Leonie, ever practical, had to ask.

"He lacks sufficient funds," Willa said.

"Which makes him an excellent quarry for our game," Cassandra concluded. "He will want to know us. And he is a *duke.* Father has mentioned him several times to me. I'm surprised yours hasn't," she said to Leonie.

"Since Baynton, Father has not been pleased with me. He acts as if it is my fault the duke even had a paramour."

"Then flirting with a new duke should please him," Willa said. "My father is like Cassandra's. All he can talk about is Camberly."

"Well, then, Camberly, it is," said Leonie. "One point for a glance—everyone is on their honor for this. Two points for an introduction."

"That should be easy enough," Cassandra said. "My father is already out and about on my behalf, as is Helen. I might win this game—"

"Win what game?" a female voice demanded.

Leonie, Willa, and Cassandra turned to face Lady Bettina Warwell, a slender redhead with an ambitious spirit. She was accompanied by a trio of young women. "What game are the Spinster Heiresses up to?" she laughingly said to her companions. "I wonder if it has anything to do with a certain new duke?"

Leonie hated the nickname the "Spinster Heiresses." Someone had dubbed them with it last Season and it had quickly caught on. Leonie wasn't so certain Lady Bettina hadn't been behind the taunt. She certainly used it often enough—especially against Cassandra. For some reason, Bettina enjoyed making fun of her more than Willa and Leonie. Perhaps because they could hold their own better than Cassandra, who cared very much what people thought of her.

However, Leonie was not going to let her friends be mocked. Stepping forward, she said, "Good evening, my lady. Enjoying your *second* Season?" But she really wasn't as good at delivering withering set downs as Lady Bettina and they both knew it.

Lady Bettina shrugged as if it was the nothing it was. "Tell me about your game. Perhaps we'd like to play." Her friends nodded their heads.

For all the world, they would appear as a group of young women having a pleasant chat while waiting for the receiving line to end and the dancing to begin. No one else would feel the undercurrent of malice born out of jealousy. If Lady Bettina learned about the game, then she would spread the word throughout the *ton* . . . unless she was a part of it.

Had Leonie thought this Season would be a bore?

She'd been wrong.

A delicious challenge formed in her mind. "Do you think it

wise we speak here and so openly? Perhaps we should adjourn to the necessary room?" She referred to the room set aside for the women to have a moment of privacy.

With a nod to Cassandra and Willa, Leonie began walking in that direction. A few steps along, Cassandra grabbed Leonie's arm. "Are you mad? She is the bitterest of souls and not to be trusted."

"Is she following?" Leonie asked.

"Yes, they all are."

"Then have faith in me," Leonie answered. "This will be fun."

Cassandra made a worried sound but both she and Willa marched right into the necessary room behind Leonie.

This early in the evening, the room was quiet. Leonie motioned Lady Bettina closer and said, "We have been plotting a wonderful game, a flirting game."

"A flirting game?" Lady Bettina tilted her head with interest. Her friends were paying attention as well. They were all daughters of lesser nobles and, Leonie realized, just as desperately caught up in this chase to find a husband as the Heiresses were.

"Yes, flirting, which is what we are expected to do anyway. It keeps our skills sharp," Leonie said easily. "We assign points to different actions—five points if he calls on you, three points for each dance. That sort of thing. Every participant offers five pounds, which Miss Reverly keeps as banker, and at the end of the Season the one with the most points is declared the winner."

"This is rather immoral, isn't it?" one of Lady Bettina's friends said.

"In what way? The men do it," Lady Bettina answered, surprising Leonie with her quick acceptance. "What do you think they write in the betting books at their clubs? They wager on us all the time." She looked at Cassandra. "Are you doing this?"

Cassandra's brows came together as if she wasn't certain she could trust Lady Bettina but she nodded.

"It adds a bit of interest in the Season," Willa said.

"But if anyone found out—" the girl who'd spoken up said, but Lady Bettina cut her off.

"Then they would think we were resourceful. Miss Charnock is correct. We must do these things anyway, why not have some sport with it. Five pounds, you say?"

Leonie nodded. "And the points only apply to one gentleman of our choosing. This Season the object of our affections will be the newly named Duke of Camberly."

Lady Bettina's eyes lit up at the name, as did her friends'.

Oh, this Season was going to be fun. "So, is the game on?" Leonie asked.

"Starting this evening?" Lady Bettina said.

"It must. Camberly will be making his appearance," Leonie answered.

Lady Bettina held out her gloved hand. "Then let the game begin and may the best woman win."

Leonie shook her hand, thinking she had seen her father do this over horse racing many a time. She rather liked this cool efficiency.

The door to the necessary room opened. A young matron with a velvet cap stuck her head in the room and then said in a furious whisper, "Bettina, Mother and I have been looking for you everywhere. Camberly has arrived. He is almost through the receiving line and the dancing will begin. You should be out here."

"I'm coming," Lady Bettina assured her, the light of competition in her eyes. She was out the door in a blink followed by her friends.

Willa looked at Leonie. "Well, now what?"

"Now we have a true competition going on."

Cassandra shook her head. "She won't play fair. I've known her most of my life and she cheats. She'll do anything to win."

"Perhaps we will as well," Leonie said. "When I started this evening, I feared I wouldn't make it through another Season . . . but now? You won't claim victory so handily this time, Willa."

"Men like dark haired women," Willa countered good-naturedly. "That purse is mine."

"Or *mine*." Cassandra started for the door. "I won't let Bettina win. I. Will. Not." She opened the door.

"And we will help you," Leonie promised as she went through. "In truth, it is us against them."

"Of course it is," Willa said thoughtfully. "Well played, Leonie. Bettina won't say anything about overhearing us because she is a part of it. Her friends will be quiet because she is involved."

"But she plays dirty," Cassandra said. "I'm warning you."

"Dear Cassandra, the voice of doom," Leonie teased. "But don't worry. The sticklers might be upset about our little game, but really, what harm is there? Very little. And they look down their noses at us as it is. If I had my way, I'd have every debutante participating. Think what a romp that would be."

They had reached the ballroom. Everyone was crowded inside with no one lingering in the hall. Willa shot Leonie a look as if to say this was strange to her as well.

"Follow me," Cassandra said, using her height and femininity to push her way into the room. They moved toward the front door when the crowd around them parted and Leonie had her first look at this new duke.

Camberly was young and tall and prodigiously handsome. Broad-shouldered, obviously athletic, and completely confident. It was there in the way he held his head and the ease in which he greeted those being introduced to him. And yet he did not give off an air of arrogance. His smile appeared sincere and had the power to charm even the most miserly of souls.

Such self-assurance was a powerful aphrodisiac.

Cassandra, who was the pickiest of the three of them when it came to men and just about everything else, made a soft, "Oh, my," that exactly summed up Leonie's reaction.

Nor did Leonie need to look at Willa to know she was charmed. The Duke of Camberly had all the physical virtues Willa had claimed she sought. In validation of that thought, Willa nudged Leonie and whispered, "This shall be a good game."

"Game?" Cassandra answered. "He's *mine*." There was no jest in her tone. Without waiting for her friends, she began moving in the direction of her stepmother, presumably to have the woman organize an introduction.

Willa's eyebrows raised. "Was that Cassandra Holwell who just spoke? I mean, I've never heard her so direct. She sounded serious. And he is a wonder. Excuse me, my dear Leonie, but not only do we have a wager at stake, I believe I'd like an introduction to the new duke as well. I can only pray he favors petite women." She left without waiting for Leonie's permission to search out her own chaperone.

And Leonie was once more standing alone.

She noted that Lady Bettina had secured an introduction. She made a lovely curtsey to the duke, whose eye wandered to Bettina's décolletage. They had not assigned points for eye wandering. Perhaps they should?

From the company all around where Leonie stood, there seemed to be only one word and that was "Camberly." The duke had quickly made his mark on London.

She started moving in search of her mother's friend Lady Dervish, who knew everyone and could secure an introduction for her. She knew better than to bother her father at cards over such a matter. He wanted results from his daughter, but he didn't want her to pester him while achieving those results.

Leonie was competitive. A touch of excitement replaced her earlier ennui. And, she reflected, wasn't courting really nothing more than a game? One with high stakes?

She might as well enjoy the moment. After all, once a woman was married, well, her life was mapped out for her, babies and then death . . . unless she took on lovers. Then she could play the courting game until no one wanted her.

Leonie rejected the idea. She had no desire to follow in her mother's steps.

The first dance pattern was setting up.

She glanced around to see where Camberly was and saw him lead Cassandra to the dance floor. *Three points and one for a glance and two for the introduction. Well done, Cassandra.*

Leonie had best hurry if she wished to score even one point for the evening. She spied Lady Dervish talking to some friends and began weaving her way toward her—but then stopped.

Thoughts of scoring points vanished. She was struck by a strong premonition that something momentous was about to happen. Leonie had lived too long in India to not pay attention to such a sudden stirring of her senses. Her soul wakened with the keen certainty that her life might be about to change.

Perhaps this explained her earlier restlessness? Could it be Camberly? Was he the force that made her too aware of everything outside of her own skin?

She *knew* this feeling.

Leonie turned to where she'd last seen the duke. He was on the dance floor with a beaming Cassandra. He wasn't thinking about Leonie. He didn't even know who she was.

The hair at the nape of her neck tingled as if she was being watched. Leonie scanned the people around her—and then her gaze met the intent stare of a gentleman.

For a second, she stared without recognition, but that was not quite true. She'd *known* him the moment she'd felt the disturbance in her orderly world. Here he was, her Past come back to haunt her.

Leonie's first inclination was to run. She'd struggled too long and hard to forgive herself for what had happened those years ago to give it up now. And yet, running had never helped.

In a strange way, Leonie realized that she had been waiting for Lieutenant Roman Gilchrist, ambitious and loyal officer of the King's forces in India. She'd known he would appear sooner or later.

Years ago, at another ball, he'd asked her to dance and her whole life had changed. He'd been leaner then, younger, and more uncertain.

Now, he appeared forceful, assured. Evening clothes did him justice. His was not a classically handsome face like Camberly's but an interesting one with slashing brows, a strong nose, and gray eyes that saw too much.

Her young world had been simple before meeting him. He had made it complicated.

Without a doubt, he had shattered all she'd believed of herself.

He could do that again.

The lieutenant made his way to her. Leonie waited as if rooted to the floor. He stopped in front of her. He did not bow. "Miss Charnock, we meet again."

She did not move, did not offer her hand. "What do you want?"

"The honor of the next dance."

His was not a request but an expectation, just as it had been those years ago on that fateful night in Calcutta. Their dance had set into motion a series of events that had led to another man's death.

However, this time, her answer to his request was different. She reached up and slapped him across the face with all the force of her being.

She anticipated a loud, satisfying sound and a moment of vindication. Instead, his jaw was like hitting granite. Despite gloves, pain reverberated from her palm down to her arm. She grabbed her wrist to help the throbbing subside.

He blinked at her in surprise. An angry, red strike mark in the shape of her hand formed on the side of his face—so she hadn't been completely ineffective—and Leonie had the distinct thought that now might be a good time to leave.

She took off running, shoving her way through the crowd.

Chapter 3

The good news was Leonie Charnock obviously remembered him.

Roman wasn't quite certain what had caused such a strong reaction from her. But then, he'd never understood Leonie. Even at seventeen she'd been mercurial.

Nor was she some delicate English flower. That was one of the things Roman had always admired about her. She was the sort of woman who would carry on no matter what.

What he hadn't known was that she had quite a bit of strength in her arm. He knew men who could not hit as hard.

Placing a hand against his jaw, his eye met that of a woman whose raised eyebrows and deep frown told him she'd witnessed Leonie's attack and was quite shocked. No one else around him seemed aware of the contretemps. They were more interested in the newly named duke. They eyed him on the dance floor, commenting on his courtly grace and other such nonsense that no decent man would appreciate.

"Did you deserve it?" the woman asked.

"Does any man?" he countered.

A rusty laugh gave him her opinion but he didn't linger to banter. He was off to find Leonie. He had an idea of where she was headed.

Working his way through the crowd, steadying a gent who'd already sampled too much of the punch, avoiding a lady who gestured wildly with her fan, and generally avoiding eye contact with everyone around him, Roman made his way to the card room.

Or at least he hoped she would run to her father. If she'd thought to escape to the women's necessary room, he would have a devil of a time talking to her.

And it was as clear to him as the stinging burn on his jaw where she'd slapped him that they needed to talk, preferably without making a further scene.

He strode into the side room filled with tables of men and women playing cards. He quickly spied Leonie. Her father was still at the table where Roman had left him some fifteen minutes ago.

She hovered behind her father's chair. She appeared desperate and greatly imposed upon but Roman and everyone else in the room knew Charnock wouldn't have time for his daughter until his hand had been played.

Leonie caught sight of him in the doorway. Her chin lifted. Her nostrils flared and her eyes lit up, reminding Roman of nothing less than an angry mare ready to kick. Little did she know her defiance only enhanced her beauty—and she was lovely.

Maturity had added character to her face, but all the attributes Roman remembered—the generous mouth, the high cheekbones, the thick and glorious hair—all of those were the same. Well, save her breasts. They seemed larger, fuller, and certainly more enticing.

God, he was a fool.

Charnock played the last pair in his hand, throwing them on the table with a grand gesture and then quickly scooping the money toward him.

He had to crow a bit as he did, saying to one of the players, "I knew you were going to lose that round. You played the wrong cards, my lord. But then *I* had the *right* ones." He chortled as if he had been very clever.

Leonie's gaze had never left Roman. As he approached the table, she tapped Charnock's shoulder. "I would have a word with you, Father."

He looked up from his winnings. "Not now. Can't you see I'm busy? I have a run of luck."

"Yes, now, Father. *Please.*" She leaned close to whisper furiously in his ear.

Roman stopped a few feet away, waiting.

He'd dealt with men like Charnock most of his military career, so he was not surprised when her father said petulantly, "Of course I know Gilchrist is here. And that is the *former* Lieutenant Gilchrist. He's an earl now. Rochdale, an important title. Very important."

Leonie shot Roman a look of such disbelief it was almost insulting. Her dark eyes took in every inch of his bearing. The downturn of her mouth said louder than words what she thought.

However, her father was in no mood to argue, especially when one of the players at the table, a lace-capped dowager, asked, "Are you playing, Charnock, or do we have to sit here and listen to you jabber to your daughter?"

"Of course I am playing." Charnock frowned at Leonie and gave a nod to Roman. "Dance with him. The two of you are old friends—"

"You are jesting—"

"No, I'm not," Charnock said. "Do the pretty and mind your manners. Rochdale is an important title, and Gilchrist has already asked my permission to court you."

"Court?" Her eyes widened in disbelief. "And you said yes?"

"Aye." Charnock then leaned in and said something to his daughter that straightened her back. "Now," he continued, raising his voice, "I am going to sit for this round because it is a poor winner who takes his winnings and leaves."

"That is the truth," the dowager said. She downed her sherry neat and signaled for another before slapping the table. "Let us play."

Charnock obliged, gleefully stacking his coins in front of him as the cards were dealt.

Leonie stood a moment as if carved of stone. She was not happy, but then she slowly turned in Roman's direction, the gesture reserved, tight. Her gaze met his.

How many times in the past had he caught her watching him and wondered what she was thinking? Her dark eyes could be remarkably expressive, or as cold and unrevealing as coal.

She moved toward him.

Roman braced himself. Was he about to receive another slap?

Instead, she walked right by him. "The dance floor is in the other room," she murmured without breaking step. Apparently, she assumed he would follow.

He'd be damned if he would.

Roman might not have money but he had pride. He also knew better than to dance to the pipe she was playing. He'd learned that lesson once. He watched her leave, wondering when she'd realize he wasn't following.

Charnock looked up from his cards. "I thought you said you wanted her, my lord?" He referred to the conversation Roman had managed before Charnock had sat down at his table.

Roman had been blunt about his intentions. He had a historical and respected title; Charnock had a daughter and a pot of money. Before Roman had even wasted time talking to Leonie, he'd wanted to know where he'd stood with her father.

And what he'd found out was that Charnock would have sold his daughter to Beelzebub if it would gain for him what he wanted. He liked the sound of "Earl of Rochdale" and had even taken the time to sound out his gambling companions as to the heraldry around the family name. He'd approved Roman's suit on their verdicts.

"Go on. Give chase," Charnock said, his tone bored and his

fellow card players amused. "It is what we men do. Or have you changed your mind about her fortune?"

"Mayhap I have," Roman responded coolly.

After all, he was a bloody lord now. And Charnock was one of those Roman suspected had been involved in his demotion and military humiliation in India. The bastard could wait on him—and his daughter could learn some manners.

With a nonchalance that he was far from feeling, Roman began walking in the opposite direction of Leonie. The far door of the card room opened onto the main hallway. He wasn't clear in his intentions but he was beginning to think he'd rather be home in his rented rooms with a good book and a hot toddy than playing lapdog to a spoiled heiress and her greedy father.

He'd almost reached the door when he heard his name called.

Roman stopped, turned—and saw Lord Erzy working his way around the tables toward him. Erzy clapped him on the back as if they were congenial colleagues, but then he lowered his voice to speak. "I hope you aren't in this room placing wagers without seeing that Malcolm and I are paid for what your uncle owed us."

"Some would say that a man's debts die with him."

He knew his argument would not fly but he had to try.

Erzy answered, "Not a debt of honor. It never goes away. Of course, you may not have the decency to pay but I'll see you are put beyond the pale by everyone of importance. Doors will be closed to you, even in the Lords. Is that what you wish, Rochdale? This early in the game after inheriting your title?"

No, Roman had no desire to be on the outs with anyone. He'd been there too long.

"I haven't been gambling," he informed Erzy. "I'm not a betting man."

"Pity. There is much sport in it."

"Not from where I stand. Now, if you will excuse me? Or do

you intend to hound me like a gullgroper?" Gullgropers were money lenders of the worst sort.

Erzy didn't like the term. His lip curled, but he stepped aside.

Roman cast one longing look at the hallway where he'd planned his escape and instead headed for the door leading to the ballroom. This had been the devil's own night. He'd been slapped, mocked, and dunned—and he'd be damned if he would put up with more of it. He intended to claim his dance with Leonie Charnock and she'd best behave because he wasn't in the mood for any more nonsense.

Out in the ballroom, the crowd seemed to have doubled in size. Roman worked his way through the milling mass of over-dressed, overperfumed, and overdrunken guests, searching for Leonie.

He didn't have to look far. She was on the dance floor, and her partner was no one less than the penniless Duke of Camberly. The man everyone talked about this evening. The man who needed a wealthy duchess.

Camberly was not paying attention to his steps. Instead, he was using his height to look down Leonie's bodice. He practically licked his lips as if she was a lamb chop for his taking.

Roman had forgotten the power of jealousy. He remembered it now as it ripped through him, releasing a molten stream of seething discontent.

No, he did not have a reason for this reaction. Leonie was not his.

Yet.

He started for the dance floor.

LEONIE KNEW HOW to master a dramatic exit. Women had few resources available to them to rebel.

Well, daughters had few resources. Her mother made cuck-olding her father an art. She did it every chance she could—although he didn't seem to care.

And Leonie knew her father would not be moved by her stiff back and head held high to show her displeasure as she left to do his bidding, but Gilchrist would.

Let him trail in her wake. At the first opportunity, she planned to launch into him. She'd make him regret ever approaching her or daring to ask for a dance. She'd lash him with her tongue so hard he would go running back to wherever he'd been all these years.

However, first she would have to dance with him.

The next set was forming on the dance floor. Couples were taking their places. Usually, the gentleman led the way.

Leonie turned to haughtily inform Gilchri—*Rochdale*, he now had a title. Earl of Rochdale. Huzzah.

"My lord," she started, ice around each word, "you should be—"

Her hauteur broke off.

He wasn't there.

Gilchris—*no*, Rochdale—had not followed her. He'd asked her to dance, made an issue of it with her father, and *he hadn't followed*?

For a dangerous moment, Leonie thought her eyes would pop out of her head with her very self-righteous and completely justified anger.

She took a step back toward the card room, her hands curling into fists as she thought to find him and drag him to the dance floor. But then she stopped. *She* could not go after him. Not even if he'd lost his way.

It was *his* responsibility to escort her, not *her* job to shepherd him. She should never have been left alone. Weren't unmarried women considered delicate flowers to be chaperoned and watched closely?

Of course, her mother and father had their own pursuits, but a gentleman like the newly minted Earl of Rochdale should have been right on her heels from the moment she had agreed, albeit unkindly, to dance with him.

And she would *not* hunt him down and lecture him on the responsibilities of a gentleman because she'd rather pick up one of the papier-mâché pots around the room and crash it on his head.

The image of Rochdale bashed in by glue and paper gave Leonie great pleasure, but it didn't conjure his presence from the card room.

No one had ever just left her on the ballroom floor before.

Well, save for her parents. They ignored her all the time. They had expectations of her but they didn't trouble themselves overmuch with her welfare.

Then there was the last time she had been with Gilchrist. He'd left her then as well, hadn't he? Delivered her home and walked off—

"Leonie."

The sound of her name brought Leonie back to the moment. Lady Dervish, her mother's friend, was hurrying toward her, pushing her way past the other guests with all the excitement of a hen about to lay eggs. "Leonie, I have been looking for you. *He* is begging an introduction to you."

"He?"

"The Duke of Camberly. He specifically asked for you and since we couldn't find your mother—"

"Of course," Leonie murmured.

"And why disturb your father?" Lady Dervish continued.

"He is undisturbable," Leonie agreed.

"I thought to bring you to our latest duke myself." She hooked her arm in Leonie's. "My dear, he is delicious. And so well mannered. He said he saw you across the ballroom and is most anxious for an introduction."

To both her and her dowry, Leonie could have added but held her peace. The duke had noticed her. She had scored her first point in this Season's game.

Let Rochdale wonder where she'd gone off to.

Let *him* stew about her whereabouts.

Of course, she could not resist, as Lady Dervish guided her to the dance floor, a backward glance at the card room.

Rochdale wasn't to be seen, and Leonie cursed herself for having looked.

So, it was that she was introduced to Camberly at just the moment when she was ready to defy convention.

He had finished leading Lord Vetter's daughter in a dance. The chit was practically hyperventilating from the experience and Leonie could understand why. Up close, the Duke of Camberly was even more handsome. His features were classic and even in contrast to Rochdale's rough masculinity.

Camberly had eyes so blue they reminded her of a summer sky. His nose was strong without overpowering his face. His lips were well formed and full in the best spirit of a romantic noble.

He was young, perhaps only four years older than Leonie's three and twenty years. He was muscular and strong and had a ready smile as if he was enjoying himself fully.

What was not to like?

In addition, if he asked her to dance, she would score three more points and let Rochdale know she didn't give two snaps of her fingers whether he honored his request for a dance or not. She had other admirers. *Ducal* admirers.

"Your Grace," Lady Dervish fawned. "May I introduce you to Miss Leonie Charnock?"

Leonie was never fond of curtseying but she did so now. A deep curtsey, one that she knew allowed the very tall duke an excellent view of her assets. She was usually not one to flaunt herself, but her feminine pride had been stung.

His response did much to restore her hurt feelings. "Miss Charnock." His voice was deep and warm. He took her gloved hand, helping her rise. "Those who have praised your beauty as more sparkling than the stars did not lie."

Leonie quickly stifled a laugh at his blatant flattery, which seemed false and silly, especially considering his age. Old men garbled nonsense like this to her, and yet he seemed sincere. Perhaps he was shy? She then remembered Cassandra saying he fancied himself a poet.

"Your Grace is too kind," she answered, wanting to take back the hand he still held.

"It is not kindness at all, but truth. I have heard much about you."

And my fortune.

Leonie attempted her best to look demure and affected by his praise, reminding herself that men rarely expected an answer, especially of the cynical sort. Her mother had warned her long ago that, when around gentlemen, it was always best to say nothing. They would form their own conclusions.

"Will you do me the honor of this next dance?"

The one that she should have had with Rochdale? "I would be honored, Your Grace."

He had never let go of her hand and now placed it on his arm. He led her to center of the floor. Such was the weight of an important title, the couples there made room for them, even switching groups if necessary.

The music started.

The men bowed; the ladies curtsied—and Leonie wished fervently that Rochdale could see her dancing and be eaten alive with despair for his blatant disregard for her.

That would be a great moment.

She was so caught in her imaginary and vehement triumph she mistakenly gave the duke's hand a little squeeze.

His brows rose. The keen glint of a hunter came to his eye, and the next time they came back together in the pattern of the dance, he gave her hand a squeeze in return, as well as a clench of the fingers.

Leonie shot him her most dazzling smile, knowing that somewhere in the ballroom her friends were thinking: one point for the glance, one for the introduction, three points for the dance . . . and did they notice the hand squeeze? There were no points for that, but it spoke well for a call—

She almost tripped over her feet, and not because she was clumsy, but because the Earl of Rochdale stood right at the edge of the dance floor and he was not happy.

In fact, he watched her as if he was willing some extremely nasty curse upon her person. No wonder she had tripped.

In response to his sourness, she leaned in more than proper to the duke and let her hip brush against his. Did Rochdale notice her advance? Good!

The pattern changed direction, calling for the men to place a hand on their partner's waist. The duke's hand held her waist with the weight of possession. His grin said he was enjoying himself and was eager for their dance pattern to bring them close again.

Normally, Leonie would be alarmed. She liked to keep a bit of control on the men in her sphere. Distance was a good way to keep them at bay.

However, anger and pride combined to make her flaunt the rules, just as she had that fateful night in India so long ago.

Back then, Roman Gilchrist had scowled as he watched her dance with another man.

Suddenly, past became present. Memories, mistakes, and the horror of one fateful night roiled inside her with such force Leonie stopped dancing.

The debutante next to her didn't notice and almost tripped over her with a small cry of alarm.

Leonie looked at the girl in confusion, her mind lost in a moment no one could see save herself. She took a step back and almost ran into the dancer behind her.

The duke came to a halt and, therefore, so did everyone else around him despite the music merrily playing along. There was chaos on the floor and it was all Leonie's fault.

"I'm so sorry," Leonie said to Camberly. "I don't feel well." She placed her hand to her abdomen and, without waiting for a response, she tore off the dance floor, and away from Gilchrist's disturbing presence.

The crowd parted for her. The duke called her name. She escaped to the hallway.

There, lifting her skirts, she ran as far from the ballroom as she could, opening a door and finding the marquis's library.

The room was thankfully, blessedly empty. A lamp was burning and there were chairs in front of a cold hearth. Leonie didn't think twice about closing the door behind her. She leaned against it, praying no one saw her come into the room, and then slowly sank to her knees.

She could not go back out there. The humiliation was too much to bear. Everyone would be talking about her and her father would be furious.

Minutes passed with the only sound being the pounding of her heart and her frantic breathing. Her mind would not shut off. She did feel sick. *She did.*

She lifted her hands to feel her forehead—and then gave a small gasp. In the lamp's light, they appeared covered with blood.

Dear Lord, there had been so much blood that night. She'd tried to staunch its flow and yet it kept coming . . . and she'd begged Arthur not to die, even though she'd just shot him.

The worst had been watching the light of life fade from his eyes. She could even remember his last words to her—

A knock sounded on the door. "Miss Charnock."

It was Gilchrist. Panic sent her to the other side of the room. *"Leave me alone."*

In response, just like that night long ago, the door opened and Gilchrist entered the room.

Gilchrist, who knew what she had done.

Chapter 4

*D*espite the expensive appointments of the Marquis of Devon's library, entering it eerily reminded Roman of his entrance into another room half a decade and half a world away. That room had held the meanest of furnishings and the air had smelled of the wild and of sex and blood. In this moment, the past foreshadowed the present.

With the wisdom he'd gleaned from the East, Roman knew he had always been meant to be right here, right now.

He closed the door.

"Open it," Leonie ordered, her tone imperial, but there was another edge to it, one of fear.

So. He wasn't the only one experiencing this awareness of the past. She'd been frightened of him *that* night as well.

She backed another step into the far corner. Tension radiated from her. She did not look well.

"Leonie, he deserved to die."

She shook her head so vehemently a few curls escaped their careful pins.

"What Paccard did was wrong. You were protecting yourself." He'd spoken these same lines the night he'd found her with Arthur Paccard's body in the abandoned ruins of some raja's hunting palace in the deep forest. Roman had tried to catch her and Paccard in time, but had failed.

Not every rescue in life was successful.

She looked at her hands as if she could see something he didn't. She rubbed them together. "He didn't die right away."

"I know."

"It took a long time, or so it seemed. I tried to stop the blood."

"I remember."

Tears welled in her eyes. "You do, don't you? And you told everyone that you had found me safe before there was harm. You told them you shot Arthur. That the two of you had dueled over me."

That, too, was true.

"If I was in the right," she challenged, "why wouldn't you have told them that I was the one who shot him? Why did you claim he died in a duel?"

"It was easiest." It had also saved her reputation.

"But they blamed you. Everyone thought you did it because you were jealous that I favored him. That he died because you wished him dead."

The room suddenly closed in around Roman. So, she knew.

"Leonie, we don't need to talk about this."

"Yes, we do," she said. "I knew what they said and I didn't speak up. I didn't have the courage—"

"You had just turned seventeen. You were young—"

"I was old enough to know better," she countered, "as my father told me repeatedly after it was all over. He swears my being involved with the whole incident is the reason he has never received a knighthood. If he knew the truth, he'd disown me. My only worth to him is marrying the title he could never have. No one would touch me if they knew what had really happened."

"Then we won't tell them."

"You don't understand. It is not that simple—"

"Yes, it is."

When Roman had entered the library, releasing her of her guilt had not been his plan. She owed him a debt and he intended she pay up. Otherwise, he could lose Bonhomie.

However, faced with her shame, he found himself softening toward her. She'd been so young back then. He and Paccard had also been young and randy and frustrated to find themselves in India. Their feud over Leonie's affections had been intense and heated and it really hadn't had anything to do with her. It had been about keeping a step ahead of the other.

What would she say if she knew Paccard had left Roman a note that night bragging that he'd won her?

And that Roman had set out to prove him wrong?

"You rescued me," she said. "If you hadn't arrived when you did, I don't know what would have happened."

"Actually, you rescued yourself."

SHE HAD RESCUED *herself.*

Leonie had never considered the matter that way.

At the time, all she had wanted was to stop Arthur from hurting her, and he had been going to do it again. She'd made a terrible mistake in trusting him. She'd wanted to go home but he wouldn't let her.

When she had felt the small pistol that he'd usually carried in his coat pocket buried in the folds of the blanket, she hadn't been thinking of murder. She had just wanted him to leave her alone. She had been trying to give herself room to think, and then everything had gone wrong.

Years ago, she had misjudged Arthur. Of the two men, Arthur and Roman, she'd believed Arthur to be the better. He'd had more polish, had been places she could only imagine, and paid more attention to her.

Roman had treated her as if she was seventeen and pretending a sophistication she didn't have. He'd been right.

Once her family returned to London after spending most of

Leonie's life in Calcutta, she learned how little she knew about the world. Her life in India had been a protected one. As one of the few white women close to a marriageable age, she'd been the center of attention. She had assumed everyone had her best interests at heart. She'd been that naive.

Arthur had taught Leonie that there were dangers every-where, even on the dance floor.

She reached out and touched the marquis's heavy velvet drapes covering the window. "Was it hard for you in India after my family left? Father said that you would be fine. He said officers dueled all the time but I heard rumors with your name. And don't say something noble such as you were happy to be of service or some other such rot. I know you were accused of shooting Arthur in a jealous rage."

"I said he had issued the challenge. I could not back down. You and I were the only two there."

"And I had left for London."

He nodded, conceding her point. "I said I had no choice. It was self-defense."

There was a tightness in his voice. She sensed all had not been as easy as he seemed to wish her to believe. "I wanted to speak at your hearing but my parents had me on the first ship out of India."

"It was just as well you didn't speak on my behalf. You wouldn't have been invited to this ball."

Heat flooded Leonie's face. He was right. Both of her parents had warned her not to confess to a living soul that she had eloped with Paccard.

Occasionally, the story would float around but a word from her father usually quashed it. Of course, he couldn't control Leonie's memories or the horrid dreams that haunted her. Only a nip of brandy could do that.

She wished she had some right now. She looked around the room. There were decanters on an ornamental table—but she'd not take a sip in front of Roman. She couldn't imagine what he'd make of her lifting the bottle to her lips and having a quick taste. He wouldn't understand.

No one did.

He was watching her, his gaze intent as if he weighed an important matter in his mind, and it made her nervous. She realized she knew very little about him. Even back then, he'd been a mystery.

She smiled, anxious to take her leave, but before she could speak, he said, "You and I are going to marry."

Leonie gave a start, unsure she'd heard him correctly. "I beg your pardon."

"You heard me, Leonie. I came to this ball to seek you out. I had the intention of wooing you. However, I don't have that kind of time."

"Whoa, whoooo . . ." Leonie said in confusion. *"Marriage?* You want to marry me? Are you still carrying an affection for me after all these years? You don't appear to be a smitten swain."

"I'm not," Roman admitted.

"Are you suddenly overcome with desire?"

"You are lovely."

"You say that with the same passion that our family butler announces dinner is served."

"It is widely acknowledged that you are a beauty—unusual in your features, even exotic, but attractive, all the same."

"Attractive. I've moved from lovely to merely attractive? I can imagine the love poetry you would write to me—'Your eyes could have been compared to the stars but now they look like two pebbles in the village garden.' "

To his credit, a hint of a smile lifted his lips. "I don't write poetry. You need not worry about being compared to garden pebbles by me."

"Reassuring." Her breathing had returned to normal; her

heartbeat had steadied. The room around her no longer held horrors.

She'd faced the worst, she realized. She looked to Roman. "I've always feared that someday I would have to atone for that night. I don't know what would have happened if you hadn't taken the blame. You understood the price I would have had to pay."

He bowed, acknowledging her remark.

"And it means a great deal to me to see you faring so well," she continued. "An earldom is not enough of a reward for what you did for me."

The words sounded pretty to her ears. They were kind, benevolent, humble. "However—" She kept her voice gentle. "—I cannot accept your offer of marriage." If his informing her they would marry could be considered an "offer."

And then, because he of all people deserved an explanation, she said, "It is not you, my lord. I don't wish to marry anyone."

There, she'd said it aloud. Her secret.

"Then why are you here this evening?" he said.

"Must you always challenge everything I say?" she countered.

"Apparently."

Leonie made a sound of frustration. "I'm here for the same reason everyone is—my parents. They have been plotting for me to marry well since I was in the cradle. It is the only thing the two of them can agree upon. They wouldn't hear me if I told them what I wanted. Fortunately, last year, I was jilted by a duke. That has made me 'used' goods in some people's eyes." She thought of Camberly. "Of course, my parents might still try to make me a duchess and then I would be forced to suffer through it all until he was bored with me."

"Suffer?"

Leonie met his quizzical gaze. "You *know* what I mean. That man thing."

"That 'man thing'?" he repeated. "No, I don't understand. And how can you wish to suffer through life?"

She blew out her breath in exasperation. "I *don't* wish to suffer through life. Which is the reason I don't wish to marry. I want something *more* from my life." And she wanted to be in control of what that was.

He considered her a moment. "So, you would marry Camberly?"

Leonie crossed her arms. "I suppose I would. Then I'd be a duchess."

"Is that what you want from your life?"

"It is what my parents wish."

"Camberly has a man thing."

His statement caught her off guard. "What?" Was he mocking her?

He appeared completely serious, even as he said, "You said you didn't want a man thing and I pointed out that Camberly has a man thing. At least, I believe he does. I don't know that for a fact, however, most men have a man thing."

"More's the pity," she snapped.

"Yes, but you said you were open to a ducal man thing, but how do you know an earl man thing wouldn't be better?"

"Because one belongs to a duke."

"But what if the duke doesn't know what to do with his man thing? Is that what you meant by suffering through life?"

Leonie would have dearly loved to slap him again, except her wrist still hurt from the last one. "I don't find you amusing."

He shrugged, the picture of reasonableness. "You are the one who brought up the subject of man things."

She felt her jaw tighten. "I wasn't talking about what I think you are talking about."

"Then what were you talking about?"

Leonie could have screamed. Now she remembered why she had favored Arthur Paccard over Roman. Arthur had been courtly and light. Roman had been serious and had on occasion let her know he believed her immature. His verdict had angered her. Even at seventeen she had known her own mind . . . and she didn't like being told she didn't.

Then again, Leonie had never been so happy to see someone as she had Roman when he'd come upon her and Arthur. He'd been a savior.

She changed the subject. "Do you wish that dance or not?"

"Will you accept my marriage offer?"

"You are astounding. I've done my best to be as kind as possible, my lord. However, you leave me no choice other than to be blunt—"

"I've always appreciated your bluntness more than your kindness, Miss Charnock," he interjected, matching her formality.

She could have boxed his ears. He was deliberately making this difficult. She decided to move on with it. "Thank you for your offer but I will not marry you."

He appeared far from disheartened. Instead of saying the usual proper words to gracefully accept a rejection, he said, "Oh, you will marry me. You owe me, Leonie. I lied for you once. It cost me my military career. It turns out they don't take kindly to officers shooting each other, even in affairs of honor. The time has come to pay up. I need your dowry."

The stab of disappointment confused her. She knew her dowry was all any of them, including Camberly, wanted. However, against all logic, she had expected at least a bit of earnest pretense from Roman. Instead, he behaved as if this was a business transaction—which marriage was, except she was rather offended by this attitude of his.

"I see," she said airily. "I am nothing more than a bag of money to you."

"Well, there are your 'garden pebbles.' I do have a man thing, you know."

"Then you best be careful because it may fall off from neglect," Leonie returned, matching his mock seriousness.

Roman grinned, the expression changing his face. He appeared younger and more relaxed. Ah, yes, when Roman let down his guard, no one could be more charming—

The door to the room was thrown open by a laughing young woman pursued by an amorous lord, his arms around her waist. Light flooded in from the hallway as the couple came to a halt upon discovering the marquis's study occupied.

"Oh, I'm so sorry," the gentleman said. The woman giggled her thoughts.

Leonie seized the interruption to leave. "It is of no matter," she hastened to say, crossing the room and slipping around the couple. "We were just discussing something but I must return to the ballroom." She started walking swiftly in that direction. There were other couples in the hall. The marquis's punch was having a potent effect. They were huddled together in that way of lovers. Leonie tried not to look at them as she hurried along.

She had reached the ballroom door when she sensed rather than heard Roman's presence behind her. His hand touched her elbow. "I will claim that dance now."

Leonie could refuse, or she could give a bit of her time as a peace offering.

"Very well," she decided, and took his offered arm. She did not look at him but she was *very* aware of him. *Too* aware.

"You should smile," he whispered as they were taking their places for the next musical set.

She did as bid, plastering a false sweetness across her face. He rolled his eyes to let her know he was not impressed.

Truly, the man was like vinegar in her life. To keep a bit of her own, she observed in a whisper, "Most men would not wish a dance after their marriage offer, however calculating, was turned down."

"Calculating? You wound me, Miss Charnock."

"You appear anything but wounded, my lord."

His eyes met hers. They were gray, the silver gray of coins or a bolt of lightning . . . she remembered thinking when they first met that they were the most unusual eyes she had ever seen. Eyes that could reveal everything or nothing.

Right now, they gave no indication of anything other than a mildly amused gentleman waiting with his lady for a dance.

The music began. Leonie enjoyed dancing and could often lose herself in the music and the patterns. This time, she found herself watching Rochdale.

Roman was a proud man. In India, several of the other officers had mentioned he had rather humble roots. No, not other officers—*Arthur* had mentioned that fact. Arthur had not wanted her giving even a sidelong glance to another man, and she didn't—at least not overtly. However, she had noticed the new young lieutenant and she'd been quite taken with him, especially because she was growing tired of Arthur's petty jealousies.

To be honest, Leonie didn't know why she let Arthur convince her to elope. Such a silly, foolish idea now, but at the time, she had been swept up into the excitement of being wanted, of being chosen.

Now, she could see how much she had longed to be noticed all her life. Her parents were locked in their own battles. At the time, it was over her mother's indiscretion with a clerk in the main counting office. They rarely spoke to each other, let alone their daughter. They'd been consumed with their own lives.

Arthur had offered freedom from that world and she'd grabbed at her chance to escape.

She glanced at Roman. He was a good dancer. She remembered this from the past. The other women in their set had noticed him as well. Leonie could imagine that if he and Camberly were placed side by side, she might choose Roman.

He caught her regard and gave her a smile, just as the pattern of the dance had them both turn away—and a wayward thought struck her, one she'd never considered before.

It was so startling that she missed her next step. She recovered but could not wait for the music to be over.

He bowed over her hand. "Thank you for this dance."

She didn't mince words. "Why *did* you follow Arthur and me that night? How did you know where we were? What made you come after us?"

Chapter 5

God save him from intelligent women.

Leonie Charnock had the mind of a barrister. These were the questions Roman didn't want to answer, the ones he'd thought long and hard about.

Before he could muster a response, a tall, blonde woman linked her arm with Leonie's. "I've been looking for you. What are the points for being escorted to the supper room?" Her eyes sparkled with anticipation. In fact, she was so intent on sharing her news she hadn't truly registered Roman's presence until Leonie brought him to her attention.

Pointedly, she said to her friend, "May I introduce you to the Earl of Rochdale? My lord, this is Miss Holwell."

Holwell. Another of the Spinster Heiresses.

Miss Holwell blushed prettily at her own forwardness and Roman realized this was his chance to avoid Leonie's questions. He was not ready to reveal too much to her.

He made his bow to the new heiress before saying, "Miss Charnock, may I return you . . . ?" She shook her head. "Ah, then," he said gratefully, "I will leave the two of you to your confidences." Roman walked away before Leonie could reply.

The crowd had not thinned. He used it to hide, swiftly moving away from her until, safe, he glanced back.

Leonie watched him. She knew he had evaded her . . . and he also knew the conversation between them was not over.

LEONIE COULD NOT believe that she had been so naive all those years ago to not have wondered why Roman had been there that night. She'd been too thankful he had appeared when he did to ask any questions. Indeed, she would have appreciated him even more two hours earlier, but he had been a godsend when he'd walked through the door of that hovel.

Still, *why* had he been there?

She followed his tall figure through the marquis's guests so intently she was not surprised when he stopped and looked to her. Their gazes held. She knew she was being bold, but let him be wary. Let him wonder what she was thinking—

"Leonie, who is that gentleman?" Cassandra asked.

Pulling her gaze from Rochdale's, Leonie said, "The Earl of Rochdale. I introduced you."

"You did . . . but there seems to be something between the two of you?"

"There is *nothing* between us." Leonie faced her friend. "What were you saying? You have six points?"

"Yes," Cassandra said, happily changing the conversation to herself, "and Camberly escorted me into the supper room after we danced. How many points is that?"

"Well done. Out of all the pigeons in this room, he chose you. The Vetter sisters and our dear Lady Bettina must be green around the gills with envy."

Cassandra lowered her voice to concede, "They are. Even Willa is a bit jealous. That doesn't happen often. Usually, I'm the jealous one. I saw him dance with you so you have at least five points."

Leonie nodded absently, her mind taken up with the sight of Roman leading Lady Imogen out onto the floor. Leonie had suspected he had hurried away to avoid answering her questions, but what if he'd just wanted to dance with someone else? Even though he'd told her in the marquis's library he intended to marry her?

Or was he going around the room asking for the hand of every heiress? It would be a short trip. There weren't that many.

Beside her, Cassandra prattled on. "His Grace told me you had taken ill. I was happy to see you were still here. Oh, by the by, Lady Bettina wants to be certain you don't claim points for dancing with him. She says you didn't finish the dance."

Women could be so competitive. However, Leonie had weightier things on her mind than the game. "I won't."

"So, what do you think of him?"

What *did* she think about *him*? Her mind on Roman, Leonie said, "I do not think he is being entirely honest with me."

"What?" Cassandra said with alarm, and Leonie realized she'd spoken aloud.

"I'm sorry, Cassandra. My mind was on something else. What did you ask?"

"Were you thinking about the duke?"

"No," Leonie admitted.

Cassandra frowned thoughtfully and looked in the direction Leonie had been facing. "The earl? Interesting."

"Not very." Leonie forced a smile. "He writes terrible poetry. He compared me to garden pebbles."

Cassandra stifled a laugh, and Leonie smiled, feeling they would safely move on to other topics and they did. They went back to the duke. "What did you think of Camberly?"

"I found him understanding when I had to race off the dance floor." Leonie didn't know if this was true or not, but did it matter?

It did to Cassandra. "Yes, understanding. He is, and it is such a good quality. What else do you think of him?"

Leonie really hadn't given him much thought. "He's young and attractive."

"Oh, *yes*." There was a swell of warmth in Cassandra's words. "I was stunned when he asked to escort me to the supper room. Every woman here had been making calf eyes at him and he chose me. The *tall* one. The *big* one. You know what they whisper. But do you know what? Camberly is taller than I am by several inches. Lady Bettina was eaten up with jealousy. I could see it in her eyes."

"So, what happened in the supper room?" Leonie prodded.

"He was the very picture of a gentleman. He offered to fill my plate and he didn't give just a spoonful of peas or a half of a pheasant wing like so many others do. He was generous."

"And the conversation?"

"Wonderful, except Soren York joined us."

"Soren York?"

"Lord Dewsberry. He is a family neighbor and a bigger oaf you could never hope to meet. He should have known I wished to be alone with His Grace. Instead, he invited himself to sit right down and take up the conversation. Apparently, they are great friends. I hinted to him that the duke and I were enjoying a companionable moment but he didn't pay any mind. I tell you, Leonie, if Dewsberry has ruined my chance with Camberly, I don't know what I shall do to him."

"If the duke escorted you to the supper room and filled your plate, then there must be some interest."

"I pray it is so. If he doesn't call on me, I don't know what I'll do. He's *the one*."

"The one?"

"Yes, *the one*. The husband I have always dreamed of. The man who would be perfect for me."

"And you discovered all of that in a dance and spot of supper?"

"I knew it the moment I laid eyes on him."

"Ah," Leonie said, pretending to understand. In a way, she did. Arthur Paccard had been very handsome, but looks lie. That was a hard lesson she'd learned.

She also didn't believe there was a "one." She'd never witnessed the sort of love the poets praised. Lust, yes. Love, no.

Gently, she suggested, "The handsome ones do make you feel that way, but give it time. Learn to know his character."

Cassandra grabbed Leonie's arm. "My feelings for him run deeper than that. Someday you will know how I feel when you find 'the one.' There isn't any of us who wants to be alone, not really. I mean, the three of us have all said we could manage, but when I was dancing with Camberly, I thought, yes, this is where I belong . . ." Her voice trailed off in a sigh.

"Excuse me, Miss Holwell?" a deep voice interrupted them. A strapping young man with a Viking's blond hair stood before Cassandra. He, too, was inches taller than her. "Will you give me the honor of this dance?"

Cassandra's immediate response was a frown. She made a begrudging introduction to Leonie. "This is Lord Dewsberry. He and my family have been neighbors of sorts in Cornwall forever. My lord, this is my good friend Miss Charnock."

This was the man Cassandra was avoiding. If he'd been a short, pock-faced, squeaky thing, Leonie could understand her friend's complaints about him. However, Dewsberry was certainly as handsome in his way—well, there was the nose that had obviously been broken a time or two—as the Duke of Camberly.

Dewsberry bowed over the hand Leonie offered. "Of course, I have heard of you, Miss Charnock. Those who praise your beauty have not exaggerated."

His compliment sounded a bit rote but Leonie didn't mind. She was more bemused that he seemed obviously smitten with Cassandra . . . while Cassandra appeared anxious to avoid him. Perhaps if they had not been neighbors?

"Why have we not met before, my lord?" Leonie asked. Cassandra had never mentioned him.

"I spent time in the Canadian wilderness seeing to family interests and then my father died and we have been in mourning."

"I'm so sorry."

"Thank you for your kind thoughts." He looked to Cassandra. "The set is starting. Will you come? You have not danced with me this evening."

"I haven't seen you dance at all, my lord," Cassandra complained. They spoke with the familiarity of people who had run around in nappies together.

"I am honored you noticed," he answered. "Flattered actually." Leonie almost laughed at the way Cassandra reacted, as if she could bite her tongue for having said such a thing.

Lord Dewsberry offered his arm. "Come on, Cass."

She did not take his arm. "I detest being call Cass."

"Come along, *Cassie*?" He was prodding now. Leonie rather liked his spirit because everyone knew she hated "Cassie" most of all.

"Soren, what is my name?"

He grinned as if he'd known this was the way to earn her full attention upon him. "Miss Holwell," he said easily, "will you join me on the dance floor?"

"I wish I could but then that would leave Miss Charnock alone," Cassandra announced, but Leonie would have none of that. She rather liked Lord Dewsberry.

"Please, Cassandra, don't worry. I am returning to my mother's side." Leonie had no idea if her mother was there or not. She just didn't want the handsome Lord Dewsberry to be crestfallen on her account.

"Well—" Cassandra started, ready to have another excuse, but Lord Dewsberry interrupted her.

"Capital," he answered, seizing the answer he wanted before she could give him the one he didn't.

Cassandra groaned. "Don't talk that way," she chastised as he took Cassandra's hand, practically dragging her to the dance floor.

Leonie looked at the other couples. Willa was paired with the handsome Camberly. They appeared almost comical together with him so tall and her so petite. Lady Bettina was shooting daggers at Willa with her eyes. Clearly, Cassandra wasn't Camberly's only conquest. Leonie wondered what Willa would say about him. She didn't seem impressed.

Roman wasn't amongst the dancers.

Had he left?

She didn't dare search him out. In fact, she was diligently working to not make eye contact with any other gentleman. She was suddenly exhausted. Ducking her head, she made her way to the card room.

Fortunately, her father, too, was ready to leave. His luck had not lasted. He'd lost all that he'd won. They decided to take their leave.

Her father did not inquire about her mother's whereabouts and Leonie had learned long ago not to ask questions. She might not like the answer.

"So," her father said the moment the coach door was closed. "What do you think of Rochdale?"

"He is polite."

"Ha!" her father answered. "Polite." He sat back in his seat and looked at the window. "I like him. You will receive him."

"Why bother with preliminaries? Why not order me to marry him and we will have the ceremony tomorrow?"

"I am," her father said, swinging his head around to pin her. "Unless you land something better, you'll take his offer when he makes it."

"Why are you certain he will?" And what would he say if he knew Rochdale had already made his offer? Well, his order, to be precise.

His response was to grin at her as if she was daft in the head.

"I'm not so certain," she replied, looking at her own window.

There was a long moment of silence between them and then he said, "I owe him, you know. When you eloped, he brought you back. Unfortunate that they dueled and Paccard died. If you hadn't been so foolish, it would have been better for both men."

A weight formed in Leonie's chest. She curled her fingers, feeling her nails through her kid gloves. She spoke, choosing her words carefully. "You have never said this."

"I've thought it. Everyone knew it. Two good men. One gone and the other . . . ?" He faced Leonie. "His career was ruined. You play fast and loose, daughter."

"Like mother like daughter?" she challenged.

But instead of an angry reply, her father just stretched to make himself more comfortable in the seat. "Mayhap. Your mother is never satisfied. What of you, daughter dear? Do you know when enough is enough?"

His assessment startled her. "How do I answer such a question?"

"You don't. You do as I say. I meant my words when I told you this is the last Season, Leonie. Do you know what they call you? The Spinster Heiress."

"Miss Reverly and Miss Holwell are also addressed by that term. It is not so much our unmarried state as a put-down of who we are. The other girls are jealous."

"Not any longer. The three of you have been around too long. Oh, don't protest," he said as she started to open her mouth. "I know that I'm as guilty as you are for your not marrying. I wish we'd brought in Baynton last year. We almost had him."

"You make it sound as if we are fishing—"

"We are! And you, my lovely daughter, are the bait. I should have made you accept Gentry's, Oldton's, and Phillips's offers when they made them the first year, but I let your success over-rule my better judgement. I was certain you could fetch a better title than what those lads had. And you will, if you take Rochdale."

"I'm not comfortable around Lord Rochdale."

"I'm grateful to him. Granted, I would rather he hadn't put a bullet in Paccard, but I am relieved he fetched you back."

She shifted in her seat. "All he wants is money."

"Aye, that is true. I never said he wasn't sensible."

"Then pay him off. Why make me marry him?"

"Because he asked for your hand."

"Was I to be consulted?" She knew she sounded petulant.

"I'm telling you now. I want you married. Rochdale will take you. I expect you to encourage his suit. You become a countess and he will have the money he needs to repair the reputation of the title. The old earl ran up gambling debts and bled the estate dry. It is a good bargain for both of you, and one that is fair to him."

He had also accepted the blame for Arthur's death, a small voice said inside Leonie. If anyone knew the truth, she did not know what the consequences would be. Could she be charged with murder? Certainly, there would be an inquiry.

For the shortest of seconds, she debated telling her father, of relieving herself of the burden of her secret. The horror of it.

Then again, once she'd arrived in London, a world away from Calcutta, she had put it out of her mind. She had been that shallow. With the help of her occasional nip of brandy, well, she'd managed.

No, telling her father would not be wise.

The coach slowed to a halt in front of their stately brick home. The footman opened the coach door. Leonie climbed out. Her father didn't follow. "Aren't you coming?" she asked.

"I'm not ready to call it a night. You sleep tight, daughter."

He barely waited until she reached the step before signaling the coachman to be on their way.

Leonie nodded to Yarrow, the family butler, who held the front door open. "Did you have a good evening, miss?"

"Pleasant," she replied, saying what was expected. She always did what was expected—except for the night she eloped.

Over her years in London, Yarrow had been a constant presence that she could count on more than her parents. He usually was the only one to greet her when she came in. She started up the stairs, but then stopped. "Do you believe in marriage, Yarrow?"

The butler considered the matter a moment and then said, "I believe it works for some people."

"Does it work for my parents?"

"You know I can't answer your question, Miss Leonie."

He was right. She did know he should not answer such a question. "Good night."

"Good night, miss."

Most nights she was alone in the house with the servants and yet this night was different—and that was because of the unsettling presence of Roman Gilchrist.

How simple her life would be if her father would just give Roman the money he wanted and she could be left to live her life as she saw fit.

She didn't want to see Roman's "man thing." Or carry any more guilt. Or fear . . .

Leonie didn't know what to.

But she knew one woman who might—her mother. She might have the power to change her father's mind.

Walking to her bedroom, Leonie stopped by the upstairs study to sneak a fortifying nip of brandy from the bottles kept there. She then went to her room, dressed for bed, and dismissed her maid, Minnie.

However, instead of crawling between her sheets, Leonie walked down the hall to her mother's suite of rooms. It had been some time since she'd been in here. Her family led very separate lives.

Her mother had excellent taste in furnishings and a flair for drama. The walls were painted a dark green like the most lush and vibrant vegetation. The bed linens were snow white. The furniture was upholstered in rich, gold brocade.

Over the dressing table was a mirror of hammered brass. Leonie remembered sneaking into her mother's wardrobe and trying on shawls and hats to admire herself in the glass. The scent of incense fragranced the air.

A lamp was burning and there was a small coal fire in the hearth, although her mother's maid, Anna, was not waiting up. Leonie pulled a folded blanket out of the carved chest at the foot of the bed and took the most comfortable chair in front of the hearth. She wrapped herself in the blanket and set about the tedious business of waiting for her mother.

Chapter 6

A shake of her shoulder woke Leonie. She came to her senses with a start. She was cold. And uncomfortable. She looked around, not recognizing her surroundings. Her sleep had been deep and she wasn't ready to leave it.

"Return to your room," her mother's soft voice suggested. She stood over Leonie holding a lamp. She was dressed in her evening finery except that her golden hair was loose and over one shoulder.

Leonie remembered where she was and why. Squinting in the lamplight, she asked, "What time is it?"

"Shortly before dawn."

Few women were as lovely as Elizabeth Charnock. She had been a bishop's daughter. Once, when he was in his cups, her father had told Leonie he'd spied the beautiful Elizabeth Snavely in services and had been smitten.

Since her father had rarely stepped foot in church in Leonie's lifetime, she doubted if that story was true.

What she could believe is that her father had taken one look and wanted Elizabeth. Men always did, even younger men. Whenever Leonie was out with her mother, wandering eyes would settle on Elizabeth first.

There was a natural grace to her that Leonie wished she had. Her mother's movements were always deliberate, always considered, in spite of obviously being up all night.

Her coloring was also different than the daughter's. Elizabeth's eyes were the blue of cornflowers and her flawless skin a creamy white. Even their lips were different. Leonie's mouth was wide, generous, full. Her mother's were cupid bows that could pout their way into a man's heart. Leonie had witnessed her doing it more than once and her mother's jewelry box teemed with gifts from admirers trying to make her smile.

The one thing they shared were slim figures and thick, heavy hair. Elizabeth's hair was smooth as glass; Leonie's was the burnished gold of a lion's pelt—an unusual color—and she couldn't stop it from breaking out into unruly waves of curl.

Leonie untucked her body in the chair, placing her slippered feet on the floor. "I must talk to you."

"I assumed." Her mother moved to her dressing table and began removing her jewelry. "You rarely make social visits."

"You rarely have time for them."

Elizabeth gave a small shrug. "You are right." She sat on the dressing table's bench, facing Leonie. "Come, tell me what is so important that it has taken you from your bed." She yawned, reached for her silver hairbrush, and began brushing out her hair.

Leonie tried to collect her thoughts. Words that had seemed so clear to her before she'd fallen asleep now seemed a jumble. Finally, she said what was uppermost on her mind. "Is it possible to marry and live separate lives?"

"Of course, your father and I do."

"I mean 'separate,'" Leonie emphasized.

Her mother caught her eye in the mirror. Her arm holding the brush had gone still. She set the brush in its place. "More than just different bedrooms? Different houses?"

"Different locations. And not consummating the marriage. Ever."

Her mother started to laugh, and then, seeing that Leonie was serious, sobered. "How unalike we are," she murmured. "Very well, no, there isn't a gentleman that *I* would allow my daughter to marry who would refuse to consummate the marriage. I realize as your mother I could be considered guilty of benign neglect on many occasions. However, even I have standards."

"Then I don't wish to marry."

"What would you do with your life?"

Well, that was the question, wasn't it? Leonie grabbed the first answer to come into her sleep-addled mind. "I would dedicate myself to good works."

Her mother's brows lifted. "So noble. But then, what would you do when you don't have good works to occupy your time?"

"I would read. And perhaps help Cassandra Holwell with her literary salon. She has started one."

"This sounds very French." Her mother's tone held a hint of mockery.

"Yes, it is, and if it didn't work, because it hasn't been too successful yet, then I would find something to do that is worthwhile. There are plays, the opera, museums, exhibits. London has much to offer."

"The amusements are many . . . or, my darling, you could find a husband who lets you do as you wish."

"Does Father give you complete freedom?"

There was a beat of silence. Her mother stared into space as if she could see something Leonie couldn't. Then she turned to her daughter. "I am who I am, Leonie. I make no apologies. However, I have never said no to your father. It is he who does not come to my bed. Not since you were born—Oh, here, I've shocked you. That was not my intent. But you are of an age when we should be able to speak freely, no?"

Leonie didn't know how to answer.

Her mother leaned forward. "I am not the sort of woman to toddle off and let her life be over. Am I to be condemned for that? Of course I know what the gossips say. I don't care. All marriages are subject to the whims of those involved and can be as stifling as the crypt."

"Then why would you push me to marry?"

"Because an unmarried woman has few rights. No protections. You would be an oddity and you do not want that. I know what you and your two friends say. I've heard your whispers. I hear more than people think I do. You may dream of a life where you make your own choices, Leonie, but you'll never live that life until you marry, and hopefully to a generous spouse— one who lets you do as you wish. And you had best be faithful, until after you have given him an heir, of course. Then you can take on all the lovers you wish."

"You didn't give Father an heir."

A look crossed her mother's face that Leonie couldn't decipher. Was she pleased or regretful? "It did not matter to him. He was happy with a daughter to sell off."

To sell off . . . yes, that was what her father was doing. Selling his daughter for a title for his heirs.

"And that is the problem," Leonie said, choosing her words carefully. "I don't know that I want a man's thing near me."

"His thing?" Her mother's brows came together and she started laughing. "Leonie, it is called a *cock*. If you are fortunate enough to marry a man who knows how to use his, you will be a happy woman. A 'thing,' " she repeated, and laughingly shook her head before looking up as if struck by a new thought. "Does this have anything to do with that unpleasantness in India?"

She didn't wait for Leonie's answer but said, "I feared he'd taken you. Your father refused to think on it, but *I knew*. Paccard had you, didn't he? You are no longer a virgin."

Leonie balked. "Why are you asking me such a question? Especially after so much time has passed. One would think you would have been more concerned when I returned."

"I feared the answer when you returned. Besides, what with Paccard's death, you were more than a touch hysterical. One wrong word and you turned into a watering pot."

That was true. Leonie had been horrified at what had happened to her, at what she'd done.

"But the bastard took you, didn't he?" Her mother opened a dressing table drawer and pulled out her silver flask. She unscrewed the top and took a drink. She offered it to Leonie, who shook her head. It was a point of honor with Leonie that, although she had taken a nip out of almost every bottle on display in the house, and there were many, she did not touch her mother's flask.

Well, she had one time—when Roman had returned her to her parents after her elopement. She had been frightened and inconsolable. She hadn't eaten or slept. While Roman had conferred with her father, her mother had pulled out her flask.

"Drink," she'd said, and Leonie had obeyed. That was her introduction to brandy and it had been a good one. Within minutes, the most delicious warmth had spread through Leonie and she'd been able to regain control over herself. She'd even had a second nip.

In truth, Leonie hadn't much liked the taste that first time, but she'd enjoyed the feeling brandy gave her. Whenever she felt a bit anxious, or the memories and guilt of that night became too much for her, a nip always helped. Always. Some days she couldn't go without two or three.

But she had not touched her mother's flask since that night.

Her mother had another good pull on the flask and then screwed the top back on. "At least no harm was done," she said as if reaching a decision. She opened the drawer to replace her flask.

"No harm?" Leonie was confused.

"No child." Her mother closed the drawer.

"My Indian maid at the time, Adya, had me drink a tea." It had been foul tasting. "She said it would prevent a baby."

"Adya? I don't remember her."

"You might not." Her mother didn't pay attention to servants.

Her mother pondered for a moment and then gave Leonie a small smile. "Well, everything ends well." The brandy was making her mellow. She changed the subject. "Have you seen Lieutenant Gilchrist recently? He was the man who returned you to us and was almost court-martialed for fighting a duel over you. I was told this evening that someone saw him in town."

Leonie was surprised her mother would single out Roman. "He was at the marquis's ball."

"Oh." Her mother pulled her hair over one shoulder to curl around her hand. "The world is a curious place. Whoever thought we would see him again?" Her lips curved into a sly smile. "I remember him as brawny man with the clearest gray eyes. Tall, dark haired. Interesting, especially after he shot his best friend over you. I may have to search him out to express my appreciation for what he did years ago."

Leonie didn't want to think about what she meant. She stood abruptly. The hour was too late for her spend it watching her mother moon over Roman. She'd received the answer to her questions—her parents would not support her living on her own. And she would probably not escape marriage.

"I've taken up enough of your time, Mother." Leonie bent to give her mother a dutiful peck on the cheek. "Thank you for talking to me."

"I enjoyed myself." Her mother stood and moved toward the bed. Leonie was almost to the door when she said, "Remember, daughter, a woman's power is between her legs. Don't be afraid to use it."

A picture rose in Leonie's mind of Arthur over her, his hand smelling of horses and leather a weight across her mouth to stop her screams, his "cock"—see? She could use adult words—tearing her to pieces inside.

That was power?

Her smile felt frozen. "Good night, Mother."

"Good night, lamb."

Leonie escaped the bedroom. She started for her own room, but then stopped and walked to the study. Just a nip would help ease her anxiousness. She made her way to her bed.

She climbed onto the plush feather mattress and pulled sheets of the finest linen over her. She stared at the bed canopy, wishing her mind would stop its frantic working.

A woman's power is between her legs.

After Arthur was done with her, she'd never felt so abused or powerless. She remembered her fingers finding the pistol that had fallen from his coat pocket. Then she'd had power.

Dear God, she wished she'd never shot him, and yet, what would have become of her if she hadn't?

This time, the brandy was not successful at chasing the "what ifs" from her brain . . .

If she had to marry someone, she'd rather it be Roman. He was right: she did owe him that much. But on what terms?

Hugging her pillow to her, her mind was suddenly alive with possibilities. She came from a long line of merchants and traders. She'd been taught that money had power . . . if she knew how to use it.

A plan began to form in her mind.

ROMAN PUNCHED DOWN the hard pillow beneath his head. The hour was well past dawn and he hated not having a good night's sleep. He'd had few of late. Money worries ate away at his serenity. Money worries and thoughts of Leonie.

He reimagined the scenes between them the night before.

They had unfinished business and he would have no peace until they had a meeting of the minds.

That would be difficult because Leonie had made it very clear she would not consider his marriage offer. She probably wanted what all women seemed to desire these days—love.

Roman didn't have time for love. He had people depending upon him. He had an estate to rebuild. He had so many dreams, he didn't have time for courting.

By the time his man, Duncan Barr, knocked on the door of his rented rooms with his breakfast, Roman had worked himself into a foul mood. It was too bad Erzy and Malcolm had presented their vouchers for pay yesterday rather than today. Yesterday, Roman had been intimidated by the weight of taking his seat in the Lords.

Today, he was ready to act out his frustration.

Duncan had been Roman's orderly when he'd first arrived in India and had remained loyally by his side throughout the fluctuations of his career. He now served as valet and secretary. He was a crusty Scot, twenty years older than Roman, and as ready as his master to return to Bonhomie and build a peaceful life. He was as close a friend as Roman could ever wish and didn't cater to Roman's moods. He carried a tray with covered dishes for Roman's breakfast along with a pot of tea brewed so strong a man's whiskers would pop out of his face with just one sip.

"Rough night, sir?" Barr set the tray on the desk, using the space Roman had just cleared by moving unread papers out of the way.

Roman grunted his thoughts, rubbed his eyes, and rose from bed. He reached for the offered mug of tea. It was hot as hades. The first drink woke him. The second fortified him. Roman knew by the time he reached the bottom, there wasn't any challenge he couldn't face.

He smiled his pleasure and then noticed a sealed envelope next to his silverware.

Seeing where Roman's eye had landed, Barr said, "It arrived this morning. A servant delivered it. He said no response was needed."

Roman picked up the envelope while Barr busied himself around the room, preparing to help his master dress. The handwriting on the address was decidedly feminine. There was no signet to the seal. Roman cracked it open and literally took a step back in surprise.

"Good or bad news, sir?" the unflappable Barr asked. He set impeccably polished boots out for Roman to wear.

"I don't know." Roman reread the words written in a surprisingly mature hand. He'd always imagined Leonie as one of those women who made wide loops on her "l's" and "e's." "Miss Charnock has requested I call on her concerning a matter of mutual interest to us both."

Barr froze in the act of laying out Roman's shaving instruments. "Miss *Charnock*?"

"Aye, the one and same. I didn't mention her last night because I thought she was done with me." He looked down at the note. "Apparently not."

Straightening, Barr said, "I would think you would give a wide berth to that creature. Even without her past, it is a bold, forward move to send a missive to a single gentleman." Duncan was not one to hold back his opinion.

"If I was wise, I would do as you suggest," Roman agreed, aware that while moments before he'd been tired and irritable, he now experienced a surge of energy.

He sat at his desk, pulled out a sheet of paper, and wrote an answer: *I beg leave to call upon you at four o'clock.* He sanded the letter, blew it off, and sealed it. He offered it to Barr, who did not make a move toward him.

"Are you arranging an assignation with that creature?"

"Her name is Miss Charnock, and yes."

"Do you not have a brain in your head? She ruined you the last time you helped her."

"Deliver it, Barr. This may be my only hope. Or . . . you can visit me in debtors' prison."

Duncan took the letter.

Chapter 7

Ten minutes until four.

Leonie sat in the side room located off the receiving room, waiting, her least favorite task. This was a cozy room with painted wood paneling and upholstered furniture in contrast to the larger room's formality. There was a solid double door between them. She chose to wait for Roman here rather than upstairs.

She wore a day dress of emerald-green cambric with a high-necked bodice trimmed in a lace ruffle. It was the most modest dress she had in her wardrobe. She'd chosen it because she wished to persuade Rochdale into saying yes to her proposal, but for the *right* reasons, not the wrong ones. She did not wish to tease him.

Still, she knew the color complemented her eyes and brought out the golden highlights in her hair, which she had styled high upon her head. She'd spent hours over her toilette. For this meeting, every detail had to be perfect.

Leonie picked up the glass of brandy she had been sipping and glanced again at the clock on the mantel over the small hearth. Usually, she didn't use a glass. She had no desire to leave any evidence of her occasional nips, but today was different. For what she planned to do, she needed fortification and a "nip" wouldn't be enough.

On that thought, Leonie drained the glass and set it on the

side table. The swiftness of her swallow burned her throat, but the feeling was fleeting. It was replaced with the blessed awareness and confidence that she had come to trust.

Leonie had not told anyone of her planned appointment with Roman. Her mother had wanted her to accompany her to a dress fitting but Leonie had cried off, saying she had a headache. Her father usually spent the afternoon at his club, so she was alone.

During her first Season, Leonie's afternoons after an important rout had been filled with calls from gentleman admirers. Flowers had come through her door in wagonloads. It was telling that after the Marquis of Devon's ball, no one had called, not even to leave a card. No flowers graced the tables in the receiving room—which was what she'd wanted, no? Hadn't she believed herself tired of all the courting and silliness?

Funny, but she'd never stopped to think of those young women who made their debut and received little interest. Now she knew how peaceful their lives were. Of course, they probably didn't think of it that way.

Leonie wondered how Willa and Cassandra were faring? Had the Duke of Camberly called? That would be four points in the game.

Or was he visiting Lady Bettina? Cassandra would be eaten up with envy if he did. It would also mean, to Leonie's thinking, that Camberly was not "the one," if such a paragon existed—

A firm knock on the front door echoed in through the house just as the mantel clock chimed four.

Leonie rose to her feet. She suddenly didn't know what to do with her hands. She pressed them against her skirts.

She heard the door open and Yarrow's deep voice. She couldn't hear what was being said or the answer. She listened for footsteps and could imagine Yarrow leading Roman the few steps to the receiving room. She could see him offer the gentleman a seat before he sent a footman to search out his young mistress. She knew that Yarrow, being the guardian he was, would go in search of Mrs. Denbright, the housekeeper, to serve as chaperone since Leonie's parents were not present. In fact, she had counted upon his doing so.

She waited for footsteps to go up the stairs. She opened and closed her hands and walked to the double doors, throwing them open.

Roman stood looking out the front window. He appeared every inch the Corinthian with his buff breeches, shining boots, and a midnight-blue coat that emphasized the breadth of his shoulders. He was not a terrible choice for a husband. Certainly, there was something about him that attracted her, something that had made Arthur Paccard jealous.

At the sound of the doors opening, he'd turned, and did not seem surprised to see her. Amused gray eyes took in every detail of her appearance, including her well-covered bosom.

He approached, stopping a discreet three feet from her. He gave a short bow. "Hello, Miss Charnock."

She didn't waste time on niceties or offer her hand. If she did, she'd lose her courage.

"I need to speak to you alone and I don't have much time before Yarrow or Mrs. Denbright join us. Were you serious about your marriage offer last night?"

He schooled the surprise from his eyes. "I was."

"Then here are my terms." She'd spent most of the day thinking how she wanted to phrase her demands, but words that had sounded confident in her bedroom now seemed a bit unwise in front of him. Still, with the careless defiance of the brandy, she forged on.

"I will accept your offer and you may have my dowry and eventually my inheritance, provided I am your wife in name only. And," she hurried to add, "you will not set me aside but support me, in London, in the manner I wish to live."

There, she'd gotten it all out.

She squared her shoulders, ready for his acceptance or rejection. She'd prepared herself for both.

Instead, there was silence, and then he said, "Name only? What exactly does that mean?"

His query annoyed her. "It means what I said. Now will you take my offer or leave it?"

"Have you been drinking spirits?"

That was not a response Leonie had anticipated. "Why would you ask such a thing?"

"Because I'm catching a hint of brandy breath."

Brandy breath? Was there such a thing? Or was he toying with her? Roman Gilchrist had an alarming ability to throw her off guard. Suspicious, she lifted her chin. "I don't know why you would ever make such an accusation."

He gave a half laugh as if he was somewhat sorry. "I have been in His Majesty's Service for a long time and I know when someone is foxed."

"Foxed?" Leonie literally trembled at the charge. She was in complete control of her senses. "How dare you accuse me of such?"

Roman leaned back as if to both avoid her breath and savor it as the same time. "Vanilla. A hint of raisins. Yes, I believe you have been tippling the brandy. Please tell me, my lady, that this isn't a regular occurrence? Because if it is, we might have a problem."

Leonie could stomp her feet in outrage. "How *dare* you—" she started, only to be cut off by the sounds of hurried footsteps and the appearance of her maid, Minnie, in the doorway.

"Here you are, my lady," Minnie said, looking somewhat confused. "I needed to tell you there was a gentleman caller—" She'd been so focused on finding Leonie she had failed to register Roman's presence until that moment. Like a frightened mouse who had just discovered a cat was in the room, her lips closed and she slipped inside, taking the nearest chair closest to the door. She folded her hands in her lap, pretending not to be present or notice anything the way she knew Leonie preferred, and yet serving as a chaperone because her mistress should not be alone with a gentleman.

Yarrow, too, appeared outside the door. He hovered there, the frown on his face saying he knew Leonie had managed to avoid proprieties and was most annoyed—and not necessarily with her but with her parents. He'd be truly appalled if he knew she'd been tippling. She resisted the reflex to place her hand over her mouth as if Yarrow could catch a hint of her breath from where she stood.

However, her worries were unfounded because Roman took control.

"You are right on time," he said to Minnie, including Yarrow in his buoyant declaration. "Miss Charnock has accepted my offer of marriage."

Thoughts of covering her mouth with her hand vanished from Leonie's mind. "I . . . what—I—?"

"You said you would accept it," he argued.

Well, what she'd meant is she would accept his offer if he accepted hers—but she couldn't make that statement in front of Yarrow.

"This is grand news, my lord," Yarrow said approvingly. "Congratulations, Miss Leonie."

"Yes, congratulations," Minnie peeped up, rising from her chair.

Yarrow took charge. "I must send word to your father. He will wish to be here." He snapped his fingers for one of the footmen. "Go fetch the master at his club—"

"No, *wait*," Leonie said, moving toward him with her hand up. "Let us give this a moment—"

She tripped over a footstool that she hadn't noticed in her path in her alarm to stop Yarrow from sending for her father and would have gone crashing to the ground save for Roman's quick action. He caught her and swung her back on her feet, the movement bringing them chest to chest, thigh to thigh.

"What ho! Good save, my lord," Yarrow said approvingly, although Leonie barely registered his words.

Instead, she found herself immersed in the strangest sense of being both off balance and yet safe. Of needing to push away and yet yearning to be closer. Roman's body heat surrounded her. He smelled of shaving soap and of something else she couldn't quite define. It was spicy and masculine, and she liked it very much.

It reminded her of that moment when he'd entered the room where she had murdered Arthur. She had thrown herself at him, burying her face in the fold of his coat, wishing he would whisk her away and save her from what she'd done. He'd smelled good to her then, too.

In that moment, Leonie knew she had no choice. She would marry him.

Perhaps her capitulation was the brandy . . . or how she rather liked his shaving soap . . . or just the fleeting understanding that she fought a losing battle. She did have to marry. She would not be allowed to be left alone until she did.

And as she'd decided last night, if she must trust someone, then let it be Roman Gilchrist, who had proven himself once.

He knew her secrets, even down to her taste for brandy.

Granted, all he needed her for was her money, but standing this close to him, looking up into those gray eyes that held a hint of laughter over how easily he'd outmaneuvered her, she saw something else. It wasn't Arthur's angry lust born out of jealousy, or the hungry one of those admirers who had trailed after her in the past.

It was something else.

He did want her. She could feel his manhood against her.

But there was something deeper, almost alien to her, in his

expression that she couldn't quite define, and then it came roaring into her awareness—he felt sorry for her.

Leonie jerked out of his grasp, almost stumbling over the footstool again as she broke the spell between them. No one noticed her angry movement. Yarrow was ordering footmen around and Minnie had left the room in search of her mother's maid to track their mistress's whereabouts.

Rubbing her arm where Rochdale had held it, Leonie lashed out at him under her breath. "How dare you do this? When my parents come, and they will, then I shall tell the truth. There will be no marriage between us."

His response was a shrug.

If Leonie had been a Harpy, one of those mythical birds that ate men alive, she would have flown at him with her talons bared. Instead, she retreated to the far side of the room, taking a seat in an upright, wood-backed chair, and warned him with her eyes not to take one step toward her. She clasped her hands in her lap, squeezing her knuckles, because he knew she wouldn't protest to her parents.

He'd gleaned that her feelings would be of little consequence to them, and they weren't.

In short order, her father barged into the house with one of his rare smiles across his face. He shook Roman's hand vigorously and called for Yarrow to bring whisky. "We must drink to our young countess's health!"

Which he did, several times. Roman nursed one glass, Leonie noticed. A pity. No one offered her a drop.

Her mother danced in, the footmen following her carrying boxes of purchases.

"My dearest child," she gushed, her tone dismissive. "This is wonderful news. And what a surprise! Gilchrist, right? You are now an earl." She pulled off her glove and offered her hand. "We knew each other in India." There was a warmth in her tone that Leonie did not trust. Was her mother implying there had been something between them?

"*From a distance*, we knew each other," Roman stressed as if he could divine Leonie's thoughts. He took a quick step away.

Her mother followed him. "We shall know each other better now."

"I look forward to calling you 'Mother,' " he agreed, a statement that wiped the feminine leer off her mother's face. Leonie could almost laugh.

Her father stepped forward, putting his arm around her mother's shoulders as he handed her a glass of sherry. "Look at the two of them, Elizabeth. We could not ask for a better match. Their babies will be beautiful."

"I pray I'm not so *aged* I can enjoy them," her mother muttered into the glass of sherry poured for her, obviously irritated by Roman's comment.

Leonie's father laughed. "Ignore her. She turns sour whenever the attention is not centered on her. Come with me, Rochdale. We have business to discuss. Don't worry about your drink. I have plenty in the library. This way, my lord." He directed Rochdale out of the room.

Silence stretched between her and her mother.

Her mother spoke first. "This betrothal is rather abrupt. The *ton* likes to witness events taking place. How else can they gossip?"

"Isn't it obvious he is smitten with me?" That jibe was for her mother, who frowned an answer.

"Is this what you wish, Leonie? A man who has a somewhat unsavory reputation."

"Unsavory? What do you mean, Mother? Last night you did not protest."

"I've had a chance to consider. He murdered your lover. There will be people who remember."

Her accusation jolted Leonie. "In all the time since that horrible night, you have never expressed such a thought. And then to hear it spoken in this manner . . . ? Are you using my confidences against me?"

"Such cool outrage. Well done, my daughter. You *have* learned something from me."

"And what is that, Mother? How to be cynical?"

Her mother laughed. "Yes," she agreed. "Cynical and practical. My every intuition tells me there is more to this proposal than meets the eye."

"There isn't."

"Leonie, you were never good at lying."

Better than you think, but Leonie kept that thought from her face. Instead, she rose. "I believe I will retire to my room."

"And not see your newly beloved when he leaves the house?" her mother mocked.

"Apparently, I have learned something else from you as well," Leonie answered, and went upstairs, but she did not go to her room. Instead, she went to the first-floor study. It was located over the downstairs library and shared a flue with the fireplace below it.

Leonie crouched near the cold hearth and heard her father's voice as clearly as if he was standing in the room with her.

"WHEN YOU SAID you were going to marry my daughter, I did not expect you to act this quickly." Charnock watched his butler pour drinks. "I have respect for a man who goes after what he wants."

The library contained very few books and the ones on the shelves appeared to have been in the family for ages. It was a room for men to gather.

Roman waited until the manservant had left and closed the door before answering. "It is not love, if that is what you are asking." He spoke briskly, placing the truth out in front of them.

"Of course not. It rarely is, no matter what the blithering poets say. Look at my wife. I despise her." Before Roman could think of a response to such a startling statement, Charnock raised his glass. "To your good intentions, my lord." He downed his drink.

Roman watched Charnock swallow good whisky as if it was water with a sense of wonder. He'd been around drinking in his time. Soldiers were not ones to let their thirst go unquenched, but the indulgences he witnessed amongst the fashionable set would have made even sailors admit they'd been mastered.

He thought of Leonie entering the receiving room looking like Venus brought to life . . . with brandy breath.

What was he setting himself up for?

His stepfather would warn him to apply logic. If he did not like Charnock's drinking, and he already knew the daughter had a taste for spirits, well, could he make peace with that?

"I suppose you are interested in her dowry," Charnock said.

Roman decided in that moment, yes, he could sleep with a riverfront slattern if it gave him the money he needed for Bon-homie, and Leonie was a far cry from that description. "It is of significance," he agreed.

Charnock grinned. One of his front teeth was crooked. "We could engage a lawyer for this, but why? We are both reasonable men." He walked over to a desk by the window and set down his glass. He pulled a piece of paper from a drawer and dipped a pen in ink. He began writing.

Roman could almost hear Thaddeus say he was a fool to be making any legal arrangements without him.

Blowing on the ink to dry it, Charnock said, "Actually, I am pleased that you will marry my daughter. You almost have a responsibility to do so, you know."

"And why is that?"

"Because of that bad business in India." Charnock reviewed what he'd written while saying offhandedly, "Yes, you involved her in a scandal that might have been avoided with a deft hand."

"Do you think?" Roman challenged, his voice reflecting a calmness he did not feel. What the devil was with Charnock? If he knew the truth, he'd be polishing Roman's boots in gratitude.

That is, if he knew what such an emotion was.

Charnock didn't hand the paper over to Roman. "It is almost justice that you marry her. She made a very unwise decision. Young girls will do that. However, now she will have you to keep her in line." He punctuated his words by handing the offer he'd written to Roman.

"Fifty thousand pounds dowry," Roman read aloud, almost not believing the amount. He stared slack jawed at the number.

With fifty thousand pounds, Roman could pay off his late uncle's gambling debts and do whatever he wished to Bonhomie. And he could take care of his family—his parents and his sisters. Thaddeus's suggestion to marry was genius.

"Have I made it worth your name, my lord?" Charnock asked.

Roman found his voice. "It is good."

Charnock grinned as if he knew Roman struggled to contain his enthusiasm. "I want my blood to inherit your title."

"If your blood is in your daughter, then that will happen."

Unfortunately, his statement struck the wrong chord with her father. *"Of course she is mine."* Color rose to his face and Roman realized he had insulted him.

Too late, Roman remembered the gossip that Leonie didn't look anything like her father. Even Thaddeus had mentioned how different her features were. His voice calm, he answered, "I did not mean to imply she wasn't." But he did wonder why Charnock was touchy?

Her father glared as if he trying to divine Roman's thoughts, and then he visibly relaxed. He lifted his glass to show it was empty. In a lighter voice, he claimed, "You may have misunderstood me, my lord. I was not offering a challenge." He moved back to the table with its row of decanters. "Would you like another?"

"I am fine, thank you." Roman looked down at the paper almost unable to believe his good luck.

"Don't stare at that number too hard," Charnock advised. "Your eyes will cross. Once you marry, the funds will be made available to you."

Roman could never have imagined fifty thousand pounds in his accounts. He was going to need to dream again, *big* dreams.

He was also agreeing to marry the woman who had almost destroyed his old dreams. *I will accept your offer and you may have my dowry and eventually my inheritance, provided I am your wife in name only.*

That would never happen.

Because, in this moment, Roman realized he longed to see Leonie Charnock pregnant with his child. And it wasn't that he wanted to possess her. No, he had the unsettling feeling that it was his fate to protect her.

He'd chased after her and Paccard that night because he had known she was making a mistake, that she would need him.

And she had.

Roman could recall all too clearly the smell of blood and gunpowder in the air and the look of horror in her eyes.

Glancing down at the agreement and hearing the clink of the whisky decanter against glass as Charnock poured another healthy drink, Roman sensed she needed him now as well. Indeed, at one time, she'd been one of his dreams, the one he had believed he'd lost.

Roman had bullied his way into the proposal, but he had no regrets. Watching her father drink, knowing the way her mother was, this marriage was best for Leonie. Come what may, he'd make her see the advantages. He had fifty thousand reasons to do so.

"I believe I will take my leave," Roman said. "Thank you, sir." He offered his hand. Charnock reached for it.

"We shall let the women work out the details of the wedding breakfast and all of that."

Roman hadn't even started to think about the actual details of a wedding. "When should we marry?"

"One week? Two weeks? Whenever."

Exactly what every caring father should answer. "I shall arrange for the special license," Roman answered.

"Let me have Yarrow show you out." Charnock downed his whisky.

"I can find my own way."

"Good. You are also resourceful. May you be a fertile bastard as well."

He left the room.

The butler waited in the hallway. He escorted Roman toward the door. They were almost to the foyer when the servant's step slowed. His gaze on the lacquered front door ahead, he said to Roman, "The servants and I wish to congratulate you, my lord."

"Thank you—Yarrow, correct?"

The servant confirmed the name with a small bow but then he came to a halt. Without looking at Roman, he said, "Please look after her, my lord. I—*we* worry."

"About?"

Yarrow's gaze met his, and then drifted away as a footman approached from a side room with Roman's hat and greatcoat in hand. The moment for confidences passed as quickly as it happened. "Here is your hat and coat, my lord. Thank you, Colin." Yarrow held the hat while Roman put on his coat.

Pulling on his gloves, curiosity made Roman want to press Yarrow for more information; however, the butler had retreated behind the facade of servantly duty. He would not say more.

Roman set his hat upon his head, tipping the brim to a rakish angle. He looked toward the receiving room, half expecting Leonie to be there and yet not surprised that she wasn't.

"Well, good day," he said to the servants, and started for the door Colin now held open for him. However, before he could leave, he heard a step on the staircase.

"My lord." The soft-spoken words turned him around. Leonie stood halfway down the stairs, her hand on the rail, one foot on the step behind her as if caught in indecision—and he thought he wanted to always remember her as she was in this moment.

The deep green of her dress set off the gold in the tawny waves of her hair. Her eyes, always disconcerting in their intensity, now reflected uncertainty.

She came down the stairs toward him, her step so light it was as if she floated. She walked to him and offered her hand. "You would leave without saying good-bye?"

Conscious that the servants watched, he took the hand and brushed his lips against the smooth, warm skin of the tips of her fingers.

She squeezed his gloved fingers and leaned close as if to peck him on the cheek. His heart seized in anticipation.

But her lips did not touch his skin. Instead, in a voice so low the servants could not hear, she asked, "Will you honor my terms for our marriage?"

Roman jerked upright.

Her huge, almond-shaped eyes beseeched him for the answer she wanted.

Well, she was not going to receive it.

"Until tomorrow," he said, and left the house.

Chapter 8

He hadn't agreed.

Leonie almost tore down the street after Roman. She pictured herself grabbing his coat sleeve, jerking him around, and demanding they reach an arrangement.

However, she was very conscience that Yarrow watched. She bit back her disappointment. Later, she would corner Roman. She smiled at the butler.

"Congratulations again, miss. I believe you have made a wise choice," Yarrow said.

"He is a *dandy*, isn't he?" was all she would let herself say because to speak what she was truly thinking would shock the butler.

She excused herself with a smile and a nod and went as quickly as properly possible to the side room. She sat at the cherry secretary and penned notes to Willa and Cassandra, both saying, *Come now. I need you.*

Loyal friends that they were, they did, even though Cassandra had tickets to attend an exhibition with her stepmother and half sisters.

Once they were safely tucked into the sanctuary of Leonie's bedroom, she announced, "The Earl of Rochdale made an offer and I've accepted it."

Both her friends opened their mouths to exclaim their gladness, and then stopped, puzzled.

"Who is Rochdale?" Willa asked.

"Did you introduce me to him last night?" Cassandra wondered.

"I did," Leonie answered. To Willa, she said, "He just rose to the title. It is an old and respected one."

"Oh, yes, *him*," Cassandra said. "I sensed there was something between you."

"You just met him last night?" Willa asked, puzzled. "Isn't this sudden for a marriage offer?"

"Yes," Cassandra echoed. "Last night, you weren't particularly pleased with him."

"My family knew him in India." It was a simple explanation, far easier than the complicated ones Leonie had been contemplating while she'd paced the floor waiting for her friends to arrive. It sufficed. Willa and Cassandra were not interested in background. In fact, Cassandra being overly dramatic, immediately began assuming all sorts of romantic notions about Leonie and Rochdale from years ago.

Willa, too, grew equally enthralled with the idea of young lovers reconnected again, and all Leonie had to do was nod and smile. Her friends' imaginations provided all the details.

When she'd asked them to come over, her thought had been to enlist their help in extricating herself from the marriage offer. She'd been willing to tell them that she'd wanted to arrange an agreement with Roman where he received her dowry and she received the freedom to live her life on her terms.

But now she knew she couldn't.

Willa and Cassandra yearned to marry. They wouldn't understand *not* wanting a husband. They played the game of scoring points in earnest, whereas Leonie had played it to keep from screaming in boredom.

"Tell us how your earl proposed," Willa said.

"Yes, we want those details," Cassandra agreed. "Were you surprised? You must have been. Did he say he had always loved you?"

Leonie couldn't imagine Roman making such a declaration. She cobbled together a story. "Well, he called on me today"—she left out that she asked for the call—"and barreled over me into accepting his offer." Yes, that was a good description.

"Tell me about last night," Willa said. "I didn't meet him. Were you surprised he was at the ball?"

Leonie dipped into her imagination. They wouldn't want to hear about her flares of temper or his rudeness. Actually, they might, and then they would believe she'd taken leave of her senses to marry him.

"He said he had never forgotten me. He came right up to me at the marquis's ball. I had my back to him." She stood to demonstrate. "I heard his voice first. 'Hello, Miss Charnock,' he said—and I recognized him immediately. I turned and—"

Her voice broke off as if she was really living the moment.

In truth, she really could see him as he'd been last night. Rugged, an outlier, even in his fine clothes. Rochdale was competent, something she could appreciate after years of living with her father's carelessness. Perhaps he was a touch jaded. However, he *had* searched her out last night.

He'd come for her.

"He said he would marry me."

"Just like that?" Cassandra asked.

Leonie nodded.

"Oh, my," Willa breathed. "So decisive."

"Yes," Cassandra agreed solemnly.

They were right. Roman hadn't minced words.

"Well?" Willa prompted. "What does he look like?"

Years ago, Leonie had chosen Arthur over Roman because of looks. Arthur had been tall, slender, almost beautifully made with deep blue eyes.

However, Roman had something Arthur had never possessed, that no man of Leonie's acquaintance had carried in the same quantity, and that was presence.

One knew when Roman was in the room. "He's handsome," Cassandra said. "Not as spectacular as the duke but he can hold his own."

"I want to hear it from Leonie," Willa chided.

Leonie forced a smile. "Tall, dark hair, lean face."

Willa waited for more. When Leonie didn't continue, Willa made a great show of saying, "That was informative. We'll recognize him because he has dark hair like a *hundred other men in London*." She pulled a face, letting Leonie know she wasn't satisfied.

Leonie shrugged. "You will meet him soon and then you can form your own opinion."

"I know and I will," Willa said with impatience. "But tell me what you like best about him?"

"Oh, that is a good question," Cassandra agreed.

It was. "He is loyal," Leonie answered.

"Loyal?" Cassandra echoed. She scrunched her nose in distaste and looked to Willa, who shrugged.

Loyalty might not mean anything to them, but it was everything to Leonie. Roman had never betrayed her.

Willa's imagination supplied words Leonie hadn't spoken. "Obviously, the earl is in love with you. He has traveled looking for you and you must feel something for him, or else you would not have agreed to this match so quickly. No one can make you do something you don't wish, Leonie. You are too strong. The rest of us can be cowed but never you."

Cassandra nodded agreement.

How Leonie wished what they said was true. She was the biggest of cowards, but she would not tell them that. No, this was her secret . . . along with so many others that if they knew they would race each other to the door to escape her presence.

But they didn't. And she was safe.

Only she and Roman knew the truth.

ROMAN WASTED NO time in posting the betrothal notice in the papers. Leonie could only surmise that he had walked straight from her house to the papers.

Always a touch cynical about Society, even Leonie was shocked at how quickly the ideas she had planted in Willa's and Cassandra's heads made the rounds of the gossips. It seemed everyone knew and accepted that Leonie and Rochdale had known each other at another time.

"Swept her off her feet," some said.

"A love lost, and yet found again," others whispered.

"They were meant to be together," seemed to be the verdict.

If Roman knew Society had declared him love struck, he gave no indication to Leonie. Although, she had to admit, he did play his part of attentive suitor well, especially in front of others, and they were never alone.

From the moment the notice appeared in the papers, Leonie had callers. Her mother's friends crowded around her, offering sage pieces of marital advice. Mothers brought their debutante daughters to bask in Leonie's good fortune, and to pick up tidbits of new information. Gossip opened doors amongst the *ton*. Even her father's business associates made perfunctory calls to wish her well.

There was no topic too personal. Leonie found herself listening to long-winded stories of the most intimate nature. When she said as much to her mother, she was assured it was much, much worse when one was pregnant with child.

"You will run from the house in horror," her mother promised.

Leonie didn't answer that she would run nowhere because she had no desire to have children. That was a conversation no daughter should have with her mother—or a father who now made it very clear he couldn't wait for her to give him a grandson. It was all he could wax on about.

She began to believe she had liked her father better when he ignored her.

Roman called precisely at half past three every day. *Both* of her parents were there to receive him. It was as if they had decided to transform into the parents they should have been.

Her father, the least political creature in the world, made a huge pretense of discussing with Roman the details of whatever issue was before Parliament. Leonie noted that Roman did have good ideas. He took his responsibilities to his title seriously.

Her mother seemed to enjoy telling Roman of her plans for the elaborate wedding breakfast that would follow the simple, private ceremony. Her parents were intent on making the breakfast a Society event. Leonie wondered if the house could hold all the people they had invited.

Of course Roman was her escort for the evenings' balls and routs. But her mother or her father were there as well. Her mother did not come in one door and duck out the next to meet a lover. They both behaved as if they were overjoyed Roman would be taking Leonie off their hands.

For her role, Leonie gave the appearance of being shy and dutiful. She always made certain she didn't have any brandy on her breath when Roman called. She also smiled and performed as expected, something she'd done all her life, but whenever she had the opportunity to catch him alone, whether it was in the middle of the dance floor or while he was helping her into the coach, she would hurriedly whisper, "Do you accept my terms for this marriage?"

He was quite adept at evading the question while still playing the role of attentive swain.

However, there were signs he would not let her have the life she wanted. His gaze rarely met her eye. They traveled though receiving lines side by side and yet they were as far apart as strangers. Even when they danced, he could look past her while giving the impression he was paying attention.

Willa and Cassandra thought him very charming. There was more than a little envy in their voices, especially since no one had seen the Duke of Camberly at any of the latest social events. It was as if he had disappeared from London and Cassandra, especially, was downcast.

Leonie didn't worry about the duke. She was busy wondering what game Roman played. She knew when a man found her attractive. She would have staked the dining silver that he wanted her. She'd seen signs of it that first evening at the marquis's ball, and yet now, he acted somewhat disinterested.

Oh, he was polite. Gentlemanly. She caught other women watching him, saw their jealous glances at the way he deferred to her opinion or ensured she was included in conversations. Her mother might have been the most envious of all.

What they didn't understand, and Leonie knew, was how practiced she and Roman were at only showing what they wanted others to see. It seemed as if they had already lived a lifetime this way. Marriage was just another milestone in the devil's bargain they had made the night she'd eloped with Arthur.

The night before their marriage, over a family dinner for fifty that included relatives who had traveled to take part in the wedding festivities, Leonie's aunt Ida asked Roman what his plans were for his and Leonie's future.

"We shall go to Bonhomie, my family seat," he said. He didn't look at Leonie as he spoke because he obviously knew she would not be happy—and she wasn't.

He was not going to honor her request for a separate life. She was going to have to be a wife to him. Worse, she was going to be buried in the country, never to be seen or heard from again.

She looked around the table. Everyone acted as if his was a

capital plan, and she could almost hate him for maneuvering her to where she did not want to be. She smiled, she pretended, and she was furious.

Either he feared her reaction to his plans for them. Or her opinion did not matter.

Her only solace was that, now that she was to be married, she was allowed wine with dinner and she took full advantage of the luxury, using it to dull her quiet fury.

Roman left early. After all, it was the night before the wedding. Leonie was happy to see him go. She spent the rest of the evening in the upstairs study with cousins. One of them brought a bottle of wine. Leonie was pleased to imbibe. She told herself she needed something to help her deal with Roman's deceit. She was certain he had known from the beginning he was going to take her to his estate, wherever that was. Being angry with him helped her deal with the apprehension that Roman expected her to be a wife in every way.

And then he would know the full truth of that terrible incident with Arthur.

She held out her glass for a bit more wine. Someone mentioned needing another bottle . . .

How she made it to bed, she did not know.

THE MORNING OF her wedding, rain came down in sheets.

And Minnie was far too cheerful. "Wake up, miss. You will become a countess today."

Leonie felt as if her arms and legs had turned to lead. Her mouth tasted funny. She did not want to open her eyes.

She did not want to marry today.

Minnie threw open the drapes. Leonie managed to lift one eyelid. There was no sun to liven the room.

"I'll bring a tray up with your breakfast, miss," Minnie said. "Your mother ordered a bath prepared. The footmen will be up any moment."

Leonie's response was to put a pillow over her head.

There was a knock on the door and she heard the tub being set up and pails of water being poured into it. She stayed right where she was.

The door shut.

"They are gone, Miss Leonie," Minnie said. "You need to bathe now. I've brought your breakfast. We must hurry. The hour for you to be married will be here in a blink."

Leonie groaned and sat up. That was a mistake. She must have moved too quickly. Her head felt as if two hundred bricks were sitting on top of it.

"You look as if you need a cup of tea," Minnie said. She hurried to make it the way Leonie liked and carried it to the bed.

Taking a sip, Leonie made a face. Her tongue felt fuzzy and thick.

"The water is exactly right," Minnie said, testing the bathwater.

"I will try it," Leonie said. Minnie's happy anxiousness was very annoying. "Is my dress ready?"

"Yes, miss. I pressed it myself this morning."

"Thank you, Minnie." Leonie tried another sip of tea. This was not going to help at all. Nor was Minnie's humming as she busied herself around the bath.

"Minnie, I believe I need some time alone. This will be a very big day."

"Yes, miss. I'll leave you alone. You will eat your breakfast? Your mother wished me to ensure you would."

"I will. Where is my mother?"

"Downstairs. She's with the guests in the breakfast room."

Leonie set down the cup and saucer on her bedside table. She forced a smile for her maid. "Go, Minnie. Go."

"Yes, miss." Minnie reluctantly left the room, and Leonie fell back on the bed. She would never make it through this day.

She should not have had the wine. Devil's brew it was. Her head felt terrible.

She felt terrible. Especially when she recalled Roman's announcement that they were leaving London. He would not honor her request of an agreement.

Her life as she knew it was over. And her head ached. Her bones ached. She did not like wine.

Leonie rose from the bed, needing a moment to steady herself. She took stumbling steps to the breakfast tray. Her stomach almost revolted. She sat down on the edge of the tub. That was not a wise idea. She almost fell in.

Standing again, she wondered what she should do. She had never felt this way on brandy—

An idea struck her, one that put purpose into her step.

Her parents both took a nip in the morning after nights they had overindulged. Perhaps that was what she needed. Just the thought lifted her spirits.

She put on a dressing gown and opened the door. The hall was empty. She padded toward the study—but saw her uncle inside reading the morning paper. She immediately turned around . . . and went to her mother's room. She knocked on the door.

No one answered. Not even the maid.

Leonie cracked open the door and peered inside. The room was empty. She hurried to the dressing table and pulled on the drawer. The flask was right there.

She took a nip.

The brandy cut her fuzziness. It tasted delicious.

Leonie dared to carry the flask back to her room. This time, she had more control over herself on the trip.

She knew she didn't dare keep the flask. Her mother might notice it missing. Leonie took the teapot from her breakfast tray. She lifted the window sash and tossed the contents. She then filled it with brandy.

There. No one would be the wiser. Her mother would just assume she'd emptied her flask herself.

Leonie had no trouble sneaking the flask back to its proper place.

Her headache disappeared and she was even able to eat her breakfast while sipping a cup of brandy. What a remarkable restorative.

Why, by the time Leonie was bathed, dressed, and ready to leave for the church, she was so mellow and at peace with the world she could have married a highwayman.

She chewed mint leaves for her breath, and no one was the wiser.

ROMAN FOUND HIMSELF surprisingly nervous on his wedding day.

For the last week and a half, the idea of marrying Leonie Charnock had not seemed completely real to him. He'd gone through the motions, often with her at his side—and her silent disapproval, her overpoliteness, her infernal repeated question whispered impatiently at every private moment he could manage to steal until he wanted to shout in rage.

And yet, he had maintained the pretense of doting suitor, despite it all . . . or perhaps *because* of it all.

He knew he was good for Leonie. He was the right man for her. He always had been. He was now going to prove it to her by being the husband she deserved—

The door swung open in the back of the chapel. He stood. He was alone. No friends; no family. The Reverend Davis waited on the bench across the aisle from him. He also rose to his feet.

Roman had not yet told his parents or his sisters of his marriage. He'd chosen not to because he did not want their disapproval of his marrying for money. The Gilchrists were an opinionated lot. They would speak their mind on the matter, and he'd rather hear their denouncements later rather than sooner. The letter announcing his marriage was on its way to them, posted two days ago.

Besides, he could not have managed his family and Leonie's

sullen reluctance to marry. For all he knew, his sisters Dora and Beth would have taken *her* side, God help him.

The Charnocks were not quiet people. William Charnock was complaining about something to his wife. His voice broke off when he saw Roman and the rector.

He came up the stone aisle. "I'm sorry that we are a few minutes behind our appointed time, my lord," he said, smiling and holding out his hand—blocking Roman's view of his bride. "You know how the women are."

"William," his wife chided in that bored tone of hers. "We have arrived in plenty of time."

They were a half an hour late, another reason Roman was glad his family was not here. His mother was ruthlessly punctual.

Roman took Charnock's hand, but then everyone moved and he had his first look at his bride.

His breath caught in his throat. His heartbeat kicked up a notch. Venus could not be lovelier.

Leonie wore her hair down, the way he liked it. A band of what appeared to be diamond roses held a lace and gauze veil in place that seemed to float in the air behind her.

Her dress was a marvel of delicate lace and layers of the same finely woven muslin shot through with silver. Her firm breasts rounded over the bodice and around her neck she wore a string of pearls as creamy as her skin. No woman had ever looked more enticing.

Roman let go of Charnock's hand. He took a step toward Leonie and knew the truth. He wasn't marrying her for money. He wanted her. He'd always wanted her.

She'd stopped at the first row of chairs. She gave him a tentative smile and he could have fallen to his knees and crawled to her.

Instead, she moved toward him. She walked as if she was in a dream. Her skirts emphasized long, strong legs.

This woman was to be his wife and he was very pleased.

Charnock was babbling about something to the reverend. Roman didn't pay attention. He only had eyes for Leonie.

She stopped when she was beside him and offered her gloved hand. He raised her hand to his lips and kissed the backs of her fingers.

Her smile at the small, gallant gesture was tenuous as if she, too, had been full of doubts and concerns.

"We shall do well together," he promised her.

Leonie nodded as if too nervous to speak.

"Well," Charnock said, clapping his hands together, "shall we be on with it?"

"Yes," his wife agreed, "the first guests will arrive at half past twelve."

Roman didn't care what Charnock wanted or when guests would arrive. "Are *you* ready?" he asked Leonie. He found himself anxious to be certain she was at peace with the marriage.

She nodded.

"Step this way," Reverend Davis said, taking over and directing them to the altar.

Roman took her hand and tucked it in his arm. Over the past week and a half, they had stood side by side without touching. Now, she leaned slightly toward him, the movement almost imperceptible, and yet it brought her body heat close to his.

Yes, they would be good together.

The rector opened his book and began reading, "Dearly beloved, we have gathered in the presence of God to witness and bless the joining of this man and this woman in Holy Matrimony . . ."

One word leapt out to Roman. *Joining.*

Had Leonie noticed? She gave no indication. Nor did she react as the rector read, "The union of husband and wife in heart, body, and mind is intended by God for their mutual joy and, when it is God's will, for the procreation of children."

Union in body. The procreation of children.

Roman was about to have a wife who could provide him solace with her body and could prove herself a helpmate as well as a lover.

He wanted children. Bonhomie would go to his heir and, standing in front of this altar, he prayed God blessed him with many healthy sons and daughters. He wanted the walls of his home to ring with their laughter.

And he wanted Leonie to desire those things as well.

Although she had never said so in words, he'd known Paccard had debased her. He'd seen it in her eyes that night and in the way her hand holding the pistol had trembled with fear and anger.

Now, it was up to him to treat her kindly, to undo the damage his rival had inflicted.

He repeated his marriage vows in a firm voice to let her know he meant the words. He would always be by her side. He would cherish and adore her.

Roman already believed he loved her.

She said hers quietly and with what he felt was much deliberate thought, as if she savored each word before she spoke it. He caught the scent of mint on her breath. That pleased him. She was already thinking about kisses. He certainly was.

"Do you have a ring, my lord?" the rector asked.

Roman hurried to pull the ring from his coat and proudly held it up. It was a star sapphire that he'd purchased in India years ago. The band was simple because it was all he could afford but the sapphire was a true treasure. It was an unusual stone in London and one only those who had been to India could appreciate. He watched for her reaction or some recognition of the type of stone . . . and was disappointed.

She looked at it without a hint of interest.

Her mother leaned forward. "You need to remove your glove," she prodded.

Leonie pulled at the kid leather, but she acted a bit confused.

Perhaps she was so impressed with the ring she was having nerves?

Her mother stepped in to help. Roman slid the sapphire on Leonie's ring finger. He liked seeing it there. It was the only thing of value he had to give her, other than his heart.

He would have appreciated a sign from his bride that she was impressed with the stone. Instead, she heaved a great sigh and looked to Reverend Davis as if wondering what would happen next.

The reverend took both of their hands, covering them with his own. "With the joining of hands and the giving and receiving of a ring, I pronounce that they are husband and wife." He then blessed them before announcing, "Those whom God has joined together let no one put asunder."

It was done.

Roman was married to Leonie Charnock—no, he corrected himself. She was Leonie, Lady Rochdale. His wife. His countess.

He smiled down at her. She was studying the ring with great concentration. Finally, she was noticing the gift of the stone. Her lips curved into a slow, lazy smile. "This is truly lovely, my lord."

And with the last word, Roman caught a whiff of mint . . . and brandy. His wife had been back in the bottle.

As if to confirm his suspicions, she started to lean and then began to fall. Instinctively, Roman reached out for her, catching her in his arms.

She grinned up at him. "Thank you for that," she whispered on a soft, silly sigh before passing out and turning into dead weight.

Chapter 9

*L*eonie did not wish to open her eyes. Her mind was stirring, but not her body.

Then, she discovered, she *couldn't* lift her lids.

They seemed to be either sealed shut or too heavy to move.

She drew a deep breath, released it . . . and realized she was in bed?

Snuffling against the pillow, she stretched, ready to become more comfortable and fall back to sleep, except she couldn't. Sleep was uncomfortable, worrisome even. She was also conscious that even her slightest movement created a hammering in the forefront of her brain. Why, even her head on the pillow seemed to annoy it.

She shifted her weight and discovered her legs seemed to be caught up in the heaviest of nightdresses. Dry drool caked the side of her mouth. To her horror, she had been sleeping with her mouth open. Her throat was dry and she was beyond thirsty.

Rubbing the drool away, she forced her eyes open—and then immediately shut them again with a groan. The drapes were drawn. The room was dark save for the light from the lamp across the room from her—but even that flickering brightness was too much.

A male voice said, "Good evening."

Every fiber of her being froze.

She was *not* alone. *Roman was with her.*

What time was it? Was she not in her bedroom—?

Memory returned. She had gone to the church. St. Anne's. She was to marry . . . and she had consumed a teapot full of brandy. At the last thought, her stomach suddenly revolted.

A strong hand pulled her to the edge of the bed. She wanted to warn him that she was going to be ill but he already seemed to know that. He unceremonious twisted her hair out of her way and said, "Use this."

Leonie wasn't certain what "this" was but she no longer had control over her body. She retched in the most unladylike way possible into a chamber pot.

The spicy sweetness of brandy was not as pleasant coming up as it had been going down. Again and again her stomach roiled until there was nothing left and still the heaving continued.

Tears ran down her cheeks with her exertions. She would never outlive the embarrassment. Roman kept her hair out of her face but she still managed to make a mess of herself.

When she was completely spent, she raised a hand and he released his hold. The mattress lifted as he stood. As she weakly pushed herself to sit up on the bed, she was conscious of his walking to the door. He opened it and gave the chamber pot to someone—another person aware of her humiliation!

She wiped her mouth with the edge of a bedsheet. She was still wearing the exquisite gown she'd worn to her wedding. She even had the diamond band in her hair, although it was askew and the edges of it dug into her scalp. She pulled the band off and attempted to put it on the bedside table but her arm didn't seem to have any grace. She ended up practically throwing the delicate piece with a force she had not anticipated.

Roman stood by the door. He was in shirtsleeves and had removed his boots. She remembered that he had looked very fine at the church. He wore the same shirt, the same breeches. Then again, he was the sort of man who could make a drayman's simple togs appear fashionable.

Now, he looked down on her, a handsome and disapproving guardian.

She broke the silence stretching between them first. "You always seem to catch me at my worst." Her throat hurt to speak.

"I need to know that I have not married a drunkard."

What a terrible word. Drunkard?

"You haven't," she answered, matching his clipped tone.

It had been the wine. She vowed never to touch wine again.

Trying to recover some dignity, she glanced around the room. *Her* room. "What are we doing here?"

"Instead of at the Pulteney?"

Leonie nodded, hazily remembering that he had said something about hiring a room at the fashionable hotel the night of their wedding. And then what were they to do?

She either couldn't remember or didn't know—and that bothered her. "What are we doing tomorrow? And the next day?" She glanced up at him. "Did we discuss this?"

Her line of questioning seemed to catch him off guard, and she rather liked that. She was feeling such a shambles it pleased her to at least pinch one of his nerves.

"We are going to Bonhomie," he answered.

"Bonhomie?" She tasted the word and didn't like it, although she would not have liked anything in this moment. And then she remembered—oh, yes, he was taking her to be buried alive in the country.

She realized her skirts were halfway up her legs, offering him an indecent display. She pulled them down. She'd probably embarrassed herself to no end while she slept. "Have you been here the whole time?"

"It seemed the only thing I could do. In case you haven't noticed, or perhaps can't recall"—disdain dripped from each syllable—"there is a wedding party going on downstairs."

Leonie listened a moment and realized he was right. She caught the faintest hints of boisterous voices and the plunking of the harpist her mother had insisted upon.

"I knew there was a wedding party," she answered. See? She wasn't completely ignorant. "I don't feel up to joining it."

"I didn't believe you would."

She ignored his tartness. He was out of sorts with her. Well, she was out of sorts with him. Welcome to married life. Her parents were always that way to each other.

And then she asked the question that puzzled her the most. "So, what happened?"

If he was surprised by her question, he didn't show it. "You arrived at the church foxed."

The brandy. She'd consumed far more than she normally would have. And very quickly, she recalled. It hadn't seemed to bother her until, well, she couldn't remember when she wasn't all right—but she could not confess as much to him.

"Foxed?" she challenged, ready to brazen it out. "That is an outrageous charge. I obviously fell ill."

"Yes," he agreed, moving from his stance at the door to a table with covered dishes. "You fell ill with a sickness called being cup-shot." He picked up a teapot. "Would you care for a cup of tea?"

Her stomach rebelled at the sight of the offending vessel of her intoxication. He knew what she'd done. Guilt led to panic, especially when the memory of draining the teapot threatened her fragile stomach. In a panic, lest she disgrace herself more, she looked around for something to use and didn't see anything. He rightly interpreted her distress and, reaching down to the floor beside a chair pulled close to the bed, picked up a chamber pot to offer her—from a number, she noticed, that he had stacked there.

But there was nothing in her body for her to lose. She'd already given it all up. At best, she gave a heave or two and then sat back.

Seeing that she was going to leave him standing with a chamber pot in his hand, Roman set it down with distaste, a distaste he obviously felt for her, and that bit her pride.

She found her energy. She kicked aside her skirts and sheets and clambered out the other side of the bed. Standing was almost as difficult as sitting upright. She weaved for the briefest second. Shoving her hair, which was a wild mess, back over her shoulder, she announced in her proudest voice, "I can see that I disgust you. I am thankful, then, that the wedding never took place."

Roman's brow lifted in a quizzing way. "There was a wedding. Didn't I just say there was a wedding party taking place?"

That bit of knowledge took the wind out of her. "There was? I don't remember saying vows."

"You did."

"I did not."

He shrugged. "You did."

Leonie wanted to lash out at him. Wouldn't she know if she had married him or not?

Or perhaps she wouldn't?

Her mouth had a sour taste, her stomach was still tender, and the devil inside every muscle and every joint would not go away.

"Did I speak clearly?" she wanted to know.

"Your diction was perfect."

She frowned at his offhandedness. "We were pronounced man and wife?" she wanted to clarify.

"Absolutely. Reverend Davis said the words loud and clear and then you nearly hit the floor."

"I *fell* to the floor?" Certainly, she would have remembered something like that. And wouldn't she have at least a bump or a bruise?

"No, I caught you before you could injure yourself."

"So gallant," she muttered to hide the fact that she was appalled by her behavior. She had spoken vows in a ceremony she did not remember, a ceremony that was considered the highlight of one's life. "Did I walk out of the church on my own?"

"No," he said. He poured himself a cup of tea. Apparently there was truly tea in it. It was a small victory that this time the sight of the teapot didn't make her so much as shudder. "That is why we brought you here instead of the Pulteney. I had no desire to be seen hauling my unconscious bride over my shoulder and up the hotel staircase. Your father thought it wiser to bring you here. I did carry you across the threshold as if I was the most eager of swains. You had your head buried in my shoulder. Everyone was fooled but I believe you feared you were going to be sick."

Leonie remembered none of this, and yet she did not question it had happened, especially when she squeezed her hand and then realized something was different. She looked down and was startled to see the ring on her left finger. It was a star sapphire. "I haven't seen one of these since I was in India."

"Yes, well, that is where I'd purchased it." He didn't look at her as he spoke but focused on the tea in the cup he held. It must not have been hot because he downed the contents.

Leonie raised her hand so she could see the ring in the lamplight. This was her wedding ring. The setting was simple and yet elegant. The stone was beautiful. She'd always marveled over the star in sapphires.

He had chosen this for her—just as if he knew her tastes.

And she knew nothing about him. Over the past few weeks, she'd been more preoccupied with her own concerns.

He watched her. There was no humor in his gray eyes, no warmth in the set of his mouth. She deserved his scorn.

"I don't remember any of the ceremony," she confessed. It was a humbling admission. She looked at the ring again and then closed her fingers, feeling the metal circling her finger. It made her nauseous to think she could behave in such a manner.

Still . . . "You never answered my question about our future. We *are* to be a marriage in name only, aren't we? Of course, you will wish that now?"

His answer was to set the teacup down on the tray. An angry muscle worked in his jaw—and she knew the answer.

"I won't, you know," she said.

"Won't what?" His voice was quiet.

She knew he understood exactly what she was talking about. It was there in the glint in his eye. He was not one to enjoy being challenged.

However, this was important to her. The matter should have been settled by now.

Leonie looked down at the ring and then, squaring her shoulders, met his gaze. "I have no desire to share the marriage bed." Her boldness frightened her. She'd been bold with Arthur and it had not gone well. However, she was not alone this time. If she screamed, a dozen guests and a harpist would come to her aide.

"We have no such agreement."

"I've spoken to you about this from the day you made your offer. In fact, I never accepted your proposal. You dragged me into this marriage because all you want is my dowry."

"And for that you felt it necessary to arrive at the church drunk?"

"Perhaps." It was taking all her courage to keep facing him, to not look away.

His brows came together. "And why is that, Leonie? Why do you wish to live separately from your husband?"

"It is not unusual. We are not a love match. Couples live apart all the time."

A shadow crossed his face at the words "love match," an anger, and in that moment, for some reason, her mind's eye went back to when she'd first laid eyes on him. She'd noticed him the instant he'd walked into the ballroom during the Colonial Ball. He had seemed so young then to how he was now.

The years had changed him.

However, that night had brought out the worst in Arthur. That had been the beginning of his jealousy.

"It isn't that I don't appreciate all you have done for me," she added. "It really isn't about you."

"What I've done for you, Leonie?" he repeated. "Are you talking about the night you ran away with Paccard? The night you shot him and I told everyone it was me? Do you appreciate what would have happened if the truth had come out?"

Her own culpability shamed her. "I didn't ask you to take responsibility for Arthur's death."

"No, you did not. I'm my own fool. But hear me well, Leonie, I was there when you needed me. Now, I'm holding you accountable. I have dreams, big dreams. I need you."

"You need my dowry," she corrected.

"Aye, I do. I want to make something of myself and not just for me, but for my family. I will not waste this opportunity. I will also not support a wife who doesn't honor her vows, even if she can't remember repeating them."

"What does that mean?"

"You know what that means."

Was he saying he would annul the marriage? Set her aside?

That would be a disastrous turn of events, especially after the Duke of Baynton jilted her last year. The scandal would brand her for life. Her father might even be so furious he would disown her. Especially since he wouldn't be able to marry her again. She had no illusions about how her father valued her.

She faced Roman. He had known she had no choice but to remain in the marriage, and as her husband, he now legally controlled her. She was his. A weight settled in her chest. "I am not a drunkard."

His answer was a dubious lift of a brow.

"I'm not." Her disclaimer sounded silly even to her own ears and her innate honesty forced her to say, "I have had a bit every now and then. I made a mistake this morning. I was not trying to disgrace you or back out of the marriage . . ."

Her throat tightened. The bile of feelings she struggled to keep at bay threatened to choke.

And there stood Roman in judgement of her. Roman who felt *she* had abused *him*, that she *owed* him. That he'd made a bad bargain in this marriage.

He had no idea how damaged and revolting she truly was. He looked at her face and her body and thought he knew her— just as everyone else did.

And yet they knew nothing about her. *He* knew nothing about her.

Her thoughts came out in a sharp bark of laughter. She sounded mad. She thought she was going mad—

"*He raped me.*"

Words she had never spoken before, that she'd barely allowed herself to think, blew out of her. They took form in the air between them.

She widened her eyes, startled at her audacity, and then she discovered that now she had started, she could not stop. "He raped me. I told him I'd changed my mind. I said I would take the blame. I wanted to return home. And he would *not* let me go." She cut the air with her hands, emphasizing her words, creating space for them. Creating space for herself. Protecting herself—

"*Leonie.*" Roman moved toward her.

She held up her arm as if to ward him off, or was it Arthur? Arthur who had hit her, who had pulled her hair and told to shut her mouth, to stop screaming?

Roman stopped. He held his hands out as if showing her he had no tricks.

"Leonie, I know he raped you."

She tilted her head, not certain she believed him.

"I knew that night." Quietly, in the voice one used to gentle an animal, he said, "He'd been brutal. It was not your fault. He was not a gentleman. You were protecting yourself."

Had she been? Suddenly, she could not remember.

Or recall very much of the aftermath. She tried not to think of those days. She had been thankful when her parents had whisked her away from India. It had been hard to sleep. That is when her mother had started giving her a little brandy.

There would be no brandy now, not with Roman.

She looked to him. "You took the gun from me."

"I did."

For a raw moment, Leonie let herself feel all the ugliness she'd compressed deep inside her. Tears rimmed her eyes. She blinked them back, struggling to be strong. She would not cry. *Not for Arthur. Not for herself.*

And then, abruptly, she lost the battle. The tears broke through her defenses and they were not gentle and soft. No, they burned. They were hot, angry, betrayed, and overjoyed for their release.

Strong arms wrapped themselves around her . . . just as they had that night.

She'd forgotten.

Leonie had remembered Roman walking into the room. He'd taken the gun from her—and now, in the same way as she had that horrible night, she buried her face in his chest and sobbed.

HE'D PUSHED HER too far.

Roman had been incensed that she'd had so little respect for him that she had come to their marriage ceremony drunk. He'd not been able to think of anything else.

Well, he'd had a few thoughts while he'd waited all afternoon for her to come to her senses, and they had been dark ones.

No man wanted a drunkard for a wife.

Considering her mother's behavior, he chastised himself for not being more cautious. Yes, he needed her dowry money, but he was leg-shackling himself to Leonie for the rest of his natural days, and at what cost?

He'd also berated himself for letting a pretty face erase him of his good sense.

In India, Leonie had been known as a willful brat whose almond-shaped eyes could befuddle any man's brains. The problem was, he'd believed himself unbefuddleable, and he was wrong. He had thought with his cock like every other man in breeches.

Twice she had fooled him, the first time being when she and her family had left India for him to face Paccard's death alone. And now this time.

He faced the truth: Charnock had paid him to marry his daughter—and now Roman knew why.

It also didn't help that, even drunk, Leonie was an attractive bit. What sort of perverse man was he?

And when she had come to her senses, Roman had wanted her repentant for what she'd put him through. He'd given quite a show for the servants and guests when he'd carried her into the house. He'd made it sound as if he couldn't wait to bed her. Any right-thinking man would have thought him a lothario of the first order and that had galled him, too. Why, there were a host of guests downstairs who assumed he was up here rightfully rogering his new wife and having a high time of it.

Oh, yes, he'd spent a good portion of his day in self-pity. And now?

Now he felt shame.

Her sobs were heartbreaking. Of course she'd turned to brandy to help her forget a wedding she never wanted. He might have as well.

Especially if the wedding triggered memories of Paccard's foul treatment of her. Roman had been furious that night when he'd seen the bruises on her arms, neck, and face. If Arthur hadn't already been dead, Roman would have killed him.

Now, as then, he found himself holding her, letting her cry until she exhausted herself. For a long moment, they stood together in healing silence.

She shifted, a signal that she'd had enough. She was better.

Roman let go . . . when what he really wanted to do was hold on.

"I think I will lie down," Leonie said. "And I must polish my teeth. May I have a moment of privacy?"

"Of course." Roman stepped outside the bedroom. Thankfully, the hallway was empty.

After a decent interval, he knocked on the door.

There was no answer.

Alarmed, he opened it and then relaxed.

She had climbed back into bed, wedding dress and all, and was asleep.

However, this was a different sleep from her passing out.

She seemed calmer, more at peace, like a child who has had a very hard day and was now weary beyond all cares.

Wanting to make her more comfortable, Roman debated calling for her maid to remove her dress but rejected the idea. He did not wish to involve the servants in what went on in this room. Too many rumors were spread by a careless word.

And so, he did it himself.

It was not an easy task. For a week and a half, and in truth longer, he had imagined this moment of undressing her. Now, he was setting aside his desire for her to be comfortable and to feel safe. He'd meant his silent vow at their wedding to be her protector.

That didn't stop him from admiring his wife. She was perfect in every way . . . including being human. She was also the stuff of every man's dreams. She did not wake while he removed her gown, unlacing and sliding it off her shoulders and down her legs. When she was free of it, and wearing only a camisole and petticoats, she curled up on her side with a soft sigh.

Roman didn't dare try to untie her stockings. Every man had his limits and he had reached his.

Instead, with one last glance of regretful desire, he pulled the sheet over her. He then folded the gown and placed it on the bench in front of her dressing table.

A burst of loud, raucous laughter from the party downstairs punctuated the moment. He'd not go down and join them. They would think him a strange bridegroom indeed to leave his bride upstairs in bed.

Instead, he pulled off his shirt and walked around the bed to stretch out on the opposite side.

Leonie didn't stir as his weight leaned the bed in his direction. He made himself as comfortable as he could when the woman of *his* dreams was right beside him.

Reverently, he dared to reach out and smooth his fingers along one of her curls spread out on the pillow. "You asked why I had chased after you the night you ran away with Paccard?"

She didn't answer, and he wouldn't have spoken if she'd been awake.

He rolled on his side toward her, keeping a respectful distance. The lamplight gave her skin a golden glow. He admired the perfect shape of her nose, the curve and peaks of her lips. Even her eyelashes were sacred to him.

"I went because I couldn't believe after the conversation we'd had in the garden the night before that you would run away with Paccard the very next evening. Do you remember what you said? That you, too, felt a connection to me? I was certain he had pressured you. I was jealous, Leonie. The tribunal had that right. I was jealous." He lightly pulled on the strand of her hair he'd been holding. "I loved you, Leonie, and I wanted to believe you loved me in return."

He carefully placed her hair on her shoulder. "Now, I don't know if that will ever be possible."

Chapter 10

Leonie woke the next morning feeling as if she had slept for a week. She lay a few moments in bed, orienting herself. Something was different.

She was married. She couldn't recall a detail of the event; however, she had shamed herself at it. She held up her left hand to be certain it all hadn't been a dream. The beautiful star in the sapphire winked at her. Such a lovely, simple ring and completely in her tastes—

Where was he?

Roman had been here.

She sat up, and was startled to see that she was in her undergarments. Her wedding dress was folded over a chair. She did not remember taking it off.

Outrage started to gather steam until she recalled the conversations she'd had with Roman. *She'd told him all. Everything.*

Recollection returned—his sitting in the chair, his anger, his arms around her when she'd broken down. He probably despised her. No wonder he wasn't here.

A timid knock sounded on the door. "My lady, it is Minnie."

My lady. That was Leonie.

"Yes?" she said, reaching for the sheet to cover her modesty.

Minnie opened the door and came in, shutting it carefully behind her. "My lord said not to wake you but I thought I heard you moving."

"I am awake," Leonie assured her.

"I am to pack your things. My lord plans on leaving this afternoon."

"He wants *my* things packed?"

"Why, yes, my lady. You are going with him, aren't you?"

"Did he say that?" Leonie was afraid of the answer. What if the servants assumed and then discovered Roman didn't want her? She couldn't imagine confronting them, let alone all of London.

"Yes, my lady," Minnie answered, a note of confusion coming to her tone.

Leonie didn't know what to make of this information. Part of her was relieved and another part was apprehensive. "Where is his lordship?"

"He went out. He spoke to Mr. Yarrow. Would you like me to ask for specifics?"

"No, but don't pack a thing until I've talked to my lord. And help me dress. I wish to bathe." Yes, Leonie would bathe. She wanted to be at her very best when she spoke to Roman. She was guilty of many things but she needed to know if he was going to treat her as a wife, or an extra servant. She'd witnessed many a husband regard their wives in this manner. She believed it rude. She also didn't know if she could serenely kowtow to his wishes. Such was *not* her nature.

Minnie set to work ordering water for a bath prepared and helping Leonie choose what she should wear. She also ordered a tray to be sent to the room to break Leonie's fast.

In an hour and a half's time, Leonie was dressed in a rose-colored day gown. Minnie had twisted Leonie's hair at the nape of her neck and held it in place with gold pins. Leonie was feeling she had some charge of her life. She sent Minnie to Yarrow to ask after Roman but the reply was not satisfactory. The butler was not certain of his whereabouts either.

Leonie stood in her room in indecision. Roman had said he'd

known Arthur had raped her. He knew she was damaged goods, and yet he still expected her to accompany him? What other man would do such a thing? And why?

A timid knock on the door interrupted her. "Yes?"

At the imperial command, an even more cowed voice said, "My lady, Miss Holwell and Miss Reverly are here to see you."

At the mention of her friends, Leonie started for the door, and then stopped. They had been invited to the wedding breakfast yesterday. They must be wondering what happened to her.

Her joy and relief at having her friends and confidantes call was tempered by the need to explain her absence from her own wedding breakfast. Her mind chewed furiously on the problem as she went downstairs.

Yarrow was in the front hall. He was directing servants as they put away silver and tidied up after yesterday's party. Seeing her, he stopped midsentence and gave a small bow. "Good morning, my lady." Yarrow gave great deference to her title and she knew he was pleased for her.

"Good morning," she answered, a bit shy about the title. "Where is my mother?"

"The mistress is still abed, my lady." He held two empty liquor decanters that he now handed over to a passing maid. "I found these under the chair in the receiving room." His pointed comment let the maid know that he was not pleased with the cleaning that had been done in there.

"Yes, Mr. Yarrow. I will give it another look."

"The countess has guests. You will wait until they leave."

The maid shot a guilty look toward Leonie and slinked away.

Yarrow shook his head. "It was a fine event yesterday."

"I heard," Leonie said, thinking of the music and laughter that had served as a backdrop to her confrontation with her husband.

The strangest expression crossed Yarrow's face. It was both

sly and a bit embarrassed. Leonie didn't know whether to question him or ignore the matter. She chose the latter.

"Is my father in?"

"He left last night with friends."

Friends could mean anything, especially since he had not returned home.

"Will you send refreshments to the side room?" Leonie said.

"I have already arranged for it."

"Thank you, Yarrow."

"My pleasure, my lady."

She paused before going into the receiving room. She decided to tell her dearest friends that she had taken ill, the sorriest excuse of all, but what else would account for her missing a party in her honor?

Placing a smile on her face, she opened the door.

Cassandra and Willa sat on the settee with their heads together. At her entrance, they jumped up and came rushing to her, giddy words tumbling over each other.

"Was it complete bliss?" Cassandra asked breathlessly.

"Were you frightened?" Willa wondered.

Leonie took a step back. "What are you talking about?"

"The marriage bed," Cassandra said. "Did he find your passion flower of ecstasy?"

"*My what?*" Leonie said.

"Oh, you know. You were at my salon the night Mr. Roger Edmonds read from his work on the topic. I thought I would swoon before he was finished."

Leonie frowned and then she remembered. "I do remember a poet reading about the 'passion flower of ecstasy.' However, I thought he was discussing gardening." She was joking, of course. Mr. Roger Edmonds was guilty of very bad poetry.

However, Cassandra didn't know if she was jesting or not. She glanced at Willa. "She's teasing," Willa assured her. To

Leonie, she said, "Your husband was dashing the way he carried you into the house."

"*Swept* in with her," Cassandra proclaimed. "We waited for you to return, and when you didn't, most of the women in the room were jealous."

"Yes," Willa agreed. "They were all certain your passion flower was in ecstasy."

"Willa! Edmonds's work is serious," Cassandra chastised, and Willa laughed her response.

Leonie looked over her shoulder, praying Yarrow and the other servants didn't hear this romantic nonsense, even as she herded her friends into the coziness of the side room. "Let us go in here. It is more private."

"Yes, privacy," Cassandra repeated brightly. "So you may tell us *all* the details."

Leonie closed the doors behind them. "What details?"

"About the marriage bed," Willa said. "Does it hurt? Annabelle Markham said she was in pain for weeks after Niles had her."

"Yes, and I can't imagine Niles has *anything* manly," Cassandra threw in, wagging her eyebrows as if she meant something other than she said.

Willa laughed. "However, Rochdale is a *far* cry from Niles."

"Oh, yes," Cassandra said. "He *is*. So, Leonie, the truth!"

"About?" Leonie didn't want this conversation. Oh, not at all.

"The passion flower of ecstasy," Cassandra replied with some exasperation. "Did you experience it?"

A knock on the door saved Leonie from answering. "Come in." The maid entered with a tray of fresh bread, jam, and tea. She excused the servant and then set about serving herself and her guests.

The door had barely closed when Willa pushed the subject again. "Well? Was it wonderful? Or terrible? I've heard both."

How could Leonie say she didn't know?

In the end, she didn't need to say anything because Cassandra decided for her. "It was wonderful, wasn't it? Everything the poets claim."

"The passion flower of ecstasy," Leonie murmured, taking a bite of bread spread thickly with butter and plum jam.

"Exactly," Cassandra said with a satisfied sigh, and sat back against her chair. "That is what I thought. When I saw him carry you up the stairs—" Her voice broke off as if words failed her.

"It was amazing," Willa said solemnly. "And then you didn't come back down. Who would have thought it? I had gained the impression from my limited acquaintance with him that he was rather staid."

"He's *not* staid." The words shot out of Leonie because Roman did deserve her loyalty.

What her defense elicited from her friends was snickers. "He isn't?" Cassandra teased. "Tell us more."

"I'm not going to tell you more," Leonie answered. The thought that everyone at the party yesterday had assumed that she and Roman had spent the afternoon consummating their marriage embarrassed her. No wonder Yarrow had a strange look on his face. He must think her quite wanton.

And if any of them knew the truth, it would be even more lowering.

"I don't believe this is fair or kind of you to not share," Cassandra said. "You are the first of our group to marry and it seems only right you should give us some inkling of what to expect."

"I see no need." Leonie dropped a lump of sugar in her tea. "Roger Edmonds, the poet, has already done so for you."

Willa and Cassandra exchanged glances and then burst into delighted giggles as if they could scarce believe what she was saying.

They had so much to learn.

Always before, when groups of debutantes had started speculating about the marriage act, Leonie had quickly made herself scarce. In truth, if she told Willa and Cassandra what she'd discovered about what happened between a man and a woman, they would lose the bread and jam they had been eating and swear never to marry—which had been exactly what Leonie had thought she had planned . . .

"You do seem different," Willa said.

Ah, different.

Leonie knew that wasn't true. After Arthur raped her—

She stopped, surprised by her own thoughts. She'd used the word "rape" without hesitation. She had never used it. The word sounded too horrible.

But it was the truth.

Arthur had done to her the worst thing a man could do to a woman short of murder. He'd taken away her purity, her childhood, her whole sense of herself as a good person.

Yes, she had been foolish to let him badger her into eloping with him. She'd been naive.

However, he'd been brutal.

Roman's words came back to her. *He was not a gentleman. You were protecting yourself.*

He was right. Who knows what would have happened if she had not found the pistol?

"I *am* different," she said to Willa.

"Because of Lord Rochdale?" the always dramatic Cassandra asked.

Leonie set her cup in its saucer and gave that question some thought. The answer was a surprising, "Yes."

Leonie also wasn't certain what that meant. However, twice now, Roman had come to her rescue. First, by claiming he'd shot Paccard in a duel, and secondly, by hiding her drunken state. If anyone outside of her family knew of how she'd been yesterday at her own wedding, she would be mortified.

There was a knock on the door. Before Leonie could say come in, the door opened and there was Roman as if her thoughts had conjured him—and both Willa and Cassandra almost purred their pleasure.

She understood why. He cut an elegant figure in buff breeches, a deep blue coat that seemed molded to his shoulders, and tall boots that gave him a sportsman's air.

His clear gray eyes went right to her. His gaze held an assessing look as if taking her measure. Had he spoken to her maid and learned that she was refusing to pack?

Her stomach fluttered with an unsettled feeling. Guilt wanted her to look away. Courage made her face him and it was as if she was truly seeing him for the first time. No, not as a fashionable gentleman, but as a man who had already done for her more than she had the right to ask.

And she wouldn't go to the country with him?

What was there for her here? Leonie didn't have an answer.

He had met Willa and Cassandra before. They had been a bit shy around him. However, today, Cassandra spoke in her blunt, forthright way. "My lord, you have my approval."

"And mine," Willa chimed in, a becoming blush to her cheeks as if she had been caught thinking something she shouldn't.

"Well, thank you, Miss Holwell, Miss Reverly." He shot Leonie a confused look.

"We were talking about flowers," she explained dryly, knowing he would not understand.

Her statement sent Willa and Cassandra into peals of laughter, and that confused him all the more.

"Have I interrupted something?" he asked.

"Why would you think such?" Leonie said.

"I have sisters. I know when women have their heads together."

Sisters? She had not known that. In fact, there was little she did know about this man she had married. Here he was, aware of the most intimate details of her life and she had not cared to ask if he had family.

The omission was humbling. Was she truly that self-absorbed?

Willa and Cassandra were taking their leave. Leonie rose to her feet, reaching for the duties of a good hostess to regain her balance.

Roman bowed over their hands, a gallant gesture that pleased them. Willa mouthed to her the words, "You are fortunate." That, too, gave Leonie pause.

Roman stepped out of the way to let the ladies pass so that Leonie could walk her friends through the receiving room to the front hall, but halfway there, she made a decision.

She stopped. Willa and Cassandra came to a halt as well, assuming that she wanted a moment with them in private, and she did.

"I want you to know that my lord and I will be leaving today for his country estate."

"You are going from us?" Willa said.

"He is anxious for me to see—" Leonie broke off. She knew he had told her the name of his home but she could not recall it.

"Bonhomie," he supplied easily, coming up behind her. He placed his hands lightly on Leonie's shoulders, the gesture husbands made toward wives hundreds of times a day.

She tried not to flinch. Cassandra and Willa did not notice, but he knew. She could tell because he removed his hands. He was that sensitive to her slightest gesture.

"Yes, Bonhomie," Leonie said, forcing a smile.

"When will you return?" Cassandra wanted to know. "I am having a salon three weeks from tomorrow. Will you be back for it?"

Leonie looked to Roman. *What were his plans?*

"We shall see," he said to Cassandra.

"Please come back for it. I have hopes for an interesting program and I need people to attend."

"I know," Leonie said. "Although I am relieved I did not miss the 'passion flower' poet."

Willa laughed, a laugh she stifled with the back of her hand to her lips. Cassandra shook her head with good nature. "May we see each other soon." Cassandra gave Leonie the kiss of a dear friend. Willa followed suit and, too soon, they were out the door and Leonie was alone with her husband, the footman minding the door having gone out to open the coach doors for Willa and Cassandra.

Roman spoke first. "Your maid said you told her not to pack."

"I did. But now I need to tell her *to* pack." She drew a deep breath and faced him. "When do you wish to leave?"

"I had thought in the hour."

"I will be ready. Now, if you will excuse me?" She didn't wait for an answer but moved toward the stairs, her current supply of courage spent.

"Leonie?" His voice stopped her. She hesitated, her foot on the next stair. He came around the staircase so they could see each other over the bannister. "What made you change your mind and decide to come to Bonhomie with me?"

Her husband was no fool.

He also treated her with more honesty than her parents ever had. Furthermore, other than Willa and Cassandra, she truly had no ties to London. For some reason, being alone had lost its appeal.

"You have sisters." On that cryptic answer, she hurried up the stairs to pack.

Chapter 11

$\mathcal{L}$eaving her parents' home was surprisingly simple.

On the way to her room, Leonie decided to tell her mother she was leaving. She knocked on her mother's door but her maid, Anna, answered. "Madam is indisposed." She spoke in whispers through a cracked door.

Leonie understood what was truly being said. Her mother had probably imbibed too much wine and whatever else at the wedding party . . . just as she'd had too much brandy. "Does she know I am leaving?"

"Lord Rochdale informed her that the two of you would be departing."

"Ah, well, then, tell her I will write."

"Yes, my lady." The door closed.

Leonie stared a moment at the hardwood. She then turned and looked down the hall to her father's room. He had still not returned. She debated informing his valet of her departure but dismissed the idea.

"I spoke to him earlier," Roman's voice said behind her. "He knows we are leaving."

Slowly, she turned to him. "I fear where you had to go to find him. Years ago, I left without a backward glance. I didn't think they would care. I didn't believe anyone cared."

"I'm certain they were worried when you eloped."

"My father's only worry was protecting his investment. I pray you received my dowry?"

He hesitated as if he didn't trust her mood, and why should he? She'd not behaved well the past two weeks. "I have."

"Very good. I shall pack."

She went to her room. Action felt good. Leaving London would not be a bad thing, she realized. Like Willa and Cassandra, the gossips would speculate about her reasons for missing her own wedding party. Some would be titillated, others scandalized. And herself? She didn't care. All those doubts had vanished once she'd made her decision to not fight her husband on the issue of traveling with him.

Minnie had already started the packing. Leonie watched the maid sort through her clothing for a moment before saying, "Will you come with me, Minnie?"

The servant's eyes widened and then softened. "I wish I could, my lady."

"But you don't wish to leave your Charles?" Charles was the butcher's apprentice. He and Minnie had been sweethearts since they were children.

"We will marry soon."

"Send me a note when you do," Leonie said. "I will want to know."

"Yes, my lady."

Leonie looked around at her possessions spread all over the room. "Very well, I shall be my own lady's maid—"

"You have a husband who can help you," Minnie quickly interjected.

"I have a what?" Leonie asked, the maid's response taking a moment to sink in. When it did, she felt herself blush. "So I do." She busied herself helping Minnie with her packing.

"Don't worry about those perfume bottles," Leonie said as Minnie gathered the heavy glass bottles. "In fact, here, you take them." She knew the maid tried the scents from time to time. She probably wore them more than Leonie did.

"You should keep one," Minnie protested.

"I wouldn't know which," Leonie offered, and waved the maid on.

The milled soap was a different matter. Leonie wanted to take the three bars she owned. She wished she had more but certainly she could buy it wherever they were going—

Wherever they were going? Where *were* they going?

She was startled to realize she didn't know the location. And what was the name of her husband's estate? She'd forgotten it again. Bonne Chance?

Leonie shook her head. That was not it. What decent Englishman had a French title for his home? A pretentious one—and Roman was anything but pretentious. *Bonhomie.* That was the name. She would have to learn the story behind it.

With Minnie's help, everything Leonie felt she must take was folded into one trunk. A valise was packed for her needs on the road. "I will send for the rest," she told the maid.

"Yes, my lady. I will have it prepared. Thank you for asking me to go."

"I will be sorry to lose you," Leonie answered, and then realized another concern. "Here, let me write a letter of reference. I don't know if there is a lady's maid role for you in the house." And she wouldn't count on her mother to think of those details. She would bring it up with Mrs. Denbright, the housekeeper. "And money . . . ? I should see that you have some."

"Lord Rochdale took care of me," Minnie answered.

"He did? When did he do that?"

"Perhaps an hour ago." When Leonie was with Willa and Cassandra. "He was very generous."

"Of course, he would be," Leonie answered, caught between resenting his high-handed manner and relief that he had seen to Minnie. She masked her uncertainty by writing an excellent letter of reference for the maid.

There was a knock at the door. "Yes," Leonie called.

"Lord Rochdale wishes to know if you are ready to leave?" a footman said through the paneled wood.

Leonie looked at Minnie. "Is this all?"

"That you said you wished to take, my lady."

"Very well." Leonie opened the door. "Besides the trunk, there is a valise on the dressing room bench that is my personal luggage. Please carry that down for me."

"Yes, my lady," the footman said. "I shall have two of the other lads carry your trunk down."

"Yes, please." Leonie put a green silk pelisse over her dress, gathered her shawl, her hat, and her gloves from Minnie, and took one last look around the room. She'd lived in the room, this house, for almost five years and yet it did not feel a part of her.

As she walked down the hall, she passed the study. A glance inside told her the brandy decanter was right where it always was.

She could use a nip, and that bothered her because now was not the time for such thinking. Besides, after what she'd done at her wedding, she should swear off spirits completely.

Therefore, she walked by the room. Her days of nipping were behind her. She even felt a touch noble in making her decision.

Downstairs, not only was Roman waiting for her in the front hall, but Yarrow as well. A footman was carrying a trunk out for him.

"Are you leaving my father's employ?" she asked with some dismay.

"Yes, my lady, I am." Yarrow looked to Roman before saying, "I am joining your husband's staff."

"I don't have staff, Yarrow," Roman said. "You will find we are threadbare at Bonhomie."

"I look forward to the challenge," Yarrow answered.

Leonie's first reaction was relief. She would have someone she knew with her. She glanced at Roman, wondering if he might have anticipated she would appreciate a familiar face. "I'm glad you are coming," was all she said.

They had to step out of the way as the footmen carried her trunk out the door. "Yarrow will ride with the wagon carrying your trunk and some other items I purchased."

Leonie glanced back up the stairs, wondering if all the commotion roused her mother. Apparently, it hadn't. She set her hat on her head and pulled on her gloves. Folding her shawl over her arm, she said, "Shall we go?"

And it was as easy as that.

On the way out, she dared to ask, "By the by, Roman, where are we going? Where is Bonhomie?"

"Somerset," he answered, and smiled as if the word alone gave him great pleasure. The name meant nothing to her because she'd rarely traveled outside London. She did like the sound of it.

A hired post chaise and driver waited on her parents' elegant street. Behind it was a wagon pulled by two draft horses. The wagon bed was covered with a tarpaulin so it could weather a long trip. The bed was apparently piled high. Roman had not wasted time spending money.

Yesterday's rain had given way to an overcast spring day. She hoped any further rain held off. She had no desire to be caught in a spring storm.

Leonie gave the wagon bed a curious look. "Tools," Roman explained. "We needed a new plow and other items that are of far better quality in London that what I can find in the country. There are also bags of seed."

"To grow what?" she asked.

"Corn, barley, every vegetable you can imagine, and flowers."

"Flowers?" Her valise was placed in the boot.

"My mother wishes a flower garden."

His mother. He had sisters and, of course, a mother.

The trunks were placed under the tarpaulin. The work was supervised by an officious redheaded gent. Roman introduced him to Leonie as his valet, Duncan Barr.

Barr nodded and bowed but Leonie sensed he was very protective of his master. He might even know the full story about herself and Roman. Men often used valets as confidants. She felt slightly uncomfortable around him. Barr seemed to sense her unease—and liked it.

Fortunately, he was riding with Yarrow. It would only be she and Roman in the coach.

After a few last orders, her husband helped her into the coach and climbed in after her. He shut the door. He gave a wave to the post boy and, with a cluck, the horses moved out.

Leonie turned on the hard leather seat for a last look at her home out of the window. Yarrow and the wagon had not left yet. He was speaking to the footmen, obviously giving his farewell lecture. Mrs. Denbright was in the door with Minnie but there was no one else.

Still, she found herself watching until they turned the corner.

And then, she was alone with her husband.

Leonie pulled off her gloves and folded her hands in her lap, conscious that he seemed to take up an inordinate amount of room in what were now very close quarters. His hat was on the seat between them. She realized she still wore hers. She undid the ribbon and then stopped.

"Is something the matter?" Evidently, he was as aware of her as she was of him.

"I realized there isn't much room to stow my bonnet."

"We can make room beside me," he offered, moving his hat over to his side of the coach, and bringing himself closer to her.

Leonie's chest tightened. She found she needed to think to breathe. She could well imagine Cassandra making something romantic about this situation. She would never understand Leonie's uncertainties.

"Or we can set both hats between us."

Her gaze went to his. His expression was carefully neutral, unthreatening.

She took off her hat, and then handed it to him, trusting him to decide.

Was it her imagination? Or did he lean in as if to see if she'd had a nip?

"No, I have not had anything to drink," she said.

"I didn't ask."

"You didn't need to." She shifted her weight on the seat. "I mean, I don't blame you. I was not at my best yesterday."

"It is behind us."

"Truly?" she challenged.

His gaze met hers, and then he answered kindly, "Truly. We are married. We have a future. That is all that matters."

She looked down at the ring. "It is lovely. Perfect, even. Thank you."

"I had hoped the woman I gave it to would appreciate it."

"She does," Leonie dared to admit, and was rewarded with one of his rare smiles.

She hadn't realized that he did not smile often until this moment. The expression transformed him. He was a handsome man but the smile, well, it softened the hard edges . . . and she remembered how he had been when they were younger, before all that had happened.

"Does your mother live at—?" She paused, once again forgetting the name of his estate, of her new home.

"Bonhomie."

She repeated the name. "I *shall* remember it."

"My hope is that you grow very attached to it, as attached as you are to London."

They were moving out of the city. The houses were less dense; the traffic lessened.

"I'm not that attached to London," she confessed.

"You wanted to stay here."

"True, but only because where else can I go?" She turned to him. "Tell me about your home."

"*Our* home."

Leonie wasn't quite certain he was right. To be "our" home, she would have to like it . . . and she wasn't certain of him let alone a place she had never visited. Still, she dutifully said, "Our home."

The expression in Roman's eyes said he knew she was pacifying him, but he launched into a wonderful description of this place called Bonhomie. He spoke of its manicured lawn, the deer park, the fields he would have turned with the new plow. It had been an old abbey until the house and the lands surrounding it were gifted to Lord Rochdale during the Reformation.

"I can see you as a Roundhead," Leonie told him.

He laughed. "Unfortunately, I can see myself that way as well. The house has seven bedrooms."

"Your mother and your sisters live there?"

There must have been something in her voice that caught his attention.

"On the grounds, yes," he said slowly. "And my stepfather."

"I did not know about your family," she explained. On one level of her consciousness, she was asking out of curiosity and because these people would soon mean something to her. On another level, she was becoming aware of an unexplained nervousness. She thought of the hour and how she hadn't had her usual nip . . . but that couldn't be a reason for a touch of anxiety? Could it? "They were not at the wedding."

"No." He paused. "They stayed at Bonhomie."

She caught the note of hesitation. She grasped on to it in an attempt to redirect her thoughts from the prickly uneasiness she seemed to be experiencing to something, *anything*, else. In a flash of intuition, she hazarded a question, "Do they *know* you are married?"

ROMAN DEBATED LYING. Then decided against it.

"I posted a letter to them several days ago," he said.

"Oh," was her response.

He didn't know if hers was a good "oh" or a bad one. "They will be happy for us."

"Or their feelings might be hurt."

Roman could tell her about his stepfather, David, but why? The news wouldn't mean anything to her and David would not thank him for his honesty. He would prefer to make his own impressions.

Leonie considered him with her solemn brown eyes. "You don't believe they will wish us happy?"

"They know that years ago I fought a duel over a woman. They are . . . protective. I wanted them to meet you first and then they can put together the story of how we first met."

"Oh," she said again, the word with more awareness. "I think I see."

And then, because he might as well have it all out, because surely someone in his family might mention it to her, he said, "They know I was demoted because of the duel."

Leonie sat quietly as if digesting his words. A small line of worry appeared between her brows. "I did not know about the demotion."

"Didn't you wonder what had become of me after you left?" He tried to keep his voice light. He wasn't entirely successful.

She pushed herself back into her corner of the coach. "I assume my father took care of smoothing matters."

"Just a snap of his fingers, eh?"

"No, of his purse." She turned away from him, staring out the window as if she could imagine him gone, and he wanted to laugh at the cruel jest of his life.

He'd married her because he wanted her, plain and simple. His stepfather had always warned him against thinking with his little head instead of his big one. Only a fool would do such a thing.

Well, Roman Gilchrist was a fool. But a rich one now. He didn't mention that his family would be upset that he had married for money. They believed in love. His mother had married twice for love. Beth and her husband, Lawrence, had been a love match, and Dora was still looking.

However, love could not have paid the old Rochdale's gambling debts to Erzy and Malcolm or make the repairs necessary to build Bonhomie into the estate he had described to Leonie.

Furthermore, he had the woman who had haunted his dreams. She sat next to him in these close quarters, the faint scent to her perfume on her skin in danger of driving him to madness . . . because *she* was his *wife*. This woman he'd sacrificed so much for was finally his.

And then she surprised him.

She looked to him, her expressive eyes shiny with unshed tears. "I should not have let you be blamed for what I did. I believe we must tell the truth." Her face had gone very pale.

"Tell the truth?" Roman didn't exactly understand what she was saying.

"Yes, we should tell people you were innocent of Arthur's death. We should go to your commanding officer or the officers at the Company"—she referred to the East India Company—"and explain that I killed him."

"We will not do any such a thing," Roman assured her, astounded she'd even offered.

"Why not? It isn't right that they believe a lie about you." She looked down at her hands. They seemed to tremble slightly. She clasped them tightly.

Roman placed his hand over hers. It had not been his imagination. Her hands did tremble. However, at his touch, her fingers curled tightly as if resisting him.

He could have pulled away. He did not.

Instead, he spoke words that, during the ruin of his military career, he had never believed he would say. "It doesn't matter. We both made choices that night. What's done is done and the two of us have managed fairly well, have we not?"

Her brows came together. "You can forgive me for all that happened to you?"

"I have." He forced a smile at the lie. It wasn't until this moment that he realized how deeply his resentments had run toward her. He truly had believed she had known of his fate, of what he'd done for her, and had not cared.

"I don't know if I can forgive myself. I don't know why I eloped with Arthur. He was insistent," she added as if that explained something.

However, Roman was all too aware of what had driven Paccard—he'd considered Roman a rival for Leonie's attention. He'd believed that since Roman had joined the brigade, she'd lost interest in him. Jealousy could drive a man to insanity.

God help him, Roman wanted to ask her if it was true.

But he didn't. She was his wife. And yet they were perfect strangers.

"Tell me about your family," she said, changing the subject.

"My stepfather was an Oxford fellow and tutor," he said. "My mother is a bit of a rooster."

"Rooster?" Leonie's eyes widened at the thought and then she laughed. "Your mother can't be a rooster."

"Peacock, then. Catherine Gilchrist is a proud woman who does not like to be crossed." He didn't tell Leonie his mother was also a very worried woman.

"I will keep that in mind."

"My sisters are very much like her."

"I shall keep that in mind as well. Any brothers?"

"I am the only son and I'm the youngest, which means I am accustomed to being bullied about by my sisters."

She laughed at the thought, the sound soft and light—and he wanted to kiss her. She was all but inviting him to do it.

If they had celebrated their marriage with a normal wedding night, or if their circumstances had been different, he'd be making love to her in this coach right now.

Roman had never been one to be shy around women. He usually knew exactly what they wanted from him, but Leonie was different.

No, the *stakes* were different. He was in love. Yes, he had fallen under her spell and he barely knew her—but what he was learning about her, he liked very much. Besides, he had a soft heart for the vulnerable.

The question was, could she love him?

And that was one that could torture a man's soul.

He really hadn't given her a choice about marriage, had he? He'd thought he'd known her secrets. Instead, he was learning her scars and he wanted to do everything in his power to make her happy with this marriage.

Bonhomie was the lynchpin in his plans. It would be safe ground between them.

So, he told her of Bonhomie as he saw it. He described the fields, the livestock, the mill with its rushing stream. She listened as if he was telling the grandest story in the world.

And he was.

What would she think when they arrived? Well, he'd have to convince her to see it as he did.

Chapter 12

They stopped for the night at an inn not far from the Post Road, the Hound's Breath. It was a busy house with travelers from all ranks of life.

Leonie was exhausted, hungry, and not feeling particularly herself.

While her husband arranged with the innkeeper for their rooms and hiring a vehicle for the morrow, she sat on a bench in the reception room and watched people coming and going in and out of the open doorway of a large taproom. Most were genteel folk but there was a group of soldiers who were well into their cups. They were drinking tankards of ale but they also had a bottle that they passed freely amongst themselves.

She caught herself watching that bottle as it was shared.

A gnawing discomfort grew in her. She'd noticed her hands trembling slightly earlier in the coach and she felt them tremble again now. She folded them in her lap. She didn't think Roman had noticed. She wondered if the trembling would stop if she could have a wee sip of the bottle the soldiers shared.

The bottle had stopped its movement. She lifted her gaze to the solider holding it.

He'd noticed her staring. He was a ragged sort, with several days' growth of beard along a pudgy jawline. He grinned, showing alarmingly yellowed teeth.

The whole table now turned and ogled her in the boldest way possible.

Leonie dropped her gaze to her folded hands, heat burning her cheeks. She had been indiscreet.

"Hey there, lovely," one of them called. "Come join us." He had an Irish accent.

Leonie studied the bench as if she could conjure a wall between herself and them. Where was Roman? He had stepped outside with the innkeeper.

"Don't be embarrassed, miss. There's room at this table for you." The jibe was met with laughing agreement—until Roman's boots stepped into Leonie's line of vision. He had returned and placed himself in front of her.

Silence fell.

Indeed, the whole taproom had gone quiet. Leonie feared she would succumb to the mortification. She knew better than to give any attention to soldiers. For some reason, male vanity took it as an open invitation—as if *she* would look twice at the likes of them at that table.

However, Roman's solid presence shut them up quick enough.

She was both relieved and furious.

Roman offered her his hand. "The innkeeper has a private room for our supper."

"Yes, please," Leonie murmured, and took his hand. She did not glance at the soldiers as he led her through the taproom. She prayed they would be gone by the time she and Roman finished their meal.

The good-sized private room overlooked an evening garden and a small pond. Several ducks were nestled in the reeds around its bank. Leonie spent time watching them, conscious of Roman's strong presence as the maid quickly set the table with pewter plates.

Another knock on the door and the innkeeper's wife, who introduced herself to Leonie as Mrs. Stoddard, carried in a huge tray of food. While the maid dutifully placed the dishes on the table, Mrs. Stoddard said, "We hope you enjoy your stay, my lord. If you or your lady need anything, you have only to say the word and Michael and I will come hopping."

"Thank you," Roman said. "We appreciate your service." He pressed coins in her hands.

Leonie waited for the door to close to untie her hat. Even though she had sworn off wine, she noted there was not a bottle of it on the table. Nor a pitcher of ale. Instead, the inn had served them tea.

Two pots of it.

She hated the disappointment she experienced at not seeing a bottle. It shamed her.

"I'm hungry," she said, her voice bright. A Charnock learned the best way to move forward was to do so smartly. She set her bonnet on a side table and unbuttoned her pelisse. "Are you?"

He smiled, the expression cautious as if he'd watched to tell her mood. "Actually, I am."

"Hard to believe when all we did was sit in a coach." She kept her voice light, friendly, warm. Leonie knew what was expected and she always performed.

ROMAN SAT WITH his wife for their first meal together. It had been a long day. However, the trip had released a great weight from his shoulders.

When he'd met with her father earlier at the bank, he'd thought to ask about the drinking. However, at the time, Charnock, who had left the night before and had not come home, was obviously intoxicated. The banker hadn't raised an eyebrow at Charnock's condition.

Charnock had rambled drunkenly about how pleased he was to have an earl, but he had made no apology to Roman about his daughter passing out drunk during her own wedding ceremony. He also did not ask how she fared.

Roman was no fool. Either the man knew and didn't care, or didn't know because, apparently, he and his wife suffered the same affliction.

And yet, Roman and Leonie had meshed together well in the coach. At the table, she served him. She poured them both cups of the rich, black tea and then placed pieces of the ham on his plate. She gave him several spoons of peas and also of carrots.

He noticed she served herself generously as well. Good. He liked women with an appetite. He remembered one of the things that had attracted him to Leonie was her lack of pretense. Amongst all the young women at the Colonial Balls, she had been the most herself.

Over the dinner table, Leonie laughed easily and asked him questions about his likes and dislikes. This was the stuff of his dreams. All afternoon, she had been engaged in his talk about Bonhomie. She'd even been interested in his family.

And now here they were, man and wife, sharing a meal.

Of course, he did feel awkwardness from her about touching. They were a marriage of convenience but he wanted it to be much more. The way she was now, her ease around him, her willingness to serve as his hostess, to discuss matters that meant something to him, was all he'd hoped.

Years ago, he'd been infatuated with her. Now that bond strengthened as he found himself eager for her approval and her smiles.

They talked more about Bonhomie.

The meal came to an end.

They fell into silence. Roman had been watching her, waiting for a sign that she was ready for bed.

Of course, ever since he had paid for the room he'd been more than ready to find the bed, and not because he was tired.

He wanted his wife in all ways. And yet he was acutely sensi-

tive to the emotional turmoil in her confession the night before
about Paccard's rape.

How did another man release her from that terror?

Roman considered himself a good and capable lover, but
Leonie had suffered greatly, more from the guilt of her own secrets than what Paccard had done. It was possible that Roman
hadn't done her a favor by taking the blame for Paccard's death.
He'd killed men in combat, and even when their deaths were
justified, it was never easy. Only those with no conscience or
who had never pulled a trigger could walk away unscathed.

Was it any wonder she had turned to brandy? However, she'd
not had a drink all day. She'd also not made a fuss this evening . . . so perhaps her drinking was an anomaly? Perhaps,
because they truly had not known each other well, she'd tried
to medicate her fear of the marriage bed and the wifely duties
it entailed?

He prayed that he'd eased those fears.

Leonie yawned, the gesture purely feminine.

"Shall we go to our room?" Roman asked, keeping his voice
neutral.

"Yes, I suppose we should."

He could have shouted hosanna, but then a line he was beginning to recognize as a sign of her doubts formed between
her brows.

"Is something the matter?" He invited her to confess any fears.

Instead, she looked at him with guileless eyes and shook her
head.

Did that mean she had no doubts about sharing his bed?

Or—and this idea was forming slowly in his mind—was she
one of those people who wore a mask well? There had been
times when she'd let him glimpse the real her. Last night was
a good example. That woman was a far cry from the polished
creature who sat at the table and was everything a wife should
be over dinner.

Some men might want the easier woman.

Roman was not one of them. However, he was not above a test. All the way through dinner and even during the coach ride there seemed to be an invisible barrier around her. He now leaned toward her and covered her hand on the table with his own. His movement broke that sense of space.

She startled. It was the slightest of gestures, one she quickly hid.

"I want you to know that I value you," he said, choosing his words carefully.

"I know that."

"You are safe with me," he reiterated.

"I assumed so."

Her answers were a bit too rote. Roman decided the time had come for directness. "I want to make love to you."

Her eyes widened and then shifted away from him to focus on the teapot nearest her. He couldn't help but wonder if she wished it could change into something else.

Then, visibly gathering herself, she smiled like the perfect gentlewoman and said, "I thought you might."

But there was no warmth behind the words.

Roman wanted warmth. He wanted passion.

And he was not going to give up.

"Come," he said, helping her rise. "Our bags will be in our room. They have one of those water closets. We'll stop there before we go upstairs."

When he opened the door, Leonie moved past him obediently. The innkeeper had kept an eye on them. He hurried up to Roman. "How was your dinner, my lord?"

"Very fine, Mr. Stoddard."

"Here is the key to your room. It is the first door at the top of the stairs. I started the fire in the hearth myself. It may be spring but we will have a cold night."

"Thank you," Roman said, and directed Leonie by the elbow toward the back of the inn where the stairs took guests up to their rooms. The main taproom was crowded and noisy. The table of soldiers Roman had noted earlier was still there. They watched Leonie with hungry eyes.

He pulled her close. She was his and a wise man would keep his eyes to himself.

The water closet was a room added on to the inn where at one time there had been an outside entrance. Stoddard had told him, when he'd taken Roman to check out the room, that this new convenience was not only for his guests, but to make the rooms more comfortable. Nothing was more annoying than a chamber pot left overnight.

Roman let Leonie use the water closet while he stood guard against any wanderers from the taproom. He then escorted her safely to their room, his boots echoing on the wood floor. The Hound's Breath had come highly recommended and he was pleased. The bed was a four-poster in the middle of the room with the sheets turned down. A candle was lit on a side night table and there was a cheery, warm glow from the hearth.

Of course, he anticipated that he and Leonie would make their own heat.

He looked to his wife. "Is all to your liking?"

She nodded but he didn't think she heard him. Instead, she studied the bed as if she had never seen one before.

This was not a good sign.

Or boded well for his night.

Roman said, "I shall return in a moment. Here is the key." He dangled the key in front of her, breaking her trance on the bed. "Lock the door behind me." He waited for her nod and then went out. He paused outside the door. "Lock the door, Leonie."

The key turned.

Now to see if she would let him back in.

He wondered if he should test her and then decided he would find out soon enough. He went down the stairs to the water closet to see to his own needs.

But the moments alone helped clear his thinking.

God, what a devil of a fix he was in. He was married to a woman who stirred his blood in a way that was not good for his sanity, especially since he worried a bit about hers.

She was a woman who had been hurt, damaged, and needed him to be the rock she had not known in her life.

Yes, a rock. An unfeeling, unchanging, unwavering rock. Or, at least, that was the impression she gave him. She acted unaware of how anxious he was to please her. How her well-being was his sole priority.

Roman clumped back up the stairs. He stopped outside the door, bracing himself for whatever may come . . . because he was not a rock. He was a man who wanted to fully love his wife. He wanted her to bear his children.

He tapped lightly on the door. "Leonie, let me in."

To his relief, she unlocked the door.

Opening it, he found his wife standing by the bed in the frothiest, filmiest confection of a nightdress any man could hope to see. It was virginal white and yet the thoughts that leapt into his mind were anything but saintly.

Aye, there was a good amount of lace. It flounced here and there, emphasizing her slim shoulders and the hem where bare toes peeked out to him. But it was the parts that didn't have lace that interested him most. Two dark circles formed into tight buds against the bodice. The high waist was gathered with more ribbons and lace, but the skirt's fine material left little to his imagination.

She was perfectly formed in every way, especially in the curve of her hips and the length of her legs. Good legs. Legs that could wrap around a man and hold him to her core.

Roman shut the door. He turned the key in the lock without looking and tossed it on the night table beside the candle.

Reverently, he moved toward his wife.

She watched with apprehensive eyes but did not back away.

This was what he'd expected last night. *This* was what he wanted to have happen.

They stood almost toe to toe. He bent his head and covered her mouth with his.

Their first kiss. Her lips were closed but pliant. She was not resisting him. She just needed coaxing. He slid his tongue along her lower lip. It must have tickled, because she gave a twitch, and he took full advantage, attempting to deepen the kiss. He pressed in, his hands on her waist. God, she tasted good . . . so *very* good—

Roman was conscious that her eyes were open.

He opened his eyes and they both all but jumped back, startled by the impact.

"I'm sorry," she said quickly as if she believed she'd done something wrong.

Roman placed a reassuring hand on her arm to keep her from falling back on the bed. "It is nothing. I was just caught off guard. Do you always keep your eyes open when you kiss?"

She turned red. "Was that wrong?"

"Wrong? No, I don't believe there is a wrong way to do it." He waited a beat and then offered, "Usually, I close my eyes."

"Oh." She shook her head as if she should have known. "I felt a bit dizzy staring at you so close. I had to look at the ceiling."

Roman wasn't certain how to take that statement. He was relieved of the responsibility of an answer when she said, "Shall we try again?"

"Oh, *absolutely*. But first, let me remove my coat."

"That makes sense," she said.

Dear God, could she see how tight his pants were? He could burst and he had no desire to scare her off before they started.

The thought was forming in his mind that Leonie might be more naive than he could have credited. Perhaps that was why she seemed unaware of her impact on men? Could she truly be without a clue?

Of course not. Even when she was seventeen she'd received more than her share of male attention. She had a good head. She knew.

However, when he took off his coat and untied his neckcloth, he took the opportunity to blow out the candle. Now the only light in the room was from the coals in the hearth. It cast a glow around the room. His movements in shadow danced against the wall.

Leonie watched the play of shadows. She glanced down to the apex of his thighs. She knew he was aroused.

"Do I frighten you?" he asked.

"I don't think you will hurt me."

"I won't." He reached out to smooth her burnished hair over her shoulder. "And this is not going to be something I do *to* you. What happens we do together. It is meant to be pleasurable."

Her expression said she wasn't certain. "I'll be fine," she whispered.

Roman wanted her to be more than fine. "Fine" was a flat word. Fine was keeping your shoes dry in the rain or a lukewarm cup of tea that wasn't cold enough to reheat.

This room, the firelight—it was made for seduction. *His* seduction. He almost couldn't remember the last time he'd been with a woman, and then, it had been a dissatisfying entanglement without any meaning other than a biological action.

This was different. He'd lusted after Leonie, but now, he was overwhelmed and honored to find this beautiful creature as his wife. He would care for her, protect her, and bed her.

She closed her eyes, her lashes fanning across her cheeks, and he was almost undone.

His lips found hers with a will of their own.

He'd moved a tad too fast. She gave a start. His hand at her waist kept her from moving back.

With a herculean effort, he held himself still.

For a second, they seemed to be breathing together and then her lips softened.

Now, Roman swept his tongue against the line parting lips and to his everlasting joy she opened to him. They were kissing. Actually kissing in the very best sense of the term.

Yes, he could take it deeper, but he reminded himself he wanted to go slow.

His arm circled her waist. He longed to crush her body against his, to press his hard readiness against her hips, but he held back.

If she had been a more experienced woman, his need was so great he would have had her back on the bed and be deep in by now. Instead, he held himself in check because he wanted them to be the best sort of lovers, and that called for patience from the beginning.

And they would have a lifetime of making love. He had so much he could show her, so much to share. He'd love her in every way possible.

He broke the kiss and nibbled a line to her ear. "Help me undress."

There was a pause and then she tugged at his shirt, pulling it from the waist of his breeches.

"Good, this is good," he said, discovering she liked the way he teased her ear. When he lifted her arm to encircle his neck, she willingly pressed her body against his, her breasts flattening against his chest.

Even nicer.

He ran his hand down over her buttock. She was naked under the nightdress. Deliciously so. And if he didn't get his breeches off, he was going to bust the buttons.

His fingers shook as he started twisting the first one. She rubbed her cheek against his. He had a heavy beard and he worried that his whiskers might scratch her delicate skin. He should have shaved—and then they were kissing again and he forgot he even had whiskers.

This time, she participated in the kiss. Her lips moved against his. Her arm was still around his neck and she reached up to place a hand on his shoulder.

·That was all the permission he needed to lift her up and carry her the two steps to the bed. He set her on the mattress, their lips not parting. He touched her with his tongue. She did not shy away but she flinched slightly and he immediately pulled back.

He broke the kiss and sat on the bed beside her. "I need to undress." She nodded. Roman pulled his shirt over his head. He tossed it aside. Crossing his leg, he gave the heel of his boot a yank. First one hit the floor, then the other.

Her eyes were dark, darker than he'd ever seen them before. The glow of the fire reflected in them as if she was some otherworldly creature come to earth to grace him with her presence. "Should I undress completely as well?"

Roman thought his heart would stop.

His mouth went dry. He had to swallow before he said, "That would be nice."

That would be nice. The greatest understatement in the world.

In response, Leonie whispered, "I do trust you, Roman."

"I will never let harm come to you."

She nodded as if she believed he meant those words.

And then she stood, reached for the skirt of her nightdress, and pulled it over her head.

Roman almost fell to his knees in both gratitude and wonder.

Chapter 13

Leonie had known she would have to let her husband have her. It was expected. Her mother had made that clear.

She hadn't been looking forward to it with any anticipation. Her one hope was that Roman would be not be angry and rough. Arthur had exposed her to the cruelty of this act.

Still, she'd had no curiosity about it, until now.

Roman's kisses kindled feelings she had trouble defining and yet she yearned for more. They were actually quite pleasant.

She was very conscious that he was doing his best to not frighten her. She could feel the tension in him. He was probably driven with the same intensity that Arthur had been—except Roman would never hurt her.

And it was that knowledge that unwound the anxiety inside of her, that freed her to discover she enjoyed his kisses. When he had breathed into her ear, she'd thought she would melt into his arms.

Now, she could begin to understand why her mother liked doing this so much.

Now, she found herself liking it, too.

She also wanted to give as much as she received. There was something about his body heat and the scent of his skin that made her move as close as possible to him. Roman's kisses also promised that there was so much more to experience and enjoy *if* she would allow him a bit more freedom.

It had been this last kiss that had convinced her. When she'd opened to him, it had been as if their souls touched.

She could have laughed at the poetry of the moment, except the description fit. She was seeing Roman's soul and it was generous, affectionate, and kind.

Taking off her nightdress was a bold move. It was also a sign of trust.

Everything they would become to each other would start with this night.

The room was warm but that didn't stop her flesh tightening at the exposure to the air. Leonie shook her hair down around her shoulders. She didn't drop the gown to the floor but held it in front of her, a bit shy about being so forward.

Roman beheld her as if she was a work of art. His mouth curved into one of his smiles that she was beginning to adore. His eye met hers. "You are lovely."

"Even now?" She knew men thought her a beauty with her clothes on. Clothes hid flaws.

His response was to take the nightdress from her so that she was completely open to him. "Yes, now." He dropped the gown to the floor, gathered her in his arms and, sitting on the bed, brought her to his lap. He kissed her with such passion she could barely think, let alone breathe.

And when he was done, she kissed him back in the same way. She was becoming quite good at kissing.

Then again, who knew kisses could be as heady as the richest brandy? She could kiss this way forever, morning, noon, and night. No interruptions. No meals. Just deep, satisfying kisses—

His hand ran along the inside of her thigh. Her initial reaction was to close her legs. He didn't move his hand. He just left it there. His tongue found hers, coaxing her to taste him the way he was her, and her legs opened.

He kissed her cheek, her neck, her shoulder. His hand found

her most intimate places. "Is this all right?" he breathed against her ear.

Leonie discovered she'd found a *new* favorite intimate place. The response to his breath on her ear could only be second best to where his hand was now.

Delicious hunger unfurled inside her. She would have let him do anything. When his thumb stroked her, she sang her delight in a soft sigh of enjoyment.

"Did I hurt you?" he asked anxiously.

Her answer was to grab his face with both of her hands, press her breasts, which had suddenly grown full and tight and lusty—*yes, lusty!*—against him, and kiss him with everything she had.

Her assault surprised him. He teetered back on the bed and then rolled the two of them onto the mattress. Now, he was kissing her and she was kissing him and his amazing hands made her feel more alive than she'd ever thought possible.

Leonie had her arms around his neck. She ran them down his back, delighting in the play of muscles beneath her palms. She could not have enough of the warmth of his body. Her hand slid under the waistband of his breeches. The tips of her fingers pressed in the hard flesh of his buttocks—

He slid his fingers inside her.

Her instant reaction was to tighten in alarm. *What was he doing?*

"Does this hurt?" She lay on her back and he was on his side over her. His fingers were still there.

Leonie waited for pain expectantly.

There was none.

She looked up at him and shook her head.

A slow smile slid across his face as if he was relieved. "Do you like this?"

"Like what?"

He moved his finger inside her, this thumb stroking one very sensitive, intimate spot. She liked that. Very much. Oh, dear, *yes*.

Roman knew what she needed better than she. He seemed intent on unleashing a wild surge of emotion inside her. Leonie struggled to control what she didn't understand. Her fingers curled into the bedclothes.

"Let it go," he urged her.

Leonie wasn't certain what he meant. She didn't want any of this to go. She wanted it to last forever and knew that it couldn't. Pressure was building in her. Part of her wanted to fight it, to return to where she felt safe. And then there was the fragment of her being that wanted *more*. Just more.

The word came out as a prayer and then she began repeating it until she wasn't praying but begging. Roman happily obliged. He knew sorcery. He robbed her of reason and took complete power of her being—

The pressure exploded into a starburst of unbridled sensation. She felt flushed and prickly and open and *energized*. Gloriously energized with awareness of her being.

For a long moment, the sound of their breathing filled the space. She couldn't speak. She had no words.

Roman acted as if he'd been as moved by the experience as herself. He drew her close, wrapping his arms around her. She could feel the pounding of his heart. It beat as fast as hers.

She also wanted even more.

Leonie felt his hardness against her hip. It pressed against the remaining buttons of his breeches. He was feeling the same urgent hunger she'd experienced only a few moments before.

What was *more*? If he could turn her inside out with his hand, what would it feel like to have him in her?

She no longer feared pain. Instead, she feared going through life without having all of him. And she wanted him right now. She began to unfasten his breeches.

Roman didn't stop her. No, he was too busy kissing her shoulder, her neck—another very sensitive spot!—and working his way to her breasts.

His lips covered her nipple just as she undid the last button. His manhood practically sprang out of his breeches, but Leonie was too lost to what Roman was doing to her to explore.

Every woman knew that men admired breasts.

But she hadn't understood why until now. She wished he'd never stop. More amazing, she felt the tugging of his mouth all the way to her very center.

Someone was sighing, the sound soft and very, very happy—and she realized it was her. She'd even buried her fingers in his hair to bring him closer.

Abruptly, he pulled away. She wanted him back but he stood and with journeyman efficiency finished undressing.

Had his eyes once been light gray? They had taken on the depth of storm clouds and Leonie knew what would come next. Her husband was the one pleasing here. He had to see to himself now, and the thought was exciting.

Roman kicked off his breeches. His buttocks were as perfectly well formed as one of the ancients' statues—and as hard.

He faced her and her eyes widened at the sight of his desire. He seemed to know what she was thinking. "Trust me, Leonie."

She nodded. He stretched out on the bed beside her and kissed her. As his lips explored hers, his hand found and carried her hand to his shaft. He wrapped her fingers around it.

Leonie did not know what to think.

"Touch me," he whispered against her lips before seeking out her ear. He'd already discovered how compliant she could be when he kissed her there.

She gave him a light stroke and then drew her hand back when he seemed to bob with a will of his own. Not only did it move, but it didn't feel as she had imagined it would. It was hard but velvety smooth.

"What do you think?" he asked.

"It's not very handsome," she answered. "Nothing like the rest of you." She liked the heavy muscles of his thighs, especially when they rubbed against hers. His hips were narrow and led up to a broad chest that she knew firsthand was very comfortable and inviting.

Roman chuckled at her words. "I hope you grow to like him as well. Touch me again."

Leonie didn't know if she wished to do so. Still, she wanted Roman to feel the same pleasure he had given her. She placed her fingers upon it.

"It" liked her touch. It seemed to stand up straighter as if vying for her attention. She dared to circle its tip—

Roman's hand covered hers. "Easy, lass."

"Did that hurt?"

"Oh, no, but right now, I can't take too much more."

Leonie looked into his stormy eyes. "Because you like what I do?"

"Because I like you." He punctuated his words by kissing her, rolling their bodies so that he was over her.

She slid her arms around his neck, their bodies fitting together. The earlier pressure of desire returned, only this time it was wiser, more demanding.

Her body knew things now.

When he lifted himself to nestle between her legs, they naturally opened to make room for him. She liked feeling his hips cradled against hers. She understood what was going to happen. Instead of the fear she had anticipated, she found herself eager. She wanted him inside her.

Like a spark to kindling, there was a heat between them and it was growing fast. He whispered her name. His lips brushed her temple. Her breasts pressed against his chest—and then he slid into her and Leonie thought she'd never felt anything more wonderful. Her lover was a full and able man. Her body stretched to accommodate him. She lifted her hips and he slid in deeper.

"Dear God, Leonie, you are precious."

No words could be better praise. No one had ever said she was "precious." Or looked at her as if she was to be valued and trusted.

"Finish this," she urged softly, trusting him in return. "Show me all."

He nuzzled her ear, her neck, lifted her hips with his hands, and began the rhythmic thrusting that, yes, she had seen in nature, but this was different. There was something sacred about what was happening between them. All her senses sharpened on their joining.

His movements were gaining more purpose. The heat between them threatened to consume her. At the same time, she never wanted this to end. She could spend her life in his arms. Here, the world had purpose and meaning.

The desire she'd experienced earlier began to build, but this time with a difference. It engulfed her. She was no longer just Leonie, she was Roman as well. Strong, capable, unafraid.

She tightened her legs around him and arched to bring him tighter to her core. He gave a sensual growl and she realized she, too, had the power to enflame him. This wasn't being done to her. Together, they were creating a bond that could never be broken. This was what her body had been created for—

Her release struck her with the force of a lightning bolt. One moment she strove with him, and in the next, she was lost in wave after wave of rippling wonder.

Her body had never felt so right or so perfectly used. Everything about her was centered on where they were joined.

He knew what had happened. He'd probably anticipated it. "You break me, Leonie. You bring me to my knees."

And then he brought her to hers with a deep, deep thrust, and his own release.

Leonie could feel the life force move from his body into hers. Had she thought she'd reached the pinnacle?

Oh, no. *This* was the peak, this moment of receiving him. Her release had been exquisite, but this feeling was fulfillment.

Never had she felt as much a woman as she did now.

He held himself over her as if he savored every second of this moment, as if he wanted to capture and hold it.

His breath came out with her whispered name. "Leonie." It was prayer and benediction. She'd pleased him.

And he'd pleased her . . . very much.

How could she ever have thought this act crude?

She'd not understood, but now her heart had been opened. "There *is* a 'passion flower of ecstasy,' " she whispered.

"What?" His mouth curved into the easy grin that she was beginning to adore.

She stretched beneath him, enjoying the weight of his body on hers, the warmth of him still inside her. "Cassandra had a poetry reading where the poet when on and on about the 'passion flower of ecstasy.' I thought he had to be teasing." She ran a hand over his buttock—so nice and solid. A marvel, really. "I believe we found it."

A proud gladness lit the gray in his eyes. "We shall always find it," he promised.

"We can do this again and again?" she said with wonder. "Exactly this way?"

"Oh, no," he answered. "Practice will make us better and better at it."

Deep within, she felt him begin to fill and swell. An answering tension built inside of her.

"Better?" she asked.

"Absolutely."

Leonie frowned. "Is it like this for everyone?"

"Only poets and lovers." He began moving and all questions evaporated from Leonie's mind.

Her body was already far too sensitive and his slightest touch seemed amplified. This time, her release was quick and hard and it was her voice that shouted his name.

Spent, neither of them could move. Roman held her in his arms, a finger playing with one of her curls. She could ask for no safer haven. She was content.

"I love you."

At first, she wasn't certain he'd spoken or if she had imagined the words. The fire in the hearth was dying and so it was harder to see his expression in the shadows.

"I believe I felt love for you the moment we met at the Colonial Ball," he continued. "Fanciful, I know. Except I'm not one to give way to whims."

Leonie went very still. She'd never imagined someone would love her.

"You asked why I went after you the night you eloped with Paccard. I knew you were making a mistake. Oh, not that Paccard would turn out to be the brute he was. I could not have predicted what he did. I didn't want you to be with him, until I'd made my declaration."

She listened, intent on his words.

"You scare me, Leonie."

That statement captured her attention. "Why?"

"Because after this, I know I'll never want anything as much as I want you." He ran a hand down her arm and over her hip. "And I want all of you, lass. I want to love and protect you and create a good life for us."

It wasn't about her money. He wanted *her*.

And it was a miracle.

Someone loved her. Despite her flaws. Despite her secrets.

Of course, she wasn't certain what this word "love" meant—and yet, she trusted him to teach her.

Leonie kissed the underside of his chin, the first place she could reach. She sensed the pleasure in his smile. He gathered her even closer, as if he could tuck her body safely inside his, and then he fell asleep.

She couldn't sleep.

Surrounded by his strength and body heat, she had to marvel at this gift he had given. If he loved her, then he must like her, not want to just possess her.

For so long she'd found herself unlikable—and here now, without any effort on her part, this noble, wonderful man had let her know that she was precious.

Was feeling this sort of appreciation in return "love"?

Her mother had never appreciated her father. Consequently, he barely gave her a care.

So, she and Roman were different from them? More powerful? And in "love"?

Leonie didn't feel the least bit sleepy. Her senses had been overworked and now her mind was trying to play catch-up.

She rested in Roman's arms and watched him sleep. Then she frowned as she observed the room's light diminishing with the fire in the hearth. She wasn't worried about being cold, not with her husband's body to keep her warm.

Staring at the ceiling, she knew she should be exhausted, but she wasn't. It was like that sometimes for her. Her mind could be very active even though every fiber of her being yearned for sleep.

Usually when this happened, a nip or two of brandy helped.

Her foot started to fall asleep and she eased out of Roman's arms so she could move it. She curled up beside him, but still sleep eluded her. She tried counting backward, a trick her father taught her. That didn't tire her.

She struggled to not think about brandy.

A call to nature made itself known. She glanced at her husband. He was sleeping soundly. She didn't want to wake him. Why should he be disturbed because she was awake?

Moving quietly, she slid out of the other side of the bed and tiptoed to where she'd placed her dress on a hook on the wall. She pulled it over her head. Braiding her hair, she slipped on her shoes and moved toward the door.

Roman turned over on his back but did not wake. She smiled, liking the sight of him filling the bed. "I'll be right back," she mouthed to him. Her need for the water closet had become very real. Turning the lock in the door, she let herself out. She considered locking the door behind her but decided against it.

The hall was solid darkness save for a lamp lit at the base of the stairs. Not a sound could be heard from the other rooms or from downstairs. She used her hand against the wall to feel her way to the steps until she could see them.

Beyond the lamp, she could see into the taproom where a fire glowed in the oversized hearth. Snoring figures bundled in coats and blankets slept on the floor or on the benches. These were the guests who could not afford a room.

Leonie moved silently to the water closet. No one was in there. Fortunately, moonlight allowed her to see what she was doing.

Feeling better, she came out intending to hurry upstairs. However, in the taproom on one of the tables, she noticed the silhouette of a bottle. The table was where the soldiers had been sitting and close to the door.

She stood riveted by the sight. She didn't know what was in the bottle, but her whole skin went alert at the thought of one small drink. Then she would be able to sleep.

And Roman would be none the wiser.

Tomorrow, well, tomorrow she'd try again to go without. It would be easier then.

But tonight, she needed a bit of whatever it was in the bottle to let her mind wind down. In the end, she knew she had no choice but to walk toward it.

Of course she was cautious. She was very quiet as she stepped around those sleeping on the floor. If someone so much as breathed differently, she paused, but then continued when she knew she was safe.

The trip really only took seconds. She leaned over a man snoozing on his back and snatched the bottle by its neck. She didn't waste time leaving the room. However, instead of turning toward the stairs, and the possibility of being caught by Roman if he came looking for her, she moved toward the inn's front door. No one was sleeping in the reception room. Leaning against the wall, her back to the taproom, she wiped the bottle's mouth and took a smell.

Gin.

Leonie made a face. Not her favorite but it would suffice. After all, she only needed a sip.

She raised the bottle to her lips. It wasn't full. She had to tilt her head way back. She'd be horrified if anyone caught her but she didn't have time to search for a glass.

Gin hit her tongue. The fragrant taste had a bite. She lowered the bottle, holding the liquor in her mouth before swallowing.

It burned down her throat. She held the bottle close to her, waiting. Gin might not be her first choice; however, it knew its job.

Her stomach tightened as the liquor hit, and then in a matter of seconds, a tension that Leonie hadn't even recognized she'd felt began to ease. Her muscles relaxed. This was why she couldn't sleep. She'd been nervous.

She took another drink, a deeper one this time, and it was as if she tasted mother's milk. Indeed, the gin gave her a buoyant feeling she had not anticipated. No wonder so many in the lower classes liked it.

Of course, there wasn't much left in the bottle. What harm could come from finishing it off—?

"Do you like my bottle, missy?"

The gruff male voice startled her. She'd been so fixated on her drinking she hadn't registered the man's presence. His form blocked the light and she couldn't make out his features in the shadows to know who he was.

She stepped away toward the front door. Before she could take more than one step, he grabbed her, his hand moving with an incredible swiftness. He slapped his other hand over her mouth before she could scream and backed her against the wall to pin her there with his body. She kicked but he was too strong and heavy for her.

"You don't receive anything for nothing," he said, his breath hot in her face. His hand was between her legs in the crudest way possible and he began fumbling with his clothing. "Now you pay for your drinks and let's do it quick."

He started pulling up her skirt.

Panic coursed through her. She remembered this. She knew it. She began struggling with fierce will. He growled at her to stay still.

His hold over her mouth lessened and she bit his finger with all she had.

He roared in rage. He stopped his fumbling and grasped her by the throat, but Leonie sensed freedom. She ducked her head and tried to run—except he had hold of her dress. His finger-nails scraped her chest as he grabbed her by the bodice. He hit her across the face with his elbow.

She tasted blood but still she tried to strike out, attempting to hit him with the bottle she held in her hand. He swore, grabbed her hair and her chest, and began dragging her toward the front door.

Leonie resisted with all her might. If he took her outside, no one would hear her scream, just like that night with Arthur. That horrible, horrible night.

And then she realized she had yet to scream. She'd been so busy struggling she'd not made a sound.

Leonie let out a scream that could have been heard in heaven. For her effort, she received another elbow to the face as he shoved the door open with her shoulder.

Chapter 14

ℛoman had woken to discover Leonie gone from his bed. He sat up, confused. Her dress was gone from where it had been hanging. Perhaps she had slipped out for the water closet?

She should have let him escort her.

In fact, he was embarrassed that she'd managed to leave the room without his being aware. He could lay the blame at her lovely feet. She'd drained him. She'd been a vibrant, demanding partner and it has been his honor to pleasure her. She'd been everything he'd hoped and more.

He'd heard men complain of wives who considered sex little more than a chore. Being a circumspect man, he'd hoped his wife would not be one of them. His sense of duty was such that he would not dishonor his marriage vows.

However, Leonie had proven herself to be very much his partner in bed. He felt blessed. Those stirrings years ago had not been just lust. His love for her had been vindicated. How could any man not help but adore such a woman? She was all he could ask.

In fact, he could have a go at her again but wouldn't. She needed rest.

So, Roman rose from bed, pulled on his breeches, and went out to search for his wife. When he found her, he would also stress that she must never fear waking him. Walking alone around even an inn such as this was never safe for a woman like herself. He'd come to realize that, though she knew her attraction, she didn't truly understand her impact on the male beast. This was part of her charm but could be dangerous.

Barefoot because he had not bothered to waste the time to put on his boots, he went out into the hall. He was on the top step when he heard Leonie scream.

Cannon shot could not move as fast as Roman did down those stairs. He heard a scuffle in the hall and saw a man trying to drag her out the door. The brute had Leonie by her dress and her hair. She was digging her feet into the floor trying to stop from being abducted.

In a flash, Roman was in front of the man. He grabbed him with both hands and, showing a superhuman strength, lifted him up and back into the inn.

Her assailant let go of Leonie with a yelp. His eyes widened to show the whites as he looked at Roman. Roman was determined that his face would be the man's *last* memory. He threw the bastard against the wall. He landed with a thud, stunned. He held up his hands. Roman recognized him as one of the soldiers who had been eyeing Leonie earlier.

"She wanted it," the man said. "Traded it for a bottle, she did—"

Roman's fist cut off the sentence.

Wanted it? Leonie had wanted this scum? Roman thought not.

He landed another blow in the bastard's gut. It wasn't just the soldier he beat, but Paccard, the man who had defiled her. He punched the bastard in his side. Another to his face. And another and another and another . . .

From a distance, he could hear Leonie crying his name.

Several pairs of strong arms tried to prevent him from battering the man more. "You'll kill him, my lord." It was the innkeeper's voice. "You must stop. He's done."

"Please, Roman. *Please.*"

Their words finally sank in.

Roman stepped back, shaking his head like a man possessed.

Leonie sobbed senselessly. He looked over to her. She was on her knees bent over as if in great pain.

The soldier fell to the floor, groaning. Roman wanted another go at him but Stoddard stepped between them.

"My lord," the innkeeper said, "he's done. Enough."

Enough? Roman wanted to tear the limbs off the man. The reception room was full of the curious. If Leonie's scream hadn't woken them, the fight did. Candles had been lit and a lamp brought in.

Roman held up his hands, a sign that he was finished. He'd leave the man to his compatriots, all of whom eyed Roman warily and didn't step to help their friend. Roman's knuckles would be bruised. There was blood on them. Not his own. The innkeeper handed him a damp towel and Roman wiped his hands as he went over to his wife.

"Leonie?"

She kept her head bowed. Her assailant had torn her bodice. She held it together.

Roman knelt and placed his hand on her shoulder. "It is all right. Everything will be fine."

She lifted her head.

The signs of her struggle almost caused him to tear into the soldier again. Instead, he raised the towel to her face and placed it gently where there was a cut by the corner of her mouth.

She flinched. He soothed her with soft words. Her lower lip trembled, but her crying quieted.

"Let me take you upstairs," he said.

Leonie nodded and allowed him to help her to her feet. She pushed her heavy hair back with her hand. The innkeeper was apologizing. Roman barely heard a word. Instead, he noticed the soldier was still doubled up on the floor. "Tie him up for the magistrate."

"Yes, my lord. Of course."

"Come," Roman gently ordered. "Let's go to our room."

She nodded and as they took a step together his bare foot struck a bottle. It rolled on the floor and the soldier's protest came back to Roman—*Traded it for a bottle, she did.*

A white heat roiled through him along with a cruel understanding.

Leonie had come down here for a drink? *His wife had exposed herself to this danger for a tipple?* No wonder she hadn't woken him when she left their bed. She hadn't wanted him to stop her.

Roman looked to the innkeeper. It took all his control to ask civilly, "Do you have brandy?"

Beside him, Leonie made a sound of protest as if she might be ill. He ignored her.

"Yes, my lord." He hurried to the taproom to fetch the bottle.

"Roman, no. That is not necessary."

"Oh, but it is," he said, unable to look at her.

The innkeeper's wife had roused from her bed. She gave an exclamation of surprise upon seeing Leonie, who tried to hide her head in Roman's shoulder.

The innkeeper came running back to them. "Here we are, my lord. And two glasses."

Roman took the bottle. "The glasses aren't necessary." He led Leonie past the curious stares of the guests who had been sleeping in the taproom and to the stairs.

Mrs. Stoddard followed them. "Do you need anything for the cuts on your hands? Or for my lady?"

"We shall be fine," Roman said, and gave her a tight smile, even though nothing could be further from the truth.

Leonie went up the stairs ahead of him. She limped slightly as if she'd hurt her foot in the ruckus. Well, the next time, she should put on shoes. Then he noticed she had one shoe on. The other was probably on the floor downstairs.

He uncorked the bottle and took a healthy swig for himself.

His wife looked back and caught him. The small worry line between her brows that marked when she was uncertain was there.

As it should be.

She reached the door first.

"It is open," he said.

Leonie went inside.

He stopped and stood for a moment, staring at the open door. What sort of hell had he entered?

Less than an hour ago he'd believed himself the most fortunate of men. Now he feared his wife would be an iron weight around his life. He'd opened his heart to her.

She had the power to pull him down, defeat him . . . she'd almost done it once.

He could not let that happen.

Roman walked into the room, shut the door, and locked it.

LEONIE WAS HORRIFIED at almost being raped again, and ashamed. Oh, yes, so very shamed.

But all would be fine. Roman had rescued her and she would learn from this lesson. She didn't like gin at all and she shouldn't have been where she was. However, she would apologize and praise him and vow never to wander off again in that manner.

She walked straight to the washbasin. There was water in the bowl from when she'd prepared herself for bed. She did not look at herself in the glass hanging on the wall. She couldn't. She knew she looked a fright with her runny nose and with bruises swelling her face. The roots of her hair hurt where that monster had tried to drag her out of the inn. She'd like nothing better than to crawl into bed and pretend nothing happened.

Still, she owed Roman an apology and an explanation. *I only went downstairs for a moment of privacy . . .*

That was true. She'd say that.

He lit a candle off the dying coals. Light filled the room.

Leonie forced a smile on her face without meeting her eye in the mirror. The cut by her lip hurt. A wall of tears threatened to overtake her. She struggled to hold them back. Roman would not admire her blubbering. She prepared to turn—

"I believed you when you said you drank to excess at our marriage ceremony because you were frightened of the wedding night. That you had to erase the memory of what Paccard did to you, but that wasn't true, was it, Leonie? You just drink."

Leonie forgot excuses. She faced her husband, her hand holding the towel dropping to her side.

"I do have bad memories of Arthur." Couldn't he see how her life had been affected? *He*, of all people, should understand because he had come to her rescue that night . . . as well as this one—

Her own culpability stunned her into silence.

Roman lifted the bottle he held in his hand. Even from here she caught a whiff of that tantalizing, sweet spiciness and felt a familiar yearning.

Her husband's gaze watched her. *He knew.*

"Your hands shook slightly earlier," he explained as if he knew what she was thinking. "I thought you had some maidenly apprehension about tonight. I didn't want to believe there could be another reason."

"I *was* apprehensive." Her mouth had gone dry. It hurt to speak. Or was that because of the tightness in her chest? *Everything will be all right*, she told herself. *Just smile.*

But everything wasn't going to be all right and both she and Roman knew it.

"What are you going to do?" she dared to ask.

"With this?" He held up the bottle. "Why, leave it here." He set it on the bedside table.

"About—?" she started, and then stopped. Perhaps she didn't want an answer.

He completed her question. "About this marriage?"

About us. But she didn't speak those words. She was wary of his mood. He seemed calm, too calm. Silence was best. She knew he was angry but there was another deeper emotion that she couldn't quite define at play, and then she recognized it—disappointment. Disillusion.

"Oh, we are married," he said. "I need your money."

Those words were like pinpoints of pain. He only spoke the truth, and yet, she was startled by the heartache. And really—why? She didn't owe him anything. They didn't know each other, not well at least.

He'd said he loved her. If he did, he wouldn't have this frightening coldness about him.

Leonie reached for her pride, her defiance, except that it was hard to hold her head high—especially since she was so aware of the brandy bottle close at hand.

Roman acted as if he waited for an answer from her. When she didn't speak, a mask dropped over his face. "I thought we had a chance." He turned away from her. "You see, I meant the vows I spoke, the ones you can't remember."

She deserved that as well. What sort of woman could not remember her marriage ceremony?

"I'm not without sin myself, Leonie. I'm not perfect and I do not expect that of you—but *this*, the drinking, I can't support this. I will not. I've seen what it does to men and to women. I've seen your mother—"

"I am *not* my mother." That brought her head up.

"Or your father?" he queried. He shook his head. "We are all products of our parents. And I am the blind fool who wanted to pretend it wasn't true."

It *wasn't* true . . . *Except,* a small voice warned her from within, *how could it not be?*

But Roman wasn't finished. "You must understand, Leonie, your shame is not that you were raped or that you killed the man who did it in self-defense. It is that *you can't look yourself in a mirror.*" He raked his fingers through his hair, pressing his lips together as if he had said too much.

And then he seemed to reach a decision.

He shrugged, his eyes bright with anger. "You can return to London. Live the life you want. But you'll not do it with the money I sold *my soul* to earn. That goes to creating a life for me and my family. A *good one*. You may have your bottle. Enjoy your night." He picked up his boots, his shirt, and his coat, and before she knew what he was about, he unlocked the door and walked out.

Leonie stared as the door closed behind him.

He'd left her? *What did this mean?*

She thought about going out into the hall and ordering him back . . . a silly idea because the man who had confronted her was in no mood for a reconciliation of any sort.

Indeed, he'd already made his judgement. She was irredeemable. She was like her parents!

Well, there were many people who admired the Charnocks . . .

Leonie's eye caught her reflection in the glass. Even in the room's shadowy darkness, she could not recognize herself.

She raised the towel to her check. The reflection raised a towel to its cheek. It *was* her.

And there, beside the bed in the reflection, was the brandy bottle. Uncorked.

If she had a sip, she would feel better.

The pulsing pain in her cheek and lip would ease.

The world, *her* world, might become a bit more tolerable.

You can return to London. Live the life you want. Hadn't that been what she'd asked?

Except, the ultimatum did not fill her with joy. He wasn't offering freedom.

She gazed at the cursed bottle. "I don't even like gin," she complained to the air around her. Her voice sounded shaky and petulant.

This was not the woman she thought herself to be. And, God help her, if she wanted to be that woman, she dared not take a drink . . . except she wanted one badly.

Still, she knew brandy would not make matters better. She knew that as clearly as she knew her name.

Leonie skirted around the bed away from the brandy bottle. She gave it her back as she sat on the bed and reached for the covers. Curling into a small ball on the mattress, she covered her head with the sheets. They smelled of Roman. His scent was all around her here.

She wrapped her arms around herself and prayed that she could either disappear or be saved. Please, oh, please let her be saved.

In this way, she fell into a fitful sleep.

A POUNDING ON the door woke her. "My lady? *My lady?*"

Leonie's eyelids seemed sealed shut and they had no desire to open. She rubbed her nose in the bedclothes. She didn't feel good. Something was not right—and then she realized where she was and what she had done.

Groggily, she forced her eyes to open and looked over at the empty side of the bed. Roman had not returned. He was true to his word.

"My lady?" The knocking had not ceased.

Leonie sat up. Her hair was a tangled mess and she was wearing the dress she'd worn yesterday.

The brandy bottle was still on the table.

She had not touched it. She had kept her resolve, a small victory.

"*My lady?*"

Leonie looked to the door. "Yes?"

The relief in the voice on the other side was noticeable. "My lady, it is Mrs. Stoddard, the innkeeper's wife. Such a hard night you had and I wouldn't bother you save the earl bid me tell you he is ready to leave. He wishes to know if you are coming with him or if you wish to take a hired chaise back to London?" The question in her voice said she didn't know if she'd got it right.

Leonie had no doubt she did. Roman would dearly enjoy sending her packing.

She looked again to the untouched bottle. Something inside of her felt its pull, but her pride would not let her bend. He expected her to hasten back to London and live on what? The man who had delivered ultimatums was not one to support an errant wife. Why, he'd set her aside—and she would not give him the satisfaction.

"Tell him—" Her voice had to be cleared. It was hard to sound proud when one's throat was so dry. "Tell him I will be down shortly to continue *our* trip to Bonhomie. I will expect to break my fast."

"Yes, my lady." Footsteps could be heard leaving the door and going down the stairs.

Leonie knew Roman would be impatient. He was done with her. If she wasn't quick, he would leave. At the same time, she couldn't let him treat her as if she was little more than a servant. She was his wife. She had pride—although now that he had her dowry, pride was all she could claim.

She pulled out a traveling dress Minnie had rolled carefully and tucked into her valise. It was robin's-egg blue with capped sleeves and rows of pleating across the bodice. She always felt very feminine when she wore it. She now dressed quickly, including pulling on clean stockings.

She brushed the snarls from her hair and twisted it at her neck, using pins to hold it in place. The splash of cold water on her face felt good and reminded her she could not put off the inevitable.

Leonie looked at her reflection in the glass.

An angry purple bruise marred her cheekbone. There was additional bruising around one corner of her mouth where the cut was. It didn't hurt anymore but Leonie was very grateful the soldier hadn't broken her nose when he'd struck her.

She lifted her chin. The marks from his fingers were on either side of her windpipe. Those bruises would fade swiftly. The ones on her face would take longer.

Stepping back from the mirror, she told herself to not be ashamed. She had not been the attacker.

From its place on the bedside table, the brandy bottle mocked her.

Leonie quickly stuffed her clothes, including her nightdress, into her valise and closed it. Roman would have someone fetch it for her. She needed to go downstairs. She put on her pelisse and picked up her bonnet and gloves.

Squaring her shoulders, she opened the door and walked briskly to the stairs and down them. She stopped at the water closet.

The sounds of a busy taproom carried down the hall. She was certain that the soldier was not there. If she'd been him, she would have run from Roman's temper with all haste. However, she didn't know who all had witnessed her attack. She had a memory of what seemed to be scores of people gathered around afterward. Certainly, some of them had not left the inn.

It took all her courage to leave the water closet and walk to the taproom. At her appearance in the doorway, the room went silent.

Mrs. Stoddard was hovering anxiously around a small table set for one with what could only be generously described as the inn's best silver. "Here, my lady." She pulled out a chair.

Over a dozen pair of eyes watched Leonie take her seat.

She was familiar with being observed by jealous mothers who considered her their daughters' rival and men of ages and sizes who enjoyed a leer, but this was different. She knew she had been the topic of conversation and it had not been flattering.

Leonie placed a napkin in her lap. The action allowed her to keep her head down and her injuries from the gawkers.

Mrs. Stoddard hurried in with a plate of eggs and beefsteak. Leonie didn't know if she had the will to eat it. However, she was not going to allow these people to intimidate her—

She felt Roman's presence before she saw him.

The air in the room literally changed. Those who stared became very busy with their own affairs. A hum of conversation returned to the room.

Of course, what Leonie experienced was this extra sense about him. She had not needed to look up to know he was there.

He stood by the door and surveyed the room. After that quick glance, she tried to keep her concertation on cutting her meat. It was hard. She feared he was coming to tell her that he'd changed his mind about her options and was sending her to London whether she chose to go or not.

The chair across from hers was pulled away. He sat in it and placed his hat on the table. "An ale," he called to the innkeeper. He looked to Leonie. "Ale for you?"

Was this a test like the brandy? "I prefer tea," she said.

"Tea for my lady."

His lady. Leonie's heart lifted at the title. Or was he being formal? She set down her knife and fork. "I'm going with you."

He glanced around the room as if seeing who still had the audacity to stare. Eyes were quickly averted. He faced Leonie. "Mrs. Stoddard said as much."

There was no hint of kindness in his tone.

Any apology she might have attempted died on her lips. Instead, she focused on her food, and did find it easier to eat. He was not going to abandon her or send her away. Yes, he was angry. Time would heal that, time and her very honest efforts to be the wife he wanted.

The tea tasted good.

"I had Mrs. Stoddard prepare a hamper for our noonday meal," Roman said.

They were going to share another meal together. A picnic. This was a good sign.

"That is an excellent idea," she murmured.

"Are you ready to go?" he asked, seeing she had finished her plate.

"I am." She picked up her hat. "When shall we arrive at Bonhomie?"

"Late afternoon." He rose to his feet, took his own hat, and motioned toward the door with it.

Leonie was only too happy to escape the taproom. She took a moment to thank Mr. and Mrs. Stoddard for their hospitality. Tears were in Mrs. Stoddard's eyes and she kept saying, "We are sorry, my lady. Very sorry."

"It is not your fault," Leonie assured them, conscious of a certain stiffness in Roman's shoulders that let her know whose fault he thought it was—and he was right.

She could blame only herself. Once they were alone in the coach, she planned on apologizing to him. The words he'd said last night came back to her—*I want to love and protect you and create a good life for us.* She would challenge him to remember them, to let her prove that they were true.

It was with a lighter step that she went out into the day. The sun was shining on a lovely early spring morning. The sky was blue, new grass was coming in, and the trees were budding. Anything was possible on a day like this one.

The post boy held the coach door open for her. Leonie climbed in. Despite the huge hamper taking up a good portion of the floor, she settled in, leaving the majority of the room for her husband. However, instead of waiting for Roman, the post boy closed the coach door. She frowned and slid across the seat to look outside.

Roman held a horse by the reins as he talked to Mr. Stoddard. Tipping the innkeeper, he then swung up into the saddle.

Leonie called his name. He frowned, but came up to her.

"You aren't riding with me?"

"I'm tired of being confined." His was a flat statement. There was no humor or warmth behind it.

"So," she said, "this is the way it is going to be?"

"Our marriage?" He snorted his opinion. "I needed money, Leonie. Now I have it." Without waiting for her response, he put heels to horse and they were on their way.

She fell back on the seat as the coach began rolling. She'd go mad riding alone all day.

But then, he knew that.

She stuck her head out the window. Her husband rode as far ahead of the chaise as he could.

They did not stop for lunch. Roman took bread and cheese out of the hamper for himself and the post boy. Leonie was left to her own wishes.

At least she was going with him.

Once they reached Bonhomie, he would not be able to escape her. One way or the other, she would make her apology and he would have to listen. He liked her. She knew that. His regard for her had lasted for years. One night couldn't make it vanish.

She hoped.

Leonie had hours to think in the coach. She relived the moments in bed last night. Roman had treated her with gentleness, the way a man who greatly cares about a woman would behave. She could not believe he could cut her out of his life so quickly.

She would win him back. She'd do whatever it took. She was heartily sorry and she would convince him of her remorse.

Of course, she could not drink. Not even sherry. The offer of ale that morning had been a trick to see if she was committed to being the wife he wanted, and she was.

It would help if he would spend even an hour with her.

Eventually, Leonie's worries tired her. She was not a person given to anxiety. Her nature was more buoyant.

She began entertaining herself by trying to remember everything Roman had told her about Bonhomie. He'd painted a vivid picture with his words. She could see the fields that would soon be planted once they delivered the new plow. The flower beds especially intrigued her. Miles of flower beds, he had claimed. Leonie adored cut flowers.

What else had he said? There were seven bedrooms? He'd also described a ballroom that he promised was larger than any she'd seen in London. That would be quite a feat.

She could picture the wide, cobblestone drive lined by the trimmed hedges and stately trees Roman had described. There were stables so guests could go riding every morning.

And she would be the hostess. She began planning her first event. Of course it would be a dance and she and Roman would lead the first set.

Suddenly, being alone in the coach did not bother her. After all, she had spent a childhood learning how to entertain herself. She had many plans to make and she made them at will. She imagined the cut flowers from the garden decorating the summer cotillion she would hold. She would make a grand entrance and come down the stairs where the three stone framed windows were.

She would be a generous lady of the house and everyone from all over England would sing her praises.

In fact, Leonie was so involved in this story of her own making it took her a moment to realize the coach was turning. She looked out the window in anticipation. They traveled on an overgrown, narrow country lane. Hawthorns and scraggly hollies bickered for space along the road. The horses did not like their sharp thorns. The post boy barely managed to keep control.

Leaning out the window, and trying not to get her head swiped by low hanging branches, Leonie called to the lad, "Where is Lord Rochdale?"

"Up ahead. He said we can't miss the turnoff." He yelped as a low-hanging branch swiped across his face.

Leonie had to sit back in the coach. This road was a travesty. She couldn't wait until they reached Bonhomie with its cobble-stone drive. It would be more pleasant to ride on.

The coach turned another corner, but instead of a smooth drive, there were ruts so deep Leonie found herself tossed and bumped as they traveled. Worse, the side of the drive was more overgrown than the road was. The horses were having a hard time of it.

And then they reached a cleared expanse. The road was still rough but branches had stopped banging against the coach.

Looking outside, Leonie expected to see an expanse of well-manicured lawn. Instead, she found herself looking at what was little more than sheep pasture. Ahead, there was the house, or what looked like a house, although it lacked uniformity.

Something was wrong with it.

As the coach drove closer, she realized that one of the walls was collapsed. A good portion of the house just wasn't there.

Furthermore, no one could tell what color the walls were be-cause ivy as thick as a man's arm had engulfed the building. Some ivy climbing walls was charming. This was alarming.

And the rooks! Big, black birds sat along what might gen-erously be described as a roofline. They were in the trees all around and jumping in the ivy on the walls. Leonie prayed there was a roof—one could not tell from this vantage—and not a gaping hole, because if there wasn't, with that many birds gathered, the insides of the house would be more ruined than the outside.

Roman had dismounted and stood in front of the house hugging people who could only be his family members. They apparently had been waiting for him. He said something to them and they all looked at the oncoming coach expectantly—and suddenly, Leonie feared she would be ill.

How could she look at that disaster of a house and meet his family with any sort of grace?

In that moment, she realized her morally superior husband had been painting rosy pictures of his assets to hoodwink her.

That she had been chastising herself for not being honest while he had been equally *dis*honest.

Leonie was no fool. There wasn't enough money in the world to repair what needed to be done to that house. Fifty thousand pounds would not even make a dent—and she was married to the folly.

A rage she'd never experienced began building inside her and grew stronger with every turn of the coach wheel leading to her husband.

Chapter 15

So, Leonie had chosen to accompany him instead of returning to London.

Roman could not lie to himself and say he was not pleased.

When he had given his ultimatum, he'd been so angry he hadn't cared which direction she chose. In fact, his life would have been easier if she had returned to the city.

That she willingly followed him to Bonhomie gave him a sense of satisfaction, and saved him from making excuses to his family about a missing wife. He knew they would already be upset at his abrupt marriage announcement. He would have plenty of questions to answer about that. Of course, Leonie really had no other meaningful choice but to join him. He certainly was not going to pay her expenses, not when he had more pressing needs in Somerset.

However, traveling alone, he had a good amount of time to think. The forty thousand pounds after paying the gambling debts was a magnificent fortune . . . until one considered all the work Bonhomie needed. He must take great care with his finances and not be overeager. Right now, the rent from his tenants brought in two thousand pounds a year. That could be increased, but only after much needed repairs had been made to yeomen's cottages and the fields replenished.

Oh, yes, there was much to do and Roman was anxious to begin. Bonhomie was his home. The future for his children.

He had been so busy with his plans for his wife's dowry he had barely registered the poor condition of the roads or the overgrown banks around them. He saw all as it could be and his chest swelled with pride.

At the sight of Bonhomie's walls, he had kicked his horse into a canter.

A shout had gone out that he was coming. His sister Dora and his mother had seen him from the front window. They'd hurried out the door to greet him. He had reined in the tired horse and hopped down in time for them to now throw their arms around him in happy greeting.

The Gilchrists were a dark-haired lot, although his mother's hair was turning white. Dora was thirty and a handsome woman with an opinionated nature. She and their mother were both of middling height and their eyes were blue instead of the gray that had come to Roman and his sister Beth by way of their late father.

"We just received this post from you—" his mother started.

"You *married*?" Dora cut in.

"Who is she?" her mother worried. "Is she with you? We've been cleaning the house to make it ready."

"Yes, she is with me. She is coming in a coach," Roman said. "And thank you for preparing the house."

"But you *married*," Dora repeated as if she could not fathom the idea. "Did you *know* this woman before you married her? You've only been gone three weeks and you never mentioned a word about courting anyone."

"Dora," their mother softly cautioned. She was a peacemaker and they all knew too well how Dora could be overbearing. She was younger than Beth by a year but one wouldn't know by Dora's behavior.

Fortunately, Roman had much practice in handling his sisters. "I did know her. I've known her for years," he answered easily, and was saved from saying more by the appearance of his stepfather, David, and his brother-in-law, Lawrence, a good-natured man with brown hair and eyes. They came from the side of the house. Lawrence carried a saw. They were both in shirtsleeves and acted as if they had been hard at it. David's hair was all white, his jaw lean, and his blue eyes keen with intelligence. Few details escaped him.

"You have a bride," David said in way of greeting as he held out his arm. Roman noted that his limp was more pronounced and he was favoring his left side. He was thankful he had been able to return from India in time to help his parents.

Giving David a hug and shaking Lawrence's congratulatory hand, Roman said, "I do indeed. She's following in the coach. I purchased a new plow and enough seed for the planting," he said to Lawrence.

"We aren't interested in plows. We want information about your wife," Dora said. "I'm surprised you didn't have Lawrence perform the sacrament. Then we could all be present."

"Dora," their mother again murmured to deter her daughter, but Roman waved her worries away.

"I would have, Dora, but there wasn't time. I wished my wife to travel with me."

That sounded so noble and fine. In truth, Roman hadn't been entirely honest with his family on how dire his financial circumstances were. He was now their sole support and he didn't want them to be uneasy.

Of course, standing here with Dora's suspicions, he realized he had been a bit naive about introducing Leonie to them. Yes, he had written that he was about to marry but he had been deliberately vague, and for good reason.

His family knew about the duel and that it was over a woman. Years ago, his stepfather had written him long lectures about the weight killing a man would have on his soul. Dueling was foolish in his opinion. No decent woman was worth that sacrifice and he had raised his stepson to rise above his temper—or so he'd thought.

If they learned too much, the truth of what had happened would help no one, especially Leonie . . . and himself.

"Here comes the coach," Lawrence said, nodding to where the drive emerged from the tree line.

All eyes turned in that direction, including Roman's.

The chaise had not been particularly well sprung. Hired vehicles rarely were. This one now rocked in and out over the uneven drive behind the hard-working horses.

Leonie had stuck her head out the window but had been forced to pull back because of the coach's bouncing—but she *had* taken a look at Bonhomie. He knew it. And in that moment, Roman saw his home as she did.

He saw the weed-filled lawn with its uneven terrain. She had to notice that a good portion of the house's southern wall was missing. He had also told her the drive was paved and she would know that wasn't true.

His impulse was to go in the house and bar the door.

Here he'd taken the high and mighty road with her. Now, he felt a bit of guilt for claiming things that were not true.

He should have been more honest with her, but damn it all, Bonhomie would be exactly as he described it to her . . . she'd just have to wait a few years.

The coach came to a stop. The post lad jumped off the lead horse. "Here we are, my lord. I thought I'd lose a wheel on that road coming in, but we managed fine enough."

Lawrence spoke. "If we had known you were coming, I would have worked on the road instead of the lane to the village."

Roman shook his head. "It is all well." To the post lad he said, "The stables are around back. There is a man there named Whiby who will help you with the horses and see that you have something to eat and somewhere to sleep." One of the blessings of this venture was that the stables and the barn were relatively intact. They were in much better shape than the house.

There was a moment of expectant silence, and then Roman realized everyone, including the post boy, waited for him to open the chaise door and present his wife. In fact, he was surprised Leonie hadn't made her presence known, although she had been very chastened earlier. Perhaps she was still feeling justifiably unworthy?

Or she could have hit her head on the coach's roof after all the rough riding and be unconscious on the floor? If that was the case, his mother would be furious with him.

He did the manly thing and stepped forward. He gave the handle on the chaise door a twist and opened it.

Leonie was in the far corner of the coach, her hands on the seat. She looked as if she had been jostled around one too many times. The jaunty crown and brim of her fashionable bonnet were hopelessly crushed. The pins had fallen from her hair. Half of it was curling down around her shoulders and the other half appeared as if it was being dragged along.

Daggers could not be sharper than the look she gave him with her brown eyes.

Roman offered his hand. "Would you like to meet my family?"

What else could he say? It was a warning of sorts that if she lost her temper, there would be an audience. An important audience.

She reached up and pulled the last of her pins from her hair and slipped them into her glove. She flipped up the crushed brim and slid across the seat. Ignoring his hand, she helped herself out of the coach.

Roman stepped back, tensing for whatever outburst might come his way.

He would have deserved it. He should not have painted such a rosy picture of Bonhomie.

She took a moment to flick out her skirts before facing his family.

Her mother gasped aloud. *"Oh, my dear.* What happened? This didn't come from the ride up the road in the coach, did it?"

Roman had been so wrapped up in his outrage with Leonie he'd forgotten her bruises from her attack, or how they must look to his family.

"No," Leonie said. "There was an incident on the road last night but all is well," she stressed without offering further explanation. "You are my lord's mother?" She offered her hand. Roman noticed that she'd carefully schooled the anger in her eyes. That would be saved for him.

His mother took the hand, covering it with her own. "You poor lass," she said, instantly creating a bond for Leonie the way she did every creature on God's earth. Roman had seen her nurse mice that lost their mother to health and birds that had broken wings. Of course her gentle soul would be moved by the bruises on Leonie's face.

"It is behind us," Leonie assured her, speaking like Lady Bountiful offering solace to the populace.

"I'm Roman's stepfather." David stepped forward. "Welcome to our family, my lady."

Roman could swear Leonie managed a tear in her eye, and he didn't know if it was real or some sort of elaborate performance for his benefit. "Thank you," she said. "And please, this 'my lady' is all new to me and not meant for family. I'm Leonie."

"And I will take pleasure in you calling me Father or David, my given name. Whatever you think best."

As if on impulse, Leonie leaned forward to give him a quick hug.

"I'm your mother now, too," his mother said. "Or you may call me Catherine. I have a salve that will work wonders on those bruises and that cut. Come with me in the house. We'll have a glass of elderberry wine to wipe away the aches of the road."

Roman almost said no to the elderberry wine but his mother had already taken Leonie's hand and would have swept her away except for Dora's stepping up.

"I'm 'my lord's' sister." She pulled a face at Roman as she said it. There was enough jealousy in Dora that she had to have a bit of fun with his title.

"The older or the younger?" Leonie asked.

"The younger."

Leonie smiled and it was as if the sun had come out behind clouds. "I've never had a sister before but I have had very good female friends in London. I pray we can be as close."

Roman couldn't imagine anyone close to Dora. Her tongue was too sharp. However, he had to admit that Leonie's speech was a pretty one, and he was confused even further.

Was she angry at him? And lying in wait until they were alone? Probably.

True to form, Dora replied, "Perhaps we shall." Neither an agreement nor a rebuttal. Dora could be tricky.

"And I'm Lawrence. I'm married to Roman's other sister, Elizabeth."

"Do you live here as well?" Leonie asked.

"No, my lady—"

"Leonie," she corrected him mildly, and smiled.

Even with bruises, Leonie had a power over men. It was innate to her. Roman had to marvel how just that simple interaction made Lawrence blush.

"Leonie," he conceded. "We have a cottage in the village. I have the living of the parish."

He spoke with pride. Roman knew how much having this position meant to his brother-in-law. Before, Lawrence had been rector of a mouse-poor church in the wilds of Scotland. He considered it a blessing to be back in England while pleasing his wife as well.

Of course, if he knew how mouse-poor Roman had been when he'd offered that living, he would have been shocked.

And that was the crux of the matter.

Roman had made commitments when he'd taken on the title. He had wanted his family around him, and now he had to make things right. That was what he did—he made things right.

"We live in a cottage, too," his mother was telling Leonie. "Oh, it is a lovely place, snug and warm."

Was it his imagination that Leonie's gaze went to the caved-in wall?

"Do you live in the main house?" Leonie asked Dora.

"No, I live with Lawrence and Beth and the children."

"*Are* there bedrooms in this house?" Leonie asked with deceptive calmness.

His mother laughed. "Of course. There is my son's—well, yours and my son's." She giggled a bit as she said it, her eyes dancing with happiness. Roman knew what she was thinking. His mother was an earthy woman who adored grandchildren.

"So, there aren't 'seven' bedrooms in this—" Leonie looked up at Bonhomie's ivy-covered walls as if she didn't know what to call it, and settled on, "Manse?"

"There is only one," Dora said flatly.

"One that is usable," David corrected. "There are seven. However, the roof leaks on that side of the house. You'll also notice that the wall is weak."

"The wall that isn't there?" Leonie asked. She was too, too calm.

"Parts of it are there," David answered.

His mother took charge. "Come, Leonie—such a lovely name and you are beautiful, too—let us have a small glass of my good wine and I'll treat you with my salve."

"Ah, an *elderberry wine*," Leonie said. She glanced back at

Roman with arched brows to emphasize the words as his mother took her arm. She led Leonie into the house.

Roman took a step after them. Afraid, angry . . . uncertain—

"My, she is a beauty," Dora said. "Even with her face all battered. What happened to her last night?"

"An incident," Roman said.

"Did she fall down the stairs? Run into a door? Trip over a stone in the walk?" Dora could badger a saint when she set her mind to it.

Roman had learned long ago, the only way to set her back was to meet her head-on. "Are you saying you don't like her?" he demanded, a touch of heat in his voice.

His sister held up her hands to ward him off. "I am saying I do like her. When she first came out of the coach, I thought she will either be a shrewish witch or so sweet I will feel syrupy every time I talk to her."

"And which is she?" Roman was genuinely curious.

"She has a spark of sass to her."

"Dora, don't stir anything up," Roman warned. He knew his sister.

"I would not," she promised. "Leonie would give it right back to me. I only use my tongue on those like you, brother. You know, the sort who are too priggish to be honest."

That statement shocked him. No one had ever accused him of priggishness. Critics claimed he tended to follow the rule book to the letter but Roman thought of that as a compliment, of sorts. "What do you mean?" he challenged his sister, but she was already heading in the front door.

"No time to talk," she called. "I'm thirsty for elderberry wine myself."

Roman started after her but Lawrence stopped him. "David and I spoke to the squire about dredging the stream."

That project was near and dear to Roman's heart. There was a lovely stream through the nearest village of Middle Pike. It was said the fishing had once been great there, but over the years, logs and debris had blocked the stream. "What did he say?"

"He'll bring his team and his men, but it will cost you. He's not one to do charity if he can earn honest coin." Lawrence had been serving as Roman's steward until one could be hired.

"Have him do it." Those words felt good to say. "We also want the pond dredged in the west field. Oh, yes, and I hired a butler. A good man. He will help organize the work that needs to be done in the house. I'll be hiring a steward next so you can return to tending your flock full-time."

"Why, this is good," his stepfather said. "The changes will be amazing."

"That is what I'm hoping."

"I can't wait to tell your mother," David said.

"Then go on and tell her," Roman answered.

"Are you coming in?"

"In a moment. I need to see the horse to the stables."

"Very good." David hurried into the house.

Roman started down the path leading to the stables. Lawrence fell into step beside him. "This new wealth doesn't have anything to do with your wife, does it?"

Here was the conversation Roman was dreading. "A bit."

Lawrence chewed on that a moment and then said, "I never saw you as the type to marry for money."

Roman stopped. "And why is that?"

"Not in your character." Lawrence started walking again. At the stable door, he said, "Then again, Leonie is one of those women it is hard not to notice." He hung his saw on a peg with other tools by the door.

"That she is," Roman said.

Whiby, an old codger who had been in the employ of the earls of Rochdale since he was seven, greeted him and took the hired horse. "You go on, my lord. Whiby has this."

"Thank you, Whiby." The post lad was busy cleaning his tack, a jug he was sharing with Whiby beside him.

Roman gave him a nod and left. Lawrence followed him a few feet to where the path led to the village. He stopped and Roman paused with him. Apparently, he had something to say and he didn't waste time in speaking.

"There is a saying in my family that I have found to be true."

"What is that?" Roman asked.

"You can marry money but you can't live with it."

That might well be the case, but Roman didn't want to admit it. "As you said, she is a beauty."

"Will that be enough?"

Roman hadn't quite decided whether to tell his family about Leonie's dowry. As his acting steward, Lawrence had gleaned enough information to form his own conclusions about the estate's finances.

However, the question was: Would Leonie be enough?

He thought of last night before the attack, of how good it had felt to be inside her, how willing she'd been. "It must be," he answered his brother-in-law. "I will see you on the morrow." He headed to the house.

Bonhomie's first floor was fairly well intact. Some of the rooms had been filled with the mildew after years of neglect but others had been dry. He and his family had worked hard to make them livable. Most of the furniture, especially the pieces with upholstery, had to be thrown out, but the rest was solid and good.

The house was laid out in the manner of all great country houses—a huge, welcoming front hall and then side rooms for reception and dining. Because of the damage to the south wall, the dining room was not used, but soon Roman planned to have a beehive of workers making things right.

His family and wife were in the reception room sitting in a circle of wooden high-back chairs.

Roman entered the room, his eye going straight to his wife. To his relief, she was sipping a steaming cup of tea while his mother painted her bruises with her salve.

His mother looked up. "Would you enjoy a glass of my wine, Roman? I offered it to your wife but she said she would prefer my chamomile."

Leonie had been watching him. She'd seen his gaze go to her cup and she now silently laughed as she toasted him with it.

"I will take a cup of the tea," Roman said. Earlier, he'd been so angry he'd baited Leonie with ale—but now? He was tired and happy to be home.

Home. This was the first one he'd known. His stepfather had been a private tutor and they had traveled with him, always living in rented houses.

Dora poured him a cup of tea. His mother sat back, surveying Leonie and proud of her work. "Does the salve sting?" she asked.

"Slightly."

"That is the mint."

"I'm surprised you are letting her cover you with one of her concoctions, Leonie," Dora said. "I spent my childhood avoiding them."

"You spent your childhood with so many scrapes you had to bathe in that salve," David said, and everyone laughed.

It was strange to see Leonie at ease with his family. She acted as if she'd always meant to be one of them. She easily kept the conversation flowing by asking his mother how she came to choose his given name.

"Roman Lancaster was in the Department of Philosophy and my late husband's closest friend, although there was a good twenty years between their ages," his mother said. She smiled with the fondness of memory when she explained, "My children's father was quite a few years older than myself. Be it as it may, Roman died shortly before this Roman was born and

Alfred wanted to honor his friend with the name. Now, in many ways, my Roman honors both men."

Leonie looked touched by his mother's sentimentality.

Of course, Dora spoiled that moment by pointing out that she, too, had one of the Latin names.

"Greek," their stepfather mildly corrected.

"Only Elizabeth escaped and that is because of Mother."

His mother smiled and confessed, "I told my late husband that if I was the one carrying the children, then I should have first choice for a name. In fairness, I let him name Dora and then I, too, loved Roman Lancaster. He was a good, good friend." For a second, a memory seemed in danger of overwhelming her. She looked over to her husband and there was one of those silent times of communication where his mother and stepfather perfectly understood each other.

Those moments always touched Roman. He longed to have that sort of deep affinity with his wife.

He felt someone watching him and looked up to see Leonie with a thoughtful expression on her face. Did she, too, long to be close to another? Had she witnessed the respect his parents held for each other and found it moving?

Roman couldn't tell in her expression. She could be a cypher, a mystery. Or a wasp's nest. She had already turned out to be vastly different than he had anticipated.

And that was part of her intrigue for him.

Dinner was a simple repast served at his parents' cottage. His mother had made a stew with bread she had baked the day before. Elizabeth, Lawrence, and the children, Edward and Jane, joined them.

Leonie proved to be good with children. Beth was taken with her to the point that his sweet oldest sister mouthed the words, "I like her," to Roman.

What surprised Roman was how Leonie could be gentle with Beth and sharp-witted with Dora, especially if Roman was the topic. She was also well read. He'd not considered her education and perhaps he should have. However, she held her own in a conversation with David. She asked intelligent questions and seemed genuinely interested in the answers.

Was it a ruse? She was a polished product of London drawing rooms. She could probably talk to diplomats and merchants alike.

The best moment was when his mother asked for stories of India. Usually, his family had no curiosity about what he'd seen and that was fine with him. Some of what he'd done and where he'd been would not have made respectable table conversation. However, Leonie drew out of him the good memories.

They talked of pilgrims bathing in the muddy rivers and monkeys stealing anything shiny. Leonie brought up the heat and everything was either very dusty or very green.

He'd forgotten that. He could almost smell the heat and recall vividly how the Indian women preferred vivid colors in their dress that seemed to make the sun brighter.

"More cider?" Dora asked everyone as the meal was coming to an end. It was sweet, potent stuff made by the villagers. Everyone save for Beth, Lawrence, and the children had been drinking it.

Beth shook her head, and then noticed Leonie's thoughtful expression. "We are Methodists," Beth explained to her.

"And?" his wife prompted, not understanding.

"We are temperate," Lawrence answered.

Leonie's brows came together. "What does that mean?"

"We don't drink spirits or ale or cider," Lawrence said.

"Or elderberry wine," his mother chimed in.

"By choice?" Leonie asked.

Beth laughed. "Of course."

"My father didn't drink well," Lawrence explained. "He, too, was a man of the church until they asked him to leave after sampling too much of the communal wine."

"Interesting," Leonie said. She smiled at Roman but there was no humor in her dark eyes. She had been poured a glass of cider but she hadn't touched it. Roman had been watching.

Beth stood. "We need to be off for bed."

"How far is the walk into the village?" Leonie asked.

"Not far from here. Just ten minutes down the path," Lawrence answered.

Beth leaned down and gave Leonie a kiss on the cheek. The affection seemed to surprise her as did Beth's next words. "Here, children, say good night to your new aunt. Come along, Dora. If you won't help me teach, then you must help me plan lessons."

Jane and Edward dutifully kissed Leonie's cheek before moving to their grandparents, and finally Roman. This was his favorite part about having his family with him.

"I believe we have had enough as well," he announced. He looked to Leonie. "Are you ready to retire?"

"It has been a long day. The stew was delicious." Leonie stood. She started to hold out her hand, but then changed her mind and kissed his mother on the cheek as if it was the most natural thing in the world to do.

David kissed *her* cheek.

And Roman knew that against his better judgement, his wife had been accepted into his family.

They all left his parents' cottage at the same time, Dora going with Beth and Lawrence. The moon was high in the sky, but he and Lawrence carried lanterns to light the way.

Dora had imbibed a bit too much of the cider and was pleasantly tipsy. Roman could hear her laughter through the woods. Apparently, she was racing Edward and Jane, because Dora was shouting, "I'm ahead of you."

"She'll fall and break her neck," Roman said.

Leonie did not answer.

He looked over to his wife. She walked with her back straight, her head high. Moonlight highlighted the delicate planes of her face beneath her bonnet, the same one that had been smashed. She'd molded it back into a semblance of shape.

"Do you wish to talk about our argument this morning?" He *had* enjoyed several glasses of the cider along with a sample of his mother's elderberry wine and was feeling a touch conciliatory . . . and, maybe, amorous? Aye, very amorous.

In fact, in between watching whether or not Leonie drank her cider or worrying about how she was being accepted into the family fold, he'd thought about how much he had enjoyed making love to her.

And how much he'd like to do it again. In fact, that topic was never far from his mind.

Of course, one could interpret by the set of her chin that she might be out of sorts with him, but why? He'd said what he'd said this morning because it needed to be said. He liked to have all opinions out in the open, especially his own. He could not call his words back. His doubts had been honest. It might be best to change the subject.

"Whiby brought your valise up to the bedroom."

Again, silence.

"Yarrow and Duncan should be here tomorrow or the next day with your trunk."

They had reached the stables. One of the hired horses nickered to them. Leonie didn't pause but went marching by, heading for the house as if she owned the place.

Well, in a way she did.

And then, just as his long legs caught up with her, she stopped. They were at the edge of the path. Bonhomie appeared silver in the night with the overgrowth of ivy cutting huge swaths of darkness on its walls. However, on the fourth side, the south side, the crumbling wall and open rooms for two floors could not be ignored.

It was the south side they faced.

Leonie spoke her first words since leaving his parents' cottage. "One must admire the architecture."

Now it was Roman who was quiet, uncertain of her mood.

"Do you think the abbey's monks took these stairs?" She nodded to the remnants of a stairway that could be clearly seen in the moon's beauty of light and shadow. "Perhaps the abbot slept in that room on the right, the one that would be overlooking the gardens *that do not exist*. He must have enjoyed the calling of rooks every morning since they seemed determined to line the trees."

"I have nothing to do with the rooks," Roman murmured. "And perhaps I exaggerated the state of the house."

"*Exaggerated?*" Leonie tilted her head up to him. "You lied."

"I thought you were over being out of sorts," Roman complained. He had a suspicion that if he wasn't cautious, there would be no love play for him tonight.

"No, I'm just starting," Leonie remarked, moving toward the house. She took several steps and then whirled on him. "I was heading to the front door, but really, why? We can go in right here." She picked her way through the rubble, twisting her ankle on a rock and almost falling.

"Careful." He took her by the waist, lifting her up and swinging her around, carrying her to the front door where it was safe to walk.

Her response was to shake off his help the moment her feet touched the ground. She even batted at his hand as if he was an annoyance and began moving toward the door—but then she, again, abruptly stopped to confront him.

"You made me feel small. You presented yourself as this holier than thou person who had been saddled with my weakness and lack of character. I despised myself when I saw who I was through your eyes. And now—" She waved her arms to encompass Bonhomie and all its grounds. "Now I learn you were misrepresenting yourself."

"I was not," Roman answered, stung more by her picture of him as some sort of judgmental overlord than her criticism of his beloved home. "Bonhomie will be everything I said it was . . . someday."

"There isn't enough money in my dowry to repair everything that is wrong with this house. Or pave the front drive." She scuffed her shoes on the ground to kick up the dust. "And if that's your idea of a manicured lawn," she continued, "then you are done before you started. But the worst part is that you carry on about honesty and yet you weren't honest about the most basic things to me. You didn't even tell me about your family and *they are lovely people.*"

On those words, she flounced into the house, leaving the door open.

Of course, the joke was on her, because the house was dark inside. Roman waited a moment, certain she would not like stumbling around in a strange house. He was right.

She appeared in the doorway. "Please give me the lantern." She spoke with dignity, as if she was Queen of the World.

He wasn't giving her anything. Instead, he walked past her into the house. "You don't know where the bedroom is, do you?"

There was a hesitation and then she said, "No."

Roman snorted his opinion. The problem was, the truth hurt and he did not thank her for pointing it out to him. He started up the stairs expecting her to follow.

She shut the front door and did.

"You never asked about my family before we married," he said as he reached the landing and the second set of steps leading to the first floor. "You never asked about me. But if you must know, I didn't see a need to haul them to London. As you can tell, my stepfather is not well."

"Because he limps?"

"His legs are failing. One day, he may not walk at all."

There was a beat of silence and then she said, "I'm sorry. Roman."

She sounded sincere.

"*And*," he continued, "your dowry and the money I take in from tenants will be enough for us to live very nicely at Bonhomie."

"Do you mean Rook Haven?"

He stopped on the top step, raising the lantern to frown down at her. "Rook Haven?"

She took the opportunity to march right past him saying, "If my money is building it, then I believe I should name it. And this is a rook haven if ever I saw one. I'd wager they come down the chimneys."

"No, they don't," he answered, moving swiftly to overtake her.

Bonhomie's hallways were wide. His boots echoed on the stones as he led her to the room on the northern wall that served as his bedroom.

"What is wrong with the other rooms?" She nodded to the doors down the hall.

"Some of the walls have huge cracks. Others are without windows. And then there are the leaks in the roof over them."

"How did it fall into this state of disrepair?"

"That is a good question," he said, opening the door. "The damage was done by Cavalier cannon when the earlier Rochdale refused to admit defeat. Unfortunately, subsequent Rochdales spent their money on other things than the house. The structure here is sound but be careful when you walk on the other side of this floor."

He'd set down the lantern on the desk by the window as he spoke and now turned to find her inside his room and looking as he had pictured her.

She'd removed her bonnet. Her hair fell around her shoulders and it did not take much imagination for him to picture her naked and willing. Exactly how she'd been last night.

"Leonie," he said, her name like a blessing on his lips.

She smiled—she had a heavenly smile—and looked to the bed. It was a four-poster and built for a big man. Roman liked it and had recently had the bed ropes replaced so that the cotton stuffed mattress was quite comfortable. Her gaze swung back to him. "Where are you going to sleep? Because I assure you, my lord, you will *not* be in my bed."

Heavenly? She was the devil.

"I beg to differ, wife. If you want to move—by all means move, but I plan on sleeping in that bed tonight and it is the only bed in the house. If you stay in this room, we will be sharing it."

Chapter 16

*L*eonie was exhausted.

It had been a long day.

However, she was not going to let Roman run roughshod over her.

She'd meant what she'd said about being thoroughly chastened this morning . . . and then to discover he hadn't been genuine? Well, it raised her hackles.

"May you have your cold bed, and be welcome to it," she announced. She reached for the counterpane, an ugly thing of blue figured material, and pulled it off. She started for the door, dragging it behind her.

"Where are you going?" Roman demanded.

"To find somewhere to sleep."

"There isn't anywhere else to sleep," he answered. "The other rooms on this floor are not safe."

"Then I shall find somewhere else." Leonie opened the door, but then realized how dark it was. Instead of reaching for her valise, she picked up the lantern and marched out into the hall before he knew what she was about.

He shouted, "Hey!" in protest of her leaving him in the dark, but she ignored him.

Because of the size of the bed, the counterpane was huge and a bit of a trial to carry, especially when it came to the stairs. Leonie reached down and grabbed her skirt to lift the hem.

There would be no honor in tumbling down the stone stairs and breaking her neck.

Of course, Roman might be happy if she did. Then he'd have all her money and no *imperfect* wife to bother him.

Just the thought of him celebrating her demise sent her stomping into the receiving room. The chairs were still arranged in the circle where Roman's family had enjoyed meeting her earlier. Something else was there as well—the bottle of elderberry wine. The glasses and tray were on a side table.

Leonie glanced behind her. All was dark.

She set the lantern on the floor, crossed to the bottle, and lifted it to her lips. There was not that much left but she had two swallows. She *had* to drink it, she realized. She'd been so good, so circumspect.

The bit of wine could not hurt anything.

Wiping her mouth with the back of her hand, Leonie quietly placed the bottle on the tray. She backed away from it, as if she could deny what she'd done by standing on the other side of the room.

Today had been hard. Being with his family and watching them enjoy cider, which she adored but was afraid to touch because of Roman's presence, had been a challenge. Leonie was not accustomed to denying herself anything.

Guilt over what had happened last night had kept her humble. However, her body was comfortable with a nip or two. Well, perhaps more than that but it wasn't like she was a *drunkard*.

Her behavior at her wedding ceremony had been an aberration. She'd never had that reaction before and might not ever have it again.

In fact, right now . . . after those few swallows of wine, why, she felt herself. She knew where she was. She understood what was happening.

She just didn't feel as irritable as she had a moment before. That was a good thing, wasn't it?

Leonie set aside troubling thoughts by giving her attention to devising her bed. There might be a better room to use but she'd never find it in the dark. Besides, she'd already given her ankle a twist. Who knew what other dangers could be lurking in this house?

She also did not intend to sleep on the floor. She dragged two of the largest chairs together to face each other and form a bed of sorts. It would be more comfortable to change into a night-dress, but she refused to go upstairs for her valise. Instead, she took off her dress and decided to sleep in her chemise and petticoats. She would be comfortable enough with the heavy counterpane around her. She placed the lantern on the seat of another chair. She welcomed the wan light. The house was very dark.

Wrapping herself in the blanket, she seated herself in one chair and raised both legs to place her feet in another. This was not *that* uncomfortable. Then again, she was sitting upright, which was not conducive for sleeping.

Leonie wiggled her way down, feeling a bit like an inchworm as she settled in the chair. She didn't fit. Her head was against the chair back. She'd end up with a crick in her neck.

What she needed was a bit more width between the chairs.

She pushed the other chair back with her feet. Her body finally stretched out and fit between the chairs, until her bottom fell between them and she found herself in a V shape with her bum on the floor.

Male laughter greeted this new indignity.

Leonie dropped her legs and rolled onto her knees to confront her spectator. Shame made her angry. Had he witnessed her drinking from the elderberry wine bottle?

Roman leaned against the doorframe. He was in stockinged feet and he had removed his neckcloth and coat.

"How long have you been there?" she demanded. "Are you spying?"

He held up his hands as if to ward her off. "No, of course not spying. I live here, remember? I'm the master of the keep?"

"Then why didn't you tell me you were there?"

"I intended to let you know . . . until you took off your dress and then, well, words died in my throat." He gave her a rakish grin.

"You are a beast." She was so relieved he hadn't caught her drinking her words were without heat.

"You bring that out in me." He pushed away from the door-frame and entered the room. *Her* space, she wanted to inform him, but then, he was the master of the keep.

Instead, she focused on immediate problems. She needed to rethink what she was doing. However, untangling herself from the counterpane was a bit confusing. She'd wrapped herself well.

His feet were beside her. "Here, let me help."

Before she could coolly insist she didn't need his help, he bodily picked her up, threw her over his shoulder, grabbed the lantern by its handle, and started for the stairs.

"What are you doing?" Leonie demanded, arching her back and trying to raise herself up.

"Taking you to bed. Duck."

"What—?" She hit her head on the top of the doorframe. It was a light bump because he stopped before she could truly be thumped.

He took a step back. "Are you all right?"

She rubbed her head. "Yes."

"Good, then duck."

This time she listened.

Roman strode up the stairs. He seemed to be taking them two at a time. Leonie didn't fight. It would be useless. No, instead, she plotted. He would have to put her down sooner or later.

He carried her into the bedroom and plopped her down on the mattress. The counterpane had loosened and she quickly freed herself, not caring that she was showing her legs as she kicked the covers away.

She had to admit, the mattress did feel good.

And she was tired. Exhausted actually—and yet, energized. He could do that to her. It had been rather thrilling to have him carry her so easily up the stairs.

It was also thrilling to have him begin shucking off his clothes as if he couldn't wait to bed her.

To bed her.

A yearning formed between her legs. Her breasts took on fullness. What sort of wanton creature was she? Had she lost all pride?

Yes, parts of her screamed. Her body longed for the closeness she had found in his arms.

Leonie struggled for sanity and she did so by reaching for complaints. "You described a much different house."

He paused in unbuttoning his breeches. The lantern light made his body appear as if it had been cast in molten metal. His clear gray eyes met hers. "What I told you is what I know it will become. Bonhomie will be everything I said and more."

"And more?"

"Yes, Leonie. Those were only *my* dreams for Bonhomie. I hope in time you will add your mark to it. Then it will be *our* home and it will be even more magnificent. We can make this house whatever we wish. I want you to be happy here."

To be happy here . . .

Leonie didn't know if she had ever been happy anywhere. She wasn't certain she knew what happiness was.

"Come here." Roman sat on the bed and motioned for her to join him. He was naked and very much ready for her.

And she was ready for him.

Yes, he'd made her furious, but this joining between them, well, it could right many wrongs. She'd felt content in his arms last night. She'd even been happy to let him carry her up the stairs because, instinctively, she had known it would lead to this.

Leonie came up on her knees and pulled off the thin chemise. She untied her petticoats and tossed her clothing aside.

"That is exactly what I was hoping you would do." His voice was a husky purr. "Come here." He smoothed the place next to him.

Leonie crawled on the bed toward him. His eyes lit up at the sight. She had only traveled a foot when he met her halfway. Taking her by the arms, he lifted her against his body and kissed her with such force, such passion, any resistance melted. She wanted to wrap herself around him, take him into her, and hold him forever—

He broke off the kiss.

His brows came together. He leaned into her as if sniffing her breath. "You have had something to drink."

"No, I—" Dazed from the onslaught of his kiss, Leonie had trouble grasping the accusation, until he released his hold—and then she understood. He had smelled the wine on her breath.

He placed his legs over the side of the bed, giving her his back. "Where did you find something to drink? And why?" He reached for his breeches.

"What are you doing?" she asked. She came up on her knees. "I'm fine." She was. She wasn't at all tipsy. She was clear of eye and mind.

"*Have* you had something to drink?" He fastened the top button of his breeches.

"You were at dinner with me—"

"You *didn't* drink any cider at dinner but you've *had* something."

"No—" Leonie broke off. She had been about to deny it, but then realized it would be an outright lie.

Roman would not appreciate a lack of honesty. That was not the sort of man he was. She was better off to say nothing. She sat back on her heels, her hair falling around her shoulders.

He started for the door. "Where are you going?" she asked.

"To find the bottle."

There is no bottle, she wanted to shout.

And he would listen to her and come back to bed and everything would fine—except it wasn't true. The damning bottle was downstairs waiting for him. He charged from the room, not bothering to take the lantern with him.

She listened to him move down the hall away from her. She doubled her fingers, clenching them so tightly her nails dug into her palms. She'd only had a sip.

Of course, if there had been more left in the wine bottle, she would have finished it, but there hadn't been that much—

The sound of a bottle being thrown against the wall reverberated like the last of a gun. Leonie jumped, and then brought her fists to her stomach. She was going to be ill. He knew. He'd known all along. It was uncanny how perceptive he was about her.

And then there came a crash and another crash as if more things were being thrown.

Or were they under some sort of attack? Was Roman downstairs needing her help?

Leonie scrambled out of the bed to her valise. She quickly pulled out her nightdress and threw it over her nakedness. Picking up the lantern, she rushed down the stairs to see to her husband.

There was no attack.

He sat on a chair in the middle of the receiving room, his elbows on his thighs, his head buried in his hands. Around him were broken chairs. In the cold hearth were the fragments of the elderberry wine bottle.

Leonie froze, stunned by the power of his anger. He did not raise his head, although he had to know she was there. She held the lantern.

The tears she'd been holding back escaped. "I'm sorry."

He didn't move at first. Instead, he seemed lost in his own world.

She set the lantern on the floor. She took an uncertain step, then another, toward him.

When she was in front of him, he pushed himself up. The lines around his mouth were tight, and yet, there was confusion and, yes, compassion in his eyes.

"Oh, Leonie, what am I going to do with you?"

"Hold me."

Her words were a plea. She'd never asked anything of anyone before. She'd managed on her own.

But now? She feared being alone. Or what could become of her.

He wavered in indecision. She understood his struggle. If he was wise, he would run.

Instead, he opened his arms and Leonie fell into them. She wrapped herself around his shoulders and buried her face in his neck. Her thighs were around his hips, her breasts against his chest. This felt right. It felt safe. "Help me, Roman. Please help me."

"I would that I could," he whispered fiercely.

"Then it will be enough," she said, praying she was right. "I don't want to be my mother. *I don't.*"

"I know. I believe you."

"You said you thought you loved me. Please, don't stop," she begged.

His hands came to her shoulders. He pushed her back so that he could look in her face. "I do. God help me, I do. Even though you may be the ruin of me."

She placed her hand on his chest, just over his heart. "I'll be better."

The lines of his face softened as if he feared that would not be true.

In answer, she kissed him, a frantic, questing meeting of their lips.

To her joy, he responded. He took charge. He still knew better than she what it was they needed. What she wanted.

His hands raised the skirts of her nightdress.

He was aroused. He had been from the moment she'd climbed into his lap. She'd felt the prodding, the heat. After all, he'd only buttoned the top one of his breeches and it was a small matter to release him.

Their kiss deepened; she stroked his shaft while his hands beneath her dress sought her breasts.

This was good. So good. He was forgiving her. And she would behave. She told him with her kiss—she would try to be what he wanted. She would.

His hands lifted her hips and sat her down upon him. Leonie gasped in pleasure as he buried himself deep within her.

He liked it this way, too. "Ride me," he ordered quietly. "Do as you wish."

At first, she didn't understand his meaning. She wiggled her hips. The movement sparked a laugh from him that she felt roll through his body and to her deepest core. She tried it again, delighted with the sensation.

"You are going to make it too fast," he warned, using his hands at her hips to show her what he wanted.

She wanted it, too.

He pulled her nightdress off, letting her determine the pace. His lips found her breasts and she thought she had discovered bliss. Her fingers combed his hair, wanting to keep him to her forever.

And yet that would not be possible, not with the heat pounding through their blood.

She understood more about how to please him. Now, he was teaching her what it meant to please herself.

Leonie moved faster, marveling at the desire spiraling tighter and tighter inside her. His lips found hers. His kiss was wild and uncontrolled. It was as if he wished to breathe her in, to possess her—and she would let him. She wanted him to have all of her.

They came at the same time.

Nothing could have prepared Leonie for the experience of meeting her peak with his. Waves of exquisite sensual gratification rolled between them.

Leonie lost track of time because it didn't matter. Only this moment was of importance and it centered on this man.

She fell forward, her head finding that nestling spot between his shoulder and his neck. It was all too, too good.

His arms hugged her to him. She felt his breath in her hair. She could feel the blood beat in his veins.

Her mother claimed that a woman's body was power. Leonie didn't see it that way. She was as hungry for Roman as he was for her. And she knew there wasn't another man walking this earth who could satisfy her and help her make sense of the world.

She knew that as clearly as she knew her own name.

"Roman, I need you." There, she'd said it. She admitted she did not want to be alone and that, for him, she would let down her guard.

"Leonie, need is not love."

There was a sadness in his voice.

She tightened her hold around him. What did she know about love? Had she ever seen it?

Yes, it held her now.

But could she trust him? Could she trust anyone?

That was the question she could not answer, even as, with the trust of a child, she nestled into his body and fell into a peaceful sleep in his arms.

THE NEXT MORNING, Leonie woke up in the big bed.

The day was well advanced. She stretched, her body feeling good, and she remembered what had happened in the middle of the night.

She rolled over, expecting to see her lover. Her husband.

His side of the bed was empty. There was no indentation of someone's head on the pillow next to hers, no sign that another body had warmed the sheets.

Need is not love, Leonie.

She wanted his love . . . she just didn't know if she was worthy of it.

Nor did she know where to start to become not just the woman he wanted, but the one she wished to be.

She knew one thing—she must not ever take another drink.

Chapter 17

$\mathcal{R}$oman had held Leonie a good long time after she'd fallen asleep. She was precious to him; she was also a danger.

He'd carried her to the bed. She'd been so tired and sated she hadn't even stirred except to nuzzle her nose in his palm when he had laid it beside her cheek.

For years, she had occupied too large a place in his mind. Even when he'd cursed her, he'd tied himself to her. Now, she might well be carrying his child and they would be forever linked.

What if she couldn't rid herself of this terrible obsession with drink?

Every fiber of his being wanted to lie beside her. He wanted to wake in the morning holding her. However, for his own sanity, he must place some distance between them, at least until he understood what he wished to do.

He could not make *any* decision until he knew she was not carrying his child.

Roman took himself to the stables. He made a bed in the fresh hay but he did not sleep well.

He woke at dawn when Whiby and the post boy began moving about. He helped with the horses and then saw the hired vehicle off with a meal of bread, cheese, and some dried apples for the driver. Both Whiby and the post boy had kept their thoughts to themselves upon discovering Roman so newly married and sleeping in the stables.

Roman broke his fast with more of the bread and cheese. He brewed a big pot of tea, thinking it would be good for when Leonie woke. He also took the opportunity to search the kitchen for anything that could cause her to indulge. Since most of his meals before leaving for London had been taken at his parents' cottage, he couldn't find anything. His mother must have brought the celebratory bottle of elderberry wine from her home. He also cleaned up the damage he'd done in the receiving room.

He had a full day ahead of him. Hopefully, Yarrow and Barr would be arriving with the plow and goods he'd purchased in London. He wanted to contact the squire about buying some of his newborn lambs and Roman would pick those out himself. He also needed to take a quick walk through the village to let them know he'd returned.

However, right now, he was too wound up in conflicting emotions to be of use to anyone.

He'd always been capable of tying himself into knots and the only way to unravel doubts and uncertainty was with hard, manual work. His stepfather had taught him that lesson over a decade and a half ago and it was as true when he was a lad as it was now.

Roman sought out the axe. He took a moment to sharpen the blade and then walked to the far field where there was a pile of wood from the clearings Lawrence had been making to the paths. Roman decided to cut it into kindling and split logs.

Within the hour, despite the cold spring morning, David found him.

"I heard the axe and had to come see who was out this early finishing what Lawrence and I started." He was walking better today, but then his affliction, whatever it was, came and went.

He noticed Roman's concern and shrugged. "I must walk while I can." He sounded almost content with a prognosis from his physician that would make most men weep.

"You should still take it easy."

"I'll be sitting out my days soon enough."

That was not an answer Roman liked, and only added to the weight he already felt. Unfortunately, David was feeling talkative.

"Your mother and Dora left fifteen minutes ago to take a basket to the Poole family on the far side of the parish. They have two children down with a fever."

Roman grunted an answer before swinging the axe and burying it in a good-sized log. The axe went in but it was not easy to pull out. He had to put his boot on it and that didn't make him any happier.

"The log is too green for splitting," his stepfather observed. "All of them are."

"Well, I've a mind to split them whether they wish to be or not."

"It will be hard work on unseasoned wood. You'd be best to stack it and wait."

He was right. But Roman wasn't in the mood for reason. "Excuse me, weren't you a lecturer? And not a woodsman?"

"Even lecturers know not to fiddle with green wood. Indeed, I would imagine captains in His Majesty's Army would also know as much. You are doing it the hard way."

"Sometimes that way is best."

"Marriage problems, eh?"

Now he had Roman's attention. "Why would you say that?"

David sat on a piece of log that made for a handy stool. He stretched out the leg he favored. "Because you are newlywed and out here in the morning air instead of snuggled in bed with your bride."

"I have things to do."

"Aye, and you should be doing them *to* her. When I married your mother, we didn't leave the bedroom for a month. We even took all our meals there.

That comment truly annoyed Roman.

"I'm sorry if I take my responsibilities seriously." He had freed his axe and now gave it a swing on the same hapless piece of wood. The axe head dug in deeper, and was more stuck than before.

Roman swore. He jerked on the handle. The log would not let go. He stepped on it and pulled. The axe barely moved and Roman could have thrown the wood and the axe to the other side of Bonhomie.

Instead, he stomped a step or two and then faced his step-father. "I believe I should set Leonie aside."

David's brows raised to his hairline. "Oh, that is a concern."

"Aye."

"You seemed happy with her last night."

Roman looked down at the axe stuck in wood and thought about the love he'd made to his wife. "I was."

"We knew you couldn't have known each other well. When we received your letter, we feared you were marrying her for money. Thaddeus mentioned his suggestion in the last letter he wrote to us." There was a beat and then he said, "Your mother and I had hoped you wouldn't listen to him."

So, they had known. "Her money is the reason I'll be able to rebuild this estate."

David looked in the distance a moment and then said, "We were surprised at how lovely she is. And she has a kind manner as well. I thought heiresses a man could marry quick were ugly as trolls . . . unless there is something that we don't see."

Roman walked back to the wood pile. He righted another piece of log and sat. "She was once important to me in India."

"Oh, now this is an interesting piece of information. Was she the one you dueled over? She would have been young, wouldn't she? Too young?"

"Seventeen."

"Young but of an age."

"Leonie is actually more beautiful now than she was then," Roman admitted. "There is something about her that attracts men. Certainly, she attracts me." Roman fell into silence, his mind busy with how he himself had orchestrated his own demise when it came to Leonie.

David interrupted his thoughts. "Why don't you make a clean breast of it? Tell all and then, perhaps, we can understand why you are out here instead of in bed with your wife."

Roman's stepfather was right; his mind was a confused mess—and so he told the story he'd not shared with anyone, including Leonie's shooting Paccard.

"There was no duel?" David repeated as if needing to realign his thinking.

"No, I fabricated the story to save her reputation."

"Do you truly believe any court would charge her for murder if this Paccard had treated her the way you say he did?"

"It wouldn't have mattered. Her reputation would have been in tatters. I don't know what would have happened to her."

"So, you sacrificed yourself."

"I took a risk. I've managed."

"Without the lady. That would have made me angry. But also, you may have unwittingly given her a burden that she has found too great to bear."

"Are you suggesting I should have let her be charged with murder?"

"You don't know if it would have come to that."

Roman looked across the field to where Bonhomie's roof could be seen above the just-budding treetops. "She was too young."

"But then your paths crossed in London?"

He faced David. "Thaddeus mentioned her name. He said her father was most anxious to marry her off to a title in exchange for a generous dowry."

"And you thought to claim her money?"

"In theory." Roman stood and paced a step, stabbing his fingers through his hair. *What had he been thinking when he first saw Leonie again?*

"My attraction to her is strong," he admitted. "She is the only woman I have ever wanted." There was truth. He'd attempted to court others but nothing had ever come of those liaisons. "The night I saw her at the ball, I was angry and yet I had a knowing that, all along, we would meet again."

"She agreed to the marriage?"

Leave it to David to find the heart of the matter. "She told me she would marry me, provided I let her live her life separate from mine."

"What did you say?"

"No."

"And here she is. That must mean something. I watched her last night. She'd look to you from time to time as if needing reassurance, and you couldn't take your eyes from her."

"She drinks."

His stepfather frowned. "Drinks?"

"Aye, she has a problem. I was watching to see if she touched her glass of cider." He ended up telling David the whole story, including the attack in the inn.

When he was done, his stepfather gave a low whistle. "She is so young. It is a shame."

"I can't decide what to do. I could send her back to her family, but her father wants grandchildren and has paid well for them."

"And if you keep her?"

"I don't know if I can trust her. Last night, she refused cider and yet when we returned home she found something to drink. I don't want to live this way, always being suspicious. I want the trust that you and Mother have."

"It took years of marriage to build what we have."

"Her mother drinks. Her father as well. A more selfish fool has never walked this earth than William Charnock. He has money and a name but he lacks what really matters."

David leaned forward. "What of the daughter?"

"I don't know yet. I want to believe she is unlike her parents, except reason tells me I'm deceiving myself."

"But you really haven't decided?"

"No." Roman paused a moment and then admitted, "Sometimes I believe I am overreacting. Other times I believe I'm mad. And still others—" He stopped, unsure whether to continue.

"Still others?" David prompted.

"I love her. I would forgive her anything. I should resent her. She's already cost me my reputation. I am fortunate I inherited this title so I have a chance to begin anew. And yet, here she is—in my life again."

"Two things, son," David said. Roman looked at his stepfather expectantly. Out of respect for Roman's true father, David rarely used the word "son," even though he'd had a hand in raising Roman since he was a babe. Roman had also learned that when he heard that word, he'd best listen. "The first is that love knows no logic. That is why the poets are good at it and the philosophers are failures. You will have to reach your own decision."

"I know that."

"Whichever way you choose, it will be right."

"I pray that is true."

"The second is that no marriage, no love, can survive resentment and a lack of honesty. If you keep her, then it is as she is. Not as you would have her, because otherwise, she will feel she must lie to you. You would be happy to have her return the favor if the situation was different."

He was right.

But could Roman make peace with who Leonie was?

He wasn't certain, and until he knew, he needed to protect his heart.

WHEN AT LAST Leonie saw Roman later that morning, she could tell he had reached the decision to keep a distance between them. She might have picked an argument with him but Yarrow and Roman's valet, Duncan Barr, arrived. She was overjoyed to see her butler. He was familiar and she needed that right now.

However, she could not help but note that the butler had a deep respect for her husband. Nor did Yarrow see Bonhomie as some crumbling ruin. He appeared excited to be part of the rebuilding.

He and Roman spent several hours that day circling and touring the house and discussing what would be needed in the way of household staff. Yarrow also had suggestions for reconstruction of different rooms.

Leonie trailed after them. She'd not had a full tour of the house and was interested in what they had to say, although Roman did not ask her opinion.

Drinking the elderberry wine had apparently taken her across some imaginary line in his mind. He was telling her with his distance that making love was not enough. The hopeful anticipation was gone from his voice when he deigned to speak to her.

What hurt most was that Yarrow didn't notice this slight.

The noon meal was taken at Catherine and David's cottage. No cider or ale was served for the meal. Everyone drank spring water, which was very sweet and refreshing, or hot tea with cream. They all treated her with respect, but Leonie was more than sensitive to the possibility that her in-laws were aware of her weakness.

Nor did it help later in the afternoon, when Roman, David, Yarrow, Barr, and even Whiby went to the squire's to choose lambs, and Leonie found herself almost obsessed with the thought of drink. After all, Roman had evidently decided her soul was black. He might enjoy her body, but that didn't stop him from disapproving of her.

At loose ends, she debated walking to the village. She might be able to find a bottle there . . . but at what cost? If her husband found out, and he would, she didn't know what she would do.

Then again, she didn't know what she would do anyway because she wasn't feeling very good. Her insides felt shaky and her nerves were stretched thin. But she stayed at Bonhomie. She managed to hold her own.

Still, it was the greatest trial of her life and by night, even though she was beyond exhaustion, she did not sleep well. Especially when she learned Roman slept in the stables. If anyone thought it strange that the earl did not share his countess's bed, they did not comment.

The next morning, Leonie was again left to her own concerns. Yarrow and Roman had gone off to the county center to hire staff.

She would have liked to hire staff.

She wanted to play some role at Bonhomie, if Roman would let her. He was so busy being all things that he didn't leave anything for her.

Perhaps it *would* help if she found a drink. Then she would feel steadier.

This time, Leonie was convinced that she could not survive the day without some fortification. She put on her bonnet and set off for the village. She hadn't been there yet but she'd been told if she followed the path she would find it. How she would manage a bottle with her lack of coin, she had not quite considered, but she would think of a good excuse. She could be clever that way.

Just like her mother.

That last thought brought her to a halt.

Tears threatened. She swallowed them back.

She had to be strong. She couldn't let this defeat her. Her will needed to win, because if it didn't, she wasn't certain what Roman would do—

"Leonie?"

Leonie swung around to see her mother-in-law coming out of the woods to her. She pasted a smile on her face and Catherine smiled back.

Catherine was wearing obviously worn clothes, a wide-brimmed bonnet, and her hands were frightfully dirty. A smudge of dirt darkened her forehead. "Were you coming to see me?" Catherine asked expectantly.

What else could Leonie say except, "Yes, I am here for a visit. But how did you know I was right here?"

"Let me show you." As if sharing a great secret, Catherine motioned to follow her and led Leonie into the woods lining the path to show her a trail that led to the cottage's back garden. From this direction, Catherine and David's cottage was not that far off the path at all.

"Would you like a cup of tea?" Catherine asked.

Leonie would have preferred the elderberry wine. She'd had her fill of tea. "I'm fine."

"It won't be any trouble."

"I understand but I'm not thirsty." Pride. Leonie must cling to her pride.

"Would you like to help me?" Catherine said.

"Help you do what?"

"Why, garden." Catherine laughed, the sound happy and a thousand years from how Leonie felt. "Do you believe I would be this dirty for any other reason?"

Leonie didn't know her mother-in-law well enough to answer that question. In truth, Catherine was a bit of an enigma. She brewed her own wine, made salves that had worked miracles on Leonie's bruises, and even baked bread. She didn't mind doing the things that servants did. In fact, she seemed to enjoy herself.

"I've never gardened before." And she didn't think she'd like it. Leonie took a step back, but Catherine would not let her go.

Showing that she was as persistent as her son, she hooked her arm in Leonie's and said, "Oh, come. I need company. There is no joy in gardening alone. If you try it and you don't like it, then no harm will come out of the venture."

"I'm not dressed for playing in dirt."

"You aren't," Catherine agreed. "I have an apron you can wear." She was directing Leonie into the cottage's back garden. There was a patch of overturned dirt in the middle of the yard.

"Is Dora here?"

"No, she is helping Beth at the school today. Did you know she was a governess? She hated it, but she knows how to help children learn. Beth and Lawrence have both been after her to work with them at the school. She digs in her heels every time Beth begs for her support. David and I thought teaching was in her blood like it is for my late husband. We may have been wrong."

"What, then, shall she do?"

"That is a very good question, my lady. I would like to see her married but she is a strong personality. I don't know if there is a man who could go toe to toe with her. Stay a moment and I'll fetch the apron from the house."

She didn't wait for Leonie's answer but hurried to the cottage's back door.

Leonie walked over to the open patch of turned soil. There were some plants by their roots in a bucket. They didn't look very appealing, or alive.

Catherine came outside with a huge apron that would cover Leonie's skirts. "How do you like this?" She shook it out.

Leonie accepted the fact that to please her mother-in-law she would garden. What else was she doing?

It was also true that since Catherine had come upon her, she'd not thought about needing a drink.

Catherine said, "I brought these gloves out as well. They are David's. He will be most pleased that you are helping me. He likes the result of the garden but he does not enjoy the work."

Casting a doubtful eye on the fresh turned earth, Leonie tied the apron around her waist and changed her good gloves for David's. They were well-worn leather and too large for her hands; however, they would suffice. "What do I do?"

Catherine beamed her approval and handed her a rake. "We must continue to smooth out the big clumps of dirt until they are the size of peas."

What seemed an impossible order.

Catherine picked up a hoe and started breaking up the clods. Leonie decided she should at least try.

The work was not that demanding, but within an hour of the two of them being diligent, they had created a relatively smooth piece of earth. It had not been a difficult task and Catherine's company had been enjoyable, although they had been so busy they had not spoken much.

"This is good," Catherine said.

"What do we do now?" Leonie asked.

"We turn the soil again and then smooth it with the rake."

"We just did that." Leonie leaned on her rake. "It looks very good."

"Yes, but the secret to a good garden is in the soil. It needs air and a shaking up, just like people do."

Leonie had never thought she could use a shaking up. Nevertheless, she had enjoyed having something to do. So, when Catherine gave her the spade and told her to dig and "lift" the soil, she did.

"The hard part was cutting through the sod," Catherine said. "Lawrence did that for me—"

Leonie gave a shout of alarm. "Look at the worms. This soil

is full of them." She frowned her disgust but Catherine was elated.

"Aren't they fat and beautiful? I knew this was a good place for a garden. Look at the sun it shall receive. Everything will happily grow, just like those worms. We should tell Roman about them."

"Why would he want to know about worms?"

"He is a passionate fisherman. Worms are good bait."

"Roman likes to fish?" Leonie had never heard him say anything about the sport. Then again, he wasn't speaking to her.

"As a boy, he would throw a hook in the water every chance he could. They say the fishing in the streams through the village was once very good. Roman is using the squire's men to dredge the waterways and see if he can bring the trout back."

That seemed an ambitious project, as was this garden, and yet, they had made progress. "What sort of garden will this be?"

"Herbs and vegetables."

"That is practical."

"If one likes to eat." Catherine smiled.

"If I grew a garden, I would plant flowers," Leonie said. "That isn't very practical." Her arm ached a bit from lifting and turning dirt but she didn't stop. It was good to be out in the air and doing something constructive.

"Flowers are always practical," her mother-in-law declared. "People need beauty. What sort would you plant at Bonhomie?"

Leonie didn't have to think hard. "Roses. Big full ones. I also like daisies and those flowers that have the tall spires. I don't know the name."

"Delphinium?"

"Perhaps. However, I would mostly plant roses. Lady Bedford has a rose garden in London. She said she modeled it after the descriptions of the Empress Josephine's. She held a party in her garden last spring and I thought I'd never been anywhere so lovely. Or fragrant."

"It sounds delightful. You should have Roman plow a bed for you. Make certain they have plenty of sun."

"And worms."

Catherine laughed. "Yes, fat ones."

They took a moment to share a glass of spring water. It was cold and good. Leonie drank thirstily. They had been at their work for two hours and she was rather proud of how good their bed looked. She'd even taken off the oversized gloves and broken up clumps of dirt with her fingers in the same way Catherine did.

"Now what?" she asked her mother-in-law.

Catherine smiled. "We plant. This is the best part."

It was. Catherine had received the plants from several women in the village. She explained to Leonie what the plants were and showed her how to put them in the ground. Of course, it was simple, but very satisfying. They planted rosemary, thyme, and mint for Catherine's salves. They placed the mint in the far corner of the garden since Catherine told her it liked to spread. They also planted something called coneflowers. "These will bring the bees," her mother-in-law promised. "David wants to set up a hive."

"Who wants to keep bees close at hand?" Leonie wasn't certain of the idea.

Catherine just laughed. "I enjoy listening to the bees' hum. You will, too. I promise you."

Leonie didn't know if that was true. She had a shyness about being stung by any insect—however, she had to admit she was enjoying herself. Here she was, William Charnock's daughter in her fashionable cambric day dress, covered in dirt, admiring worms—and happy.

Yes, happy.

It was a startling realization.

She had also not thought of her problems over the past several hours or worried about where Catherine might keep the cider or elderberry wine.

Catherine was telling her the plans for the vegetable garden to be planted on the other side of the herbs when Leonie had a sudden desire to confess to this very kind woman. "I have a problem with drink."

Her mother-in-law stopped speaking in midsentence. She'd had her arm flung out to describe her plans for another bed by the cottage back door. She now lowered it. "I know."

"Do you think badly of me?"

Catherine considered a moment and then said, "I believe we all have challenges in life. David is losing strength in his legs. I don't know what will happen. The doctor suspects the worst. I'm glad we are here with Roman and my daughters."

"Do you mean he may be unable to walk?"

"No, Leonie, the worst."

"He could die?"

Catherine bent to rub a mint leaf between her fingers before answering. "Yes, he could. The doctor believes he has a wasting disease"

The information was startling. "Are you afraid?"

Her mother-in-law struggled a moment with emotions Leonie could only imagine. Then she said, "My dear girl, it is not how we die that is important, but how we live. David is good right now. We are both happy here and this moment is all that matters. Besides, I keep hoping the doctor is wrong." She paused and then asked, "Are you good right now?"

"About drinking?" Leonie had been so caught up in David's story she'd forgotten herself. "I had a moment this afternoon. I was on my way to the village in search of something. If I had found it, I don't know what would have happened between Roman and myself."

"What would you *have* happen?" There was a carefulness in Catherine's voice, as if she knew she treaded on dangerous ground.

"I'd have him forgive me—again. But he wouldn't. He isn't

the sort to give me my lead and not finally decide he'd had enough."

"Would you mind?"

Leonie looked at the good dirt she had been combing through with her fingers. "Yes," she replied so quietly she was speaking more to herself than Catherine.

But her mother-in-law had heard. She leaned over and covered Leonie's hand with her own. "I've known people who have your penchant. They had to learn how to stay away."

"And how did they do that?" There was the crux of the matter.

"I never asked. It always seemed such a personal question." Catherine thought a moment and then said, "They found something they loved more than the drink."

"Something they loved more." Leonie looked at the fledgling plants. "I enjoyed this. I haven't thought about a drink."

"That is a start." There was another pause. "What about my son?"

"What about him?" Leonie asked, confused.

"Do you love him enough to change?"

Did she love Roman? "He said he loves me," she admitted. "Or he did. He has made it clear he does not wish to spend much time with me anymore. He is very angry."

"I didn't ask what he thought of you, Leonie. I asked what you thought of him."

"I don't know that I understand what love is, especially the way your family talks about it. Already my marriage is nothing like my parents'." She studied the coneflowers' leaves and then said, "I think he is the most honest, brave, and considerate man I know. That I've disappointed him tears me apart inside. Is that love, to be sorry that I failed him? Or is it love that I miss him? We don't speak and I hate that most of all. It's as if I've had glimpses of what it could be like between us, and yet, each time, I fail him."

Catherine leaned toward. "I think my son cares for you

deeply. But I'll tell you a lesson I had to learn, and that is, unless I loved myself I would never understand my worth to David or my children. It had to start with me. Love yourself enough to save yourself, Leonie." She brushed Leonie's hair back from the temple. "Then you will know how to love others. I will give you a hint. It isn't all about what happens in bed. It has more to do in how we honor each other."

"Such as my not drinking and doing as he wishes?"

"Perhaps he is more frightened for you, Leonie, than angry with you. However, he can't be more afraid than you are for yourself. The imbalance would destroy the two of you."

Leonie reached over and gave her mother-in-law a spontaneous hug. She would never have done this to her mother.

Or have received such reasoned and personal advice.

"Thank you," she whispered.

"I want you and Roman to be happy. I want grandchildren from you, but I know all of this is not in my hands."

Leonie nodded. She rose to her feet. She needed some time to digest this. "I should return to Bonhomie. I shall see you this evening."

"I have a chicken stew cooking right now."

"That sounds good." Leonie took off the apron, folded it, and placed the gloves upon it. Even with the apron, her dress had dirt on it. The walking shoes she wore would need a good brush and polish and her fingernails had a rim of dirt beneath them, but she did not mind. These matters could be taken care of. "I enjoyed my afternoon in the garden."

"Feel free to return. David and I like this cottage. I plan on several more beds."

"Thank you. I will."

Leonie walked back to Bonhomie, taking the shortcut through the woods. Her mind weighed what Catherine had said. Leonie had always believed she thought highly of herself . . . but now she wondered.

The sense of being fine with the way things were continued all evening. She joined others for dinner and felt relaxed. That night, she fell into bed, again, without Roman. Only this night, she was so tired from hours spent outdoors in the fresh air, she slept deeply.

The next morning, an hour before dawn, she woke with a bit of pain in her shoulder and what looked to be some new muscles forming in her arm.

She also realized that when she woke her first thought was not of how much she wished to drink.

No, she woke thinking of roses. Lush, fragrant roses raised by her own hand. Roses like Lady Bedford had in her garden, roses like the Empress of France.

The early hour didn't deter Leonie. She dressed in the oldest gown she could find in her trunk, put on the walking shoes she'd worn the day before, and headed to the stables.

She found her husband sleeping on a cot in one of the empty stalls. Yarrow, Whiby, Barr, and the two new field workers they had hired also slept in the stables, but in the loft. Leonie could hear them snoring.

Because everyone on the estate knew her husband had rejected their bed, Leonie realized she had been timid and reticent about asserting herself. However, right now, she couldn't give a care what anyone thought. She was on a mission. She wanted a rose garden.

Her husband's body filled the small, uncomfortable cot. She started to give him a little shake, but stopped, her hand hovering over him.

She sniffed the air.

He smelled of strong drink. She knew. She'd been craving that smell for the last two days, although, right now, the scent was *far* from pleasant.

Roman had been drinking? And enough so that the stench clung to him?

Guilt gave way to indignation. Her husband was not perfect himself. She wouldn't be offended except for the hair shirt he'd been having her wear.

Well, she was taking it off.

Leonie smartly tapped Roman on the shoulder. He slapped at her as one would a fly.

"Roman." She kept her voice low so as not to be overheard in the loft.

He groaned a response and rolled over, giving her his back—which was no mean feat on the rickety cot. He could not be comfortable.

Leonie stood for a moment in indecision. Outside the stables, the sun was rising. The birds had begun heralding the day, a day when she was intent on planning her rose garden.

There was an anvil against the wall close to Roman's cot. She had noticed a bucket full of worn horseshoes in the stable aisle. She thought of the other men sleeping peacefully on their cots. She regretted disturbing their sleep, but she was going to enjoy disrupting Roman's.

Oh, yes, this was going to be fun after his holier-than-thou attitude.

The bucket was heavy; however, she was determined. Leonie dragged it to the anvil. She tried to pick it up high enough to dump the horseshoes out of it.

That wasn't going to work. Instead, she grabbed handfuls of horseshoes, held them over the anvil at her height, and let them fall.

The clang of metal against metal was not as loud as she'd hoped. It still served the trick.

Roman practically fell out of the cot, coming to his feet, his fist clenched and ready for any attack—save for the fact his eyes were barely open and he wobbled a bit.

He frowned when he recognized Leonie. His fists came down. "Is everything all right?"

"Yes, it is fine," she said briskly. "But I need your help. How do you hook up the horse to the plow?"

Roman shook his head as if he didn't trust his ears. "You want to use the plow? For what reason?"

"Flower beds, Roman. I want to plant flower beds and I'm starting with roses, just like the Empress Josephine."

Chapter 18

Roman had been dreaming about Leonie sleeping by his side.

Last night, over dinner, he'd noticed she had been more relaxed than he had seen her for days. She'd readily joined in the family conversations. She'd even been less self-conscious around him.

He didn't know how he'd felt about that. If he was honest, he could admit he had rather enjoyed Leonie acting chastised. It meant his opinion mattered to her, that he could disturb her peace of mind as effortlessly as she did his.

Walking home, she hadn't trailed behind him or sheepishly tried to stay by his side or even attempted to stomp ahead of him as she had the night before. No, she'd moved with easy grace.

She'd also been full of questions, asking him about his plans for the field he and the hired men had plowed that day. What would be planted there? Why had he chosen of all things clover?

When it came time to part ways—he, nobly taking himself to the stables and leaving her the house—she'd cheerfully wished him a good night as if something else occupied her mind. Something that wasn't him.

She was planning to leave him. She must be thinking of returning to London. Roman could imagine no other reason for her behavior.

It had always been a possibility from the very beginning. Hadn't she wanted that to be their bargain? And wouldn't he be better off alone rather than spending his days and nights worrying about her tendency toward drink?

Except it *didn't* make him happy.

He understood that he shouldn't try to stop her from leaving. She had too much power over him. She could play him for a fool, just as she had in India.

But then, not everything had been her fault. Her parents had a role. They were the ones that had left him to face the tribunal. Nor could he blame Leonie for his decision to lie about Paccard's death.

David's suggestion that perhaps he should have let justice have its course nagged at him. What if his decision to take the blame for Paccard's death was part of why Leonie drank? Perhaps they wouldn't have this wall between them?

In the end, Roman had taken himself to the village and the local public house because he wasn't fit company alone—and because he feared he had a strong desire to crawl on his knees to his wife and beg her forgiveness for his churlishness. He couldn't do that. He *wouldn't*.

A half bottle of whisky convinced him he was completely right in his rigid stance.

But that hadn't stopped her from invading even his drunken sleep, and now here she was, right before him . . . and talking about hitching the plow?

Perhaps he was still dreaming?

From the way his head pounded, he didn't think so.

He watched his wife pick up horseshoes and toss them into a bucket. She appeared rested and happy while he would like nothing more than to pull his head off his shoulders.

He found his voice. "Hitch the horse?"

"Yes, to the plow." She dropped the last of the horseshoes in the bucket. She wore her hair down and loose around her shoulders, the way he liked it. Her dress was a plain, dark blue gown without embellishment, but Leonie didn't need pleats, lace, and buttons to look lovely. "I've decided where the rose garden should be. Of course, it might be best if we plow up the whole back lawn and then I can replant it the way I believe it should be."

The pounding in his head was subsiding. "*You* want to use the plow?" He spoke slowly.

"Is it hard to do? Don't you just follow the horse?"

"You have to keep the plow down." He could add he'd never seen a woman plow. And if he said that, Leonie might take it up as a challenge.

She considered his statement a moment. "I might need help."

"I believe you will."

She smiled at him, an expression so dazzling it hurt his bloodshot eyes. She'd picked up on the dryness in his tone. Perhaps she knew he was teasing slightly, or perhaps she just wanted him to feel more like the besotted fool he was.

And he *was* out of his depth. No woman had a smile more potent that Leonie's. Yes, God had gifted her with looks that could set every male imagination on fire. However, in her smile was just that right touch of uncertainty, as if what he thought of her was important.

"Come," she said. "Let me show you what I mean to do."

She started walking out of the stall.

"Wait," he called. "I need to put on my boots."

"Do you need help?"

Now there was an offer! Roman blinked a few times to be certain he wasn't still dreaming. He wasn't. She stood at the stall door looking fresh as the day's dawn.

He reached for his boots and gingerly slipped them on. It

took him a moment to rise to his feet. That cot was the most uncomfortable thing he'd ever slept on. Stretching, he found his bearings and nodded for her to lead the way. He followed her out of the stables, blinking when he stepped out into the morning light.

"When I feel as you," she said thoughtfully, "I have learned it helps to wash my face and clean my teeth."

It would help. "I will be back," he said. He started for the kitchen in the house. He'd moved his shaving kit and personal items there when he'd left their room.

"I'll be by the garden door."

Roman stopped. "The garden door?"

She laughed. "The back entrance. Wait until you learn what I have in mind."

Was this his wife? Curious now, Roman hurried to bring himself to his senses. Splashing cold water on his face in the basin in the kitchen, he reflected that she was being very generous with him. If he'd caught her in his shape, he would have been . . . cruel?

Their circumstances were different, he told himself. He'd made a mistake. Drinking was a character issue with Leonie.

Or was he the one with the character issue?

He ran a hand over his rough beard and looked at himself in the mirror. He did not like what he saw. He appeared tired, disillusioned, drink bitten.

This wasn't the man he wanted to be.

He lathered his shaving soap and quickly ran a blade over his jaw. The use of tooth powder also helped him regain a bit of his own. He put on a clean shirt and headed for the "garden" door.

Leonie stood out on the lawn looking up at the house.

Roman took a moment to savor the picture she presented. While he'd been gone, she had twisted her hair back into a knot at the nape of her neck. She stood on the rough ground that made up the back garden studying the house.

She sensed his presence and smiled her welcome. That was all it took to stoke his heart.

"What are you thinking?" he asked. His voice sounded normal despite everything inside him being a mixture of lust and wonder and wanting.

"How soon do you think it will be until you start rebuilding the side of the house?"

"Two days. Some stonemasons contacted me offering their services."

"Will you be able to copy the stone mullions in the windows like they are on the other side of the house?"

"That may be difficult." Roman joined her on the lawn. "We might have to settle for wood. It is easier to make."

"With the curved designs?" She referred to the ivy leaf design on the original windows.

"Possibly not."

"That would be a pity. Then again, that the house isn't identical on both sides could become a story of interest."

Roman agreed, then dared to ask, "Are you saying you might grow accustomed to Rook Haven?"

The lips of her generous mouth gave a rueful twist. "I call it that," she admitted. "There are no rooks this morning."

"There will be later."

"We shall see," she said with another quick smile, and then she changed the subject to her rose garden. She had many ideas. It would be a garden fit for a royal palace. She wanted the roses along the house and other flower beds in patterns across the lawn. She even had plans for an arbor with benches beneath it. "I saw it at Lady Fitzhugh's garden and thought it the most perfect place to enjoy a summer day. Is it possible?"

Her enthusiasm charmed him. He liked what she had planned. "Of course it is possible. Adams in the village is a very capable carpenter. He and his sons will do whatever you design."

"Whatever *I* design," she repeated. She looked to Roman. "I like that. It will be my mark on Bonhomie."

"Yes," he said, daring to move toward her, but then an expression crossed her face that made him stop. It was wistful but there was regret there as well.

She took a step away from him. He had not misread her.

He stopped. They stood a little less than a foot from each other. A man and his wife discussing the garden, for all the world to see. But he knew this could be much more.

"I love you." His words flowed out of him. They were a statement of inescapable fact. Doubts be damned, he felt what he felt.

Leonie crossed her arms. She attempted to smile . . . but she was not entirely successful. "I know you do."

"Then all will be well between us."

Her arms tightened against her. "I am trying to be strong."

"You *are* strong. Perhaps stronger than I—"

She crossed the space between them and placed her fingertips against his lips. "You weren't wrong to be angry," she said.

"Leonie—"

"Shh, no. Don't argue, Roman. Please, don't. I don't know if I can overcome my weaknesses. Is it love to care for your well-being more than my own? I would hate myself if I used you in such a manner. It would set me adrift, and I want something more than what my parents have."

As did he. His mind, and his heart, knew she was right. And yet, his body begged for him to shout, *Use me. Let me love you. I will do anything to keep you safe. To protect you.*

She seemed to hear his unspoken words. "This isn't about you. I am going to save myself. I must find a way to survive and I believe roses will be key. They have taken ahold of my imagination. I know this sounds silly, but look—" She held out her hand. "See? It is steady."

His response was to take her hand. He adored the warmth of her skin. He dreamed of it.

He looked out over the expanse of lawn that she proposed transforming into flower beds. *Transforming . . .*

Roman had little use for flowers. He'd intended to raise food to eat, grain to mill, and fodder for animals. His passion was for what had permanence, such as rebuilding Bonhomie's structure. Roses were fine. They smelled good, but they could not be eaten or woven.

However, if they could nourish Leonie's soul, he'd plant acres of them.

For that reason alone, he considered the back of the house. "So, you want the rose bed over here along the house. Would this be deep enough for the beds?" He drew a line in the air to roughly indicate his thoughts.

"Yes, and an herb garden by the kitchen door. Your mother will help me design it. Those beds will be the beginning." She glanced down to where their hands were still joined. She did not release her hold. Instead, she said, "I would also like a say in the hiring of the household servants."

"Absolutely," he said. "Yarrow is yours to command. I'll be busy plowing flower beds."

She gifted him with a radiant smile. "Thank you, Roman."

Dear God, she humbled him.

"Would you care for a cup of tea and toasted bread?" she asked. "My tea-making skills are fairly reliable and Dora told me how to toast the bread. I'd like to try her method. It doesn't sound difficult. The loaf is fresh from your mother, so if the first piece is too black, you can eat it untoasted."

"Who could have imagined the elegant Miss Charnock of London would be willing to toast bread?"

She blushed. "Wait until you've tasted my toast before you brag upon me."

Leonie started toward the house but Roman, still holding her hand, pulled her back. She glanced to him.

"We will share a bed," he said. Her lips parted as if to protest, but he continued. "Aye, we will. I'll not do anything you don't wish." It would be damned hard not to touch her, but he could. "I'm tired of sleeping on that cot, Leonie. I want my bed."

"And I can move?" Her chin had come up and a flash of fire lit her eye. "You are the one who left the bed, Roman. Not I."

"That is true. I'm a fool."

She looked down at their joined hands, and then her mood softened. She smiled.

He smiled back and, just like that, there was hope for them. It would take time. He understood. She was still fragile. She had set for herself a colossal task, one she must do for herself.

God, could he be patient and wait? Had he not waited long enough for her?

The answer was—he would wait for her forever.

And yes, she burned the toast.

Yes, he ate it buttered with praise.

TRUE TO HIS word, Roman had one of the field workers plow up the back garden. It was quite a chore.

Leonie didn't have the opportunity to watch the work be done because she and Yarrow were busy discussing staff for the house.

This was all new to her. She'd never run a household and realized her mother hadn't either. Her mother had other pursuits and Leonie had not paid attention to what the succession of housekeepers over the years had been doing. Besides, in such a wealthy household, there had always been plenty of servants to do even the most basic of tasks. That would not be the case at Bonhomie. Even with the wealth Leonie brought to the marriage, economies needed to be practiced to achieve all that Roman had planned.

Yarrow understood her lack of household knowledge. With infinite kindness, he helped school her in what the lady of such an estate as this should know.

Leonie also had the support and combined wisdom of her mother-in-law and her sisters-in-law. She would have hired the first cook who walked in the door if it had not been for Catherine.

"Don't you want to know how she cooks?" Catherine had asked.

Shrugging, Leonie said, "She is a cook. She has references. Why would she not cook well?"

"Because there is a great deal to know about cooking."

"I know nothing. How can I judge if she knows what she is doing? I served Roman burnt toast."

"You eat, don't you?" Dora said with her customary bluntness. "That is the only true measure of a good cook."

Encouraged by the two women, Leonie asked the woman applying for the position to prepare a dinner. The food was terrible. Catherine, her daughters, and even David understood exactly why. There had been no salt. The gravy had lacked flavor because of a lack of fat and the vegetables had been cooked to mush. And so began Leonie's education in the kitchen arts.

"Even a countess needs to boil an egg from time to time," Dora declared.

Since that might be true, Leonie attempted egg boiling to accompany Roman's burnt toast. Eggs led to chickens and Roman had the abandoned coop cleaned out. He purchased hens and a rooster to fill it and it was Leonie's task to gather eggs until they hired a girl from the village for the duties of a scullery maid.

In two weeks' time, Leonie hired, with the family's approval, an excellent cook from Yorkshire who wished to move to Somerset to be closer to her family. The woman had worked on a large estate so understood that she was not only cooking for the Earl of Rochdale's extended family, but would be expected to serve meals to the field workers, the stonemasons, the carpenters, the stable lads, and the growing number of household staff. Leonie didn't know how Cook managed the overwhelming task and yet everyone was well fed and satisfied.

Roman hired a land steward, a Mr. Briggs, who came highly recommended and knew exactly how to tame the forests about Bonhomie. The fields began to take shape. One field was sown with the clover that had seemed an odd crop to Leonie but which Mr. Briggs agreed with Roman would be good for the soil and the future. The other two-thirds were planted with corn and hay. Briggs also had a cousin who could restore an old mill that had fallen into disrepair. Soon people would not have to travel all the way to Ilminster to have their grain ground. He and Roman also began making plans for a logging mill. Now that the stream was unblocked, water flowed freely and could be put to use.

Duncan Barr, Roman's valet, discovered he preferred working with the animals instead of polishing boots. With Roman's blessing, he took over the lambs that would become Bonhomie's herder. Leonie adored watching the lambs play in the fields and was a touch sad when they matured to the point they didn't kick up their heels or jump over clumps of buttercups.

Roman had visited an apple orchard where the sheep grazed beneath the trees and he was determined to do the same at Bonhomie. He said it made sense to use the land for two purposes. Of course, right now, his apple trees were little more than twigs in the ground.

A half acre between Bonhomie and David and Catherine's cottage was prepared for a vegetable garden. His parents took on its management. Every day as spring rolled into summer, they could be found in the garden during the early morning hours. Sometimes Leonie helped with the weeding. Often Edward and Jane joined them. Leonie enjoyed their company.

Their childhoods, surrounded by doting adults, were vastly different than her own had been. Their curiosity was encouraged, and she found herself thinking about how lonely she'd been.

Contrary to her vow to avoid all children save for her niece and nephew, Dora began spending more time at the village school, taking over Beth's role as teacher. The parish was growing and Lawrence needed his wife's help. Despite detesting her years as governess, Dora found she liked overseeing her classroom and that children were not so dreadful when they went home to their parents each day.

In all aspects, Bonhomie teemed with life. Roman brought ducks for the pond and a cow for her milk. Two huge oxen were purchased to plow the fields, leaving the wagon horses for other chores.

Rabbits discovered the garden. Roman had a fence built around it to keep away the deer, but the rabbits always found a way in and that was when Chester and Soldier came into their lives.

Chester was a herding dog who helped Barr with the sheep. When he was done for the day, he performed a rabbit patrol with Soldier, a lively foxhound pup who, when he wasn't sniffing out garden thieves, wanted to follow Roman wherever he went—including into the house.

At first, Leonie refused the dogs entrance. Chester was happy in the stables with the hired men but Soldier was crestfallen. It took only one day of the poor pup sitting on the step crying in loneliness for her to relent.

And when she said yes, Soldier's tail wagged so furiously with joy it threatened to wag off his body.

Leonie was charmed.

Then one afternoon, a scrawny orange tabby came wandering onto the estate. He had one eye permanently shut from a fight. Leonie's heart immediately went out to him. She offered him fresh milk. He ate as if he was starving and then disappeared.

She worried. Roman told her cats were independent creatures and could fare for themselves. He would return if he wished.

Leonie wasn't certain. Once, when she was a child, she'd found a kitten. She'd wanted to keep it for a pet but her father had it tossed from the house. The next day, when she'd been taking a walk with her nurse, she saw its body on the street. She'd been inconsolable.

However, Roman proved to be right. The next morning, Cook was horrified to find a dead, fat field mouse on the back step. When the scullery maid came in with the milk, the tabby was trailing behind her. Leonie was overjoyed he was back and served him a saucer of cream herself. She named him Vishnu after the Hindu god for protection. Roman had laughed upon hearing the name but Vishnu lived up to it. He kept the feed room in the stables and the pantry in the kitchen free of rodents. Cook said she'd never seen a better mouser. In the afternoons and mornings when Leonie worked in her gardens, he chased butterflies or sunned himself while keeping watch over her and Soldier.

The rose garden proved to be a touch more challenging than Leonie had anticipated. No one at Bonhomie knew very much about roses. Roman sent to London for information and purchased a book, *A Collection of Roses from Nature* by a Miss Mary Lawrence, from his friend Thaddeus Chalmers. The book had delightful renderings of roses but little information.

It was up to Leonie to educate herself. Neighbors with roses let her do cuttings. She tried rooting them in water and in damp soil and in peat. She discovered that roses were remarkably sensitive. Some cuttings thrived in water, some in soil.

Word quickly spread that Lady Rochdale had a passion for roses. Leonie learned she was not alone. Rose lovers wrote to her from all over Somerset offering cuttings and advice. In this way, her little garden began to grow.

Catherine helped her with the other beds, but Leonie tended the roses herself. Every little leaf gave her great pride. When Dame Fenlon of Ilminster offered her a whole bush, Leonie almost wept with joy. She might have blooms this summer.

At least once a week, Roman made time to sit out in the garden while she worked. He said he liked seeing her with a bit of dirt on her chin and in her nails.

She knew that couldn't be true but they had the best conversations during those times. Their lives had become so busy there was rarely time for themselves. He would talk about what changes he was making to the estate that week and she would share her ideas for the house. *Their* house . . .

It was times like this that she felt guilty that she thought of her mother's hidden flask. Or that she yearned for a taste of brandy. The thought of a drink was never far from her mind. She was weak-willed and it shamed her. She was glad Roman had cleared Bonhomie of spirits in any form.

Of course she and Roman shared their bed.

Yes, he had the right to sleep in her bed, but she built a row of bedclothes between them. He had his side; she had hers.

His first act upon seeing what she had done was to toss everything on the floor.

Again, she stacked the bedclothes and, again, he destroyed her little wall.

She assumed this meant he wished to join with her, that they would go on with this act that was so satisfying. And she was not against the idea. Even with his breeches on, her husband was a large man and his arousal was difficult to hide. The sight of it was enough to inspire an answering desire in herself.

However, that was not what Roman had in mind. "I want you, aye, I do. You can see the proof of that." He indicated his body's reaction to her. "But we are not ready for 'us' in that way, Leonie. It is not the time."

What a curious thing to say. He proved his words by falling into a deep and easy sleep.

Leonie had not relaxed so easily. Her feelings were a bit hurt. She knew he wanted her. She wanted him . . . and yet he denied himself?

What did this say about her as a woman? What did it mean for them? He'd talked about sending her away, then kept her, but sleeping with her without satisfying the hunger they both felt for each other's bodies . . . ?

She puzzled over those questions most of the night until the answer came. Then she understood.

Roman didn't completely trust her not to drink. Not yet.

Leonie knew she didn't trust herself either.

And, until Roman made up his mind about her, he would not do anything that could create a child. She understood his motives as clearly as if he had spoken the words. Her husband valued responsibility.

This also meant he might still set her aside.

Leonie spent a good five minutes trying to work up her anger as a defense against his distrust—except in her heart, she knew he was being wise.

Of course, their bodies didn't stay away from each other. They were drawn together like magnets. She woke the next morning with her head on his shoulder and his hand between her legs.

"What are you doing? I thought you said we shouldn't—?" she started, and then sighed as he found his mark.

His lips were by her ear as he whispered, "I didn't say we couldn't play." He then proceeded to show her what he meant by doing amazing things with his hands and mouth.

Leonie learned she could "play" as well. She found it a heady experience to have her brawny husband at her mercy. Over the days that passed, she was free to explore every inch of his body. She delighted in pleasing him. It gave her almost more gratification than the pleasure he gave to her.

Was this love? Did giving more than receiving qualify?

Soon, they both knew Leonie was not with child. She'd also been very good and had not touched a drop. It had been her private struggle.

However, no matter how "good" she was, Roman kept a boundary between them.

She didn't understand completely. *What did he want from her? What was the key that would convince him that he could trust her?*

Working in the garden gave her time to mull over these questions and other, unsettled feelings.

She liked sleeping with her husband. She adored what he could do to her body.

And yet, she sensed a lack of permanence. A queasy feeling that she did not deserve Roman or his family, that she should *not* be loved.

It was all confusing.

Or so she thought . . . until one overcast day, as she gently planted a rose cutting, a thought she kept carefully tucked away in her mind reared its ugly head.

She'd killed a man.

It wasn't that Leonie hadn't recalled the terrible amount of blood that had been everywhere or holding Arthur while begging him not to die. She knew that if she hadn't acted, he would have continued to hurt her.

Still, everything had happened so quickly, and then she'd shut it away in her mind. Even justified, she had not let herself think on what it truly meant to take someone else's life, especially someone she'd known and had trusted.

She looked at the fragile cutting that she dearly hoped would grow into a blooming plant. She found it hard to breathe. The cutting seemed to have activated her conscience. The weight of it was almost unbearable.

Vishnu sensed her turmoil. He rubbed against her and then climbed into her lap. Soldier and Chester had been napping close. They, too, understood something was not right. They padded over to her. Chester took position as if guarding her. Soldier nudged her.

Leonie knew she could go to Roman. He would hold her and tell her all the right words to placate her conscience. Then again, she'd harmed him as well.

No, she needed to speak to someone she trusted who could give her an honest answer.

She rose from the ground and went inside. After washing her hands, she changed her clothes, put on a shepherdess's bonnet with its wide brims and yellow ribbons, and walked to the village.

Her brother-in-law was pulling weeds around the graves circling his stone church. He smiled a greeting but before he could speak, Leonie said, "Do you have a moment, Lawrence?"

"Of course. Would you like a cup of water or tea?"

"I'm fine, thank you. I have a burden on my soul and I must ask you what I should do. I may need to go to the magistrate."

Chapter 19

*L*eonie's pronouncement gained her Lawrence's attention. He led her inside the cool, dry darkness of the church. There was a silence here, as if no confession spoken would leave these walls.

They sat in the last row of chairs.

"What is troubling you, Leonie?"

She told him her story. She didn't spare details. She was done keeping secrets. Roman did know most of the story, but to Lawrence she could confess the heady feeling of playing on the two men's jealousies.

"I led both to believe they were important to me," she admitted.

If Lawrence was shocked, he gave no indication. Instead, he listened intently. He didn't even flinch when she tearfully told him about the rape, about how brutal Arthur had been.

"I had told him that I had changed my mind about running away with him. I hadn't really thought we were going to do it. I was foolish. He told me he couldn't let me go. He said I must marry him now and, when I refused, he threatened me with his pistol." She had to draw a deep steadying breath before she could continue. "I let him do what he wanted. He would have killed me. He hit me. He choked me. When he was done, he didn't relax. He wanted more and that is when my hand found the pistol." She looked to Lawrence, begging him to understand. "I shot before I realized what I was doing—and then, Roman came in the door and I let him take charge. He took me home."

"He also claimed he was the one who killed this Arthur?"

Leonie nodded. "We've discussed it. Roman says it is not my worry. And yet, it is. I wish that night had never happened and it is all my fault. What must I do? For so long, people have thought Roman was guilty for Arthur's death."

"I believe he has made peace with that. My brother-in-law would not have married you even for money if he believed you are a murderess. I'm certain of that fact."

"I don't know. He was very anxious for my dowry." She picked at her skirt a moment and then said, "He tells me he loves me."

"Then believe him."

"That is the hard task. I made such a mistake . . ."

Lawrence leaned forward. "Leonie, the hard task is forgiving yourself."

He was right.

"Roman has," Lawrence pointed out. "He has brought you into the family. He cares deeply for you."

She nodded. "He is afraid of me though."

"No, he has concerns about your need for strong spirits. That doesn't make you a bad person."

"Then what does it make me?"

"Human." Lawrence took her hand. "You can't change the past. All of us have done something that haunts us. You are responsible for your decisions that night, but not for this Arthur's. He sounds as if he received what he deserved, and I don't know if the courts would have given you justice. But I shall tell you something I have learned over my years as being a man of the cloth—none of us have the right of it. We are all doing the best we can and we have failings. But we also have choices. You can continue to carry this burden or you can start putting your attention on what truly matters to you."

Leonie nodded, although she didn't know if she could leave her regret behind. It was, she discovered, a powerful part of her life. They then prayed and she thanked Lawrence and went home.

Yes, *home*—Bonhomie had become very dear to her, even with its crumbled wall that was quickly being rebuilt.

Roman didn't know that she had been gone. He'd spent his day at the mill. He was very pleased with the repairs.

"Briggs says we shall test the grindstone in a few days."

"That is good news," Leonie said, meaning the words.

Cook had prepared venison for their dinner. Leonie barely tasted it. Her mind was on Lawrence's advice.

"We'll be grinding for every family in the parish and the next one over," Roman predicted, but then he stopped speaking.

At the silence, Leonie looked up to find him staring at her. "Is something the matter?" she said.

"I was going to ask you that question. You seem preoccupied."

He knew her so well.

Before she could muster some sort of answer, he said, "I love you." His hand covered hers on the table.

I love you, too.

She didn't speak the words aloud. She did not trust herself. Instead, she turned her hand over to clasp his as hard as she could.

He looked at their joined hands and then said, "I know, Leonie. When you are ready, I will be here."

"I fear I'll never be what you want."

A sober look came to his eye. His answer was to raise her hand to his lips.

That night, she rested her head on his chest and listened to the beat of his heart and prayed she could make right all that she'd done wrong.

THE NEXT DAY was Squire Jones's annual hunt culminating in a village dance. The event was the highlight of their country society.

Of course the Earl of Rochdale and his lady were invited as were all the members of his family. Roman told Leonie that he was just as happy to stay home but she felt they should go. "It is our first social engagement. It would be churlish after all the help he has given us with Bonhomie to refuse his invitation."

She was right.

However, Roman had his reservations. The squire liked his food and drink. The squire prided himself on his stamina when it came to strong spirits. Roman knew Leonie still struggled; after all, didn't he struggle with trusting her?

He'd unburdened himself to Lawrence a week ago. He'd confessed he wanted his wife in all ways. Lawrence understood the danger of drink, having grown up around those who imbibed too freely.

"I believe she loves you," Lawrence had said. "In time, you will have the right answer for your own heart."

In time . . . Roman hated those words. He wanted to know now. He did not know how much longer he could live like a monk around her. Their celibate games in bed were growing tiresome. He wanted to possess, to be inside her, to have his seed grow within her.

Early that morning, Roman, Lawrence, and Briggs rode in the wagon to the squire's far field to join the hunt for pheasant and whatever other bird they could flush.

Squire Jones informed them they would be eating whatever they shot for the day so the game was on to see which hunter could bag the most birds. Roman would have liked to bring Soldier for the experience but decided this might be too busy a hunt for a pup. He'd left his little friend in one of the stalls. His whining had been a pitiful sound. Roman warned Leonie to not let him loose. "He will try and find me."

She agreed.

Leonie would be traveling to the squire's later with his parents and sisters.

It was good to be out in the air. The early June day was the sort that made a man glad to be alive. The company was a mixed collection. There were several of Roman's largest tenants and neighbors from as far away as twenty miles.

Roman acquitted himself well for the hunt. He didn't bag the most birds but his number was respectable and only one was gun shot. Lawrence also managed a goodly number. Squire Jones crowed his approval. "You have earned your dinner for your family, my lord."

"I always wish them well fed."

The squire laughed. "They will be." His nose was already turning a cherry red. The spirits had been flowing freely. That was one of the reasons why the others had such poor aim. Many of their birds were inedible. There was too much shot in them.

Roman had refused the spirits. Watching Leonie's battle, he was wary of what he consumed. He enjoyed a tankard of ale but that was enough.

Shortly after the noon hour, the men started for the squire's house. They handed their birds over to the kitchen and then the serious drinking began. The squire mixed his own punch and took great pride in the ingredients.

"Arrack?" Roman questioned. He knew the liquor. It was much like rum only far more potent.

"Just a touch," Squire Jones assured him. He then added the whole bottle as well as a bottle of brandy and claret.

Roman decided he'd keep with his ale.

At that moment, he looked across the grounds and saw his family coming in the cart he'd purchased for trips around the parish. Leonie sat with her arms around Edward and Jane while Beth drove. Dora was giving instructions and his parents were laughing.

Leonie looked like a charming shepherdess with her tawny gold hair curling wildly beneath a wide brimmed hat trimmed in colorful ribbons to keep the sun from her face. Her dress was the green of new leaves. The style was simple, but his wife could wear a sackcloth and set men's imaginations afire.

Behind him, Roman heard the hum from the other male guests.

"You are a lucky man, Rochdale," one of his neighbors, Sir Charles Everett, said. He had been one of the hunters and had been matching the squire drink for drink, although he didn't show it.

The cart pulled to a halt. Roman decided he needed to stake his claim and walked to greet his family. To his surprise, Squire Jones almost knocked him over as he hurried in Leonie's direction to help her from the cart.

Roman's legs were longer and it was *his* hands that took Leonie by the waist and swung her down, leaving the squire to help Dora while Lawrence and Roman's stepfather saw to Beth and his mother.

The music for the afternoon had already started. Two local fiddlers set a lively tune.

Squire Jones bowed over Leonie's hand, ignoring his own wife, who had rushed to greet the countess as well. "It is an honor to have you here, my lady. You are a vision."

"Why, thank you, Squire," Leonie said. She shot Roman a look that said she realized the man was well into his cups. She gave a tug on her hand. He didn't want to let go, but Leonie proved she'd been in these circumstances before. She knew how to extricate her hand and then wisely turned her attention to Mrs. Jones, the squire's giggly wife.

Roman took Leonie's arm and led her to where couples were dancing. He was right to think that Squire Jones and his wife were not dancers. There was a measure of peace here.

"You look fetching, wife. I adore your hair down."

She colored prettily and glanced around to see if anyone had overheard. He didn't care if they did. He'd shout the words if he must. "Thank you," she said, and then added, "You look fetching, too."

Her words made him laugh and when the dance started he could have flown through the steps he was so happy.

The afternoon was a good one. The squire had set up tables under the trees and people ate and drank until they were full and more. Roman could see why this event was anticipated by everyone in the parish.

In the beginning, Leonie was right by his side, but as time passed, she was pulled over to join some of her rose-growing friends. They sat in a circle with his mother and sister Dora. Beth was with the other young mothers supervising the children.

Roman was called into a group of men to recount the morning's hunt. It was a good companionable time and the punch bowl never seemed to empty.

Leonie had given it wide berth. She had wisely planned ahead and had Cook make a huge pottery crock of lemonade. It had taken both Briggs and Lawrence to remove it from the wagon. Roman noticed that his sisters and mother were drinking it as well as several of the other ladies.

All in all, it was a good afternoon. The sky was clear, the company entertaining, and Roman experienced what could only be described as happiness. His life made him proud. As time went by, he would continue to prosper. The years of hardship and frustration were behind him—

Squire Jones jostled his arm, interrupting his thoughts. "You will thank me, my lord."

"I'm already in your debt, Jones," Roman said. "This is an admirable event. I believe I have been introduced to everyone in the parish."

"You have, my lord, you have." The squire weaved a bit, a silly conspiratorial smile upon his face. "The wife and I are proud to bring everyone together, but that isn't what I was talking about."

"Then why else will I thank you?" Roman said.

Squire Jones touched the side of his nose. "I noticed your lady wife had not tried my punch. I made a new batch. I can barely stand after sampling it. I gave her a cup. It will be a good night for you, my lord. That punch will loosen her lacings."

Cold fear mixed with anger in Roman. "You gave her a cup? Did she take it?"

"Of course. Said she liked brandy. I put two bottles in this last batch, I did." He waved his hand as he spoke and almost toppled over into the arms of another guest. That man attempted to right him but it was too late for the squire. He fell to the ground and, to Roman's shock, curled up and passed out.

Everyone grinned and pointed at him. "Does this every year," someone said. "He lasted longer this year than last."

Roman didn't give a damn about the squire. He looked to where he'd last seen Leonie with Dora and some other women at one of the tables . . .

She was not there.

He walked over to his mother. "Have you seen my lady?" He spoke calmly, aware of how many people could overhear him.

His mother looked around. "I thought she was right here."

Dora didn't know where Leonie had gone either. "I'll help you look for her."

"No, she's fine," Roman lied. "You enjoy yourself with your friends." He didn't wait for his sister's answer but set out to find his wife.

She could not be seen anywhere in the crowd. People were constantly moving and dancing. He feared he could miss her. Then again, his every sense told him that she was not amongst the assembled company. He walked through the squire's house. She was not there.

Desperate now, he went out the front door—and there he saw her. There was an arbor covered with ivy close to the tree line bordering the lawn. Beneath it was a bench and there sat Leonie holding a punch cup. She studied it as if working a great problem in her mind. She'd loosened the ribbons of her hat so that it hung down her back.

Roman watched her, a weight settling in his chest. He didn't think she'd seen him. With one step, he could return inside the house and pretend he'd not witnessed her with the punch.

She'd break him, she would. This habit of hers would crush his heart, and he was powerless to stop her. Nor could he leave her. He loved her too much.

And then, Leonie stood.

Holding the cup ceremoniously in front of her, she poured the contents on the ground.

She didn't drink it. She had chosen not to drink. Roman could have fallen to his knees in thanksgiving. Instead, he shouted her name and ran to her.

Leonie looked up with a start, obviously unaware that she'd been watched.

Before she could do anything, he was upon her. He swung her in his arms, twirled her around, and kissed her with the freedom of a man who loved.

At last he stopped because they both needed to take a breath, but he held on to her. He was never going to let her go. Leonie looked up at him. "How did you know I was here?"

"The squire told me he'd given you a cup of his special punch."

"And you came looking for me? You were afraid I would drink it?"

"I prayed you wouldn't."

Her dark eyes searched his for understanding. "I wanted it, Roman. I could smell the brandy. I haven't forgotten the scent."

Her words were his deepest fears for her.

"But then I thought about roses and how when they are buds the petals are all folded in on each other. They don't look like they could be anything. However, when they reach out to bloom, those same petals reveal the most amazing gifts. The center of every rose is like the heart of the flower." She leaned toward him. "I told myself I was like one of those roses, closed off from anything meaningful because if I thought too hard I'd see how ugly I was—"

"Leonie, you are beautiful."

She blushed and then said, "I am now, Roman. But not because of how other people see me, but because of you. You forgave me for what happened with Paccard."

"I never blamed you—"

"Yes, you did."

She was right. He had. When she'd abandoned him to his fate, he had blamed her for the whole of it . . . but that seemed so long ago. "If things hadn't gone as they did, we would not be here together right now," he said.

"That is true. I can't imagine my life without you. I'm far from perfect and my looks will fade with age—"

"Not in my eyes."

She laughed, the sound dear to him. She placed her hands on either side of his jaw. "I love you."

Her declaration filled him with joy. Before he could cover her with kisses, she said, "I've worked very hard to become the woman I want to be. That woman chose life over what was in the cup."

"Leonie, you are all that I could ask. I'm not perfect either."

She laughed. "I know, and yet you are perfect for me." And she kissed him.

She put her arms around his neck, pressed her breasts against his chest, her thighs meeting his, and kissed him with such love there wasn't anything he wouldn't do for her.

When she was done, he could scarce remember his name. She'd stolen his wits.

Nor was she done with him. "Roman, may we marry again? I believe I'd like to remember repeating my vows."

His answer was to gather her in his arms and kiss her again.

She was the victor. She had won.

Yes, in the future, there would be demons—his as well as hers. However, together, they could face anything because, miracle of miracles, Leonie loved him.

LEONIE AND ROMAN wasted no time finding Lawrence. They discovered him playing ninepins with a group of men and asked him to marry them that very night. After all, no banns needed to be read or special license procured for a couple already married.

Of course he said yes.

They gathered the family from the squire's party and drove to the church in the wagon, leaving the cart for Briggs to take home.

By now, evening was falling. The church was quiet and dark. Edward and Jane happily lit candles while Dora and Beth helped Leonie tidy up in a corner.

"You should have been married here the first time," Dora grumbled. "This is the way it should have been."

Beth shushed her.

Leonie took off the star sapphire and handed it to Lawrence. "We'll need this blessed."

"Absolutely," he agreed. He donned his vestments.

Leonie was surprised at how nervous she was, and yet she felt a great sense of peace. She couldn't imagine herself married to anyone but Roman. In her short time with him, she'd done more living than she had all the years before in her life.

Dora and Beth stood by Leonie and Roman's parents took their place beside him. Edward and Jane sat in the front row.

Lawrence opened his prayer book.

The words he spoke were all new to Leonie because, no, she hadn't remembered them. She was struck by their strength and blessed assurance.

When Roman repeated his vows, he did so with warmth,

gentleness, and loving generosity. He promised to love and cherish her "until we are parted by death."

Holding his hand, she vowed the same. Yes, this was what she wanted for her life. This man, his family, his dreams, *her* dreams . . . she could not ask for more.

Lawrence blessed the ring. Roman took it and, holding it over the tip of her ring finger, he said, "With all that I am, and with all that I have, I honor you." He slid the ring down her finger. Leonie hadn't realized how much the ring had already become a part of her until it was back in place.

And the moment it was there, she moved right into Roman's arms.

This, too, was good. Roman held her close as Lawrence pronounced them man and wife.

Of course, there wasn't a fancy feast. Roman and Leonie didn't need any of those trappings. They had family around them and that was enough. The family was all teary-eyed with happiness, even Dora. There were hugs all around and Leonie felt *truly* blessed.

Leonie and Roman drove his mother and father to their cottage. "That wedding was lovely," his mother kept saying. "Perfect even."

Leonie agreed. She sat on the seat beside her husband, as close to him as she could possibly be. She noticed that Catherine and David held hands.

This was how marriage was meant to be. Yes, Roman had received her substantial dowry; however, she had no doubts that he loved her. *Her*—as imperfect as she was.

Would they have no future trials? Leonie only had to look at Catherine and David to know that they could. Trials came in many forms. She also knew that with Roman by her side, they would weather them.

It was dark by the time they reached Bonhomie. Whiby sent a

stable lad with a lantern to take care of the wagon. There were many servants around the estate now. She took pride on how well it was run.

Yarrow opened the front door in welcome.

"Hold it there," Roman said. Before Leonie knew what he was about, he swung her up in his arms, her skirts sweeping around her with the movement, and carried her over the threshold. She laughingly grabbed hold of him for safety and then held him because she liked the strength in his arms and being this close to him.

"I take it the squire's party was enjoyable, my lord?" Yarrow observed, a hint of a smile on his face.

"Better than enjoyable," Roman informed him. "We are to bed for the evening, Yarrow. No need to wait on us," he said as he carried Leonie up the stairs. "You may do as you wish."

"Yes, my lord," Yarrow answered, the hint of a smile turning into a wide grin. He knew where Roman was taking her. He knew what they were going to be doing.

As Roman reached the stairs' landing and started up the second set, Leonie looked down at this man who had been more than a servant, and he winked at her.

She blushed but it was not with embarrassment. No, she was happy. All was very, very good.

Roman kicked open the door of their room. He still had not replaced Duncan Barr and she had yet to hire a suitable lady's maid, so they were alone.

He carried her to the huge four-poster and sat her down upon the mattress. "Now, I'm going to celebrate the wedding night I should have had in London."

"*We* should have had," she corrected, and he laughed, his gladness matching her own.

And celebrate they did. They made quick business of shedding clothing. They were comfortable with each other now so there was no hesitancy.

Better, she knew what he liked and he had always known what she wanted.

Their "play" over the past weeks had been agreeable, but nothing made Leonie happier than once again accepting her husband into her body.

He held her as if he, too, relished the moment.

His gray eyes sought hers. "I love you, wife," he whispered.

She reached up to brush the hair from his brow. "Not as much as I love you, husband."

Roman laughed as if nothing could please him more. He began moving in her. Leonie wrapped her body around his, whispering his name and her love for him. His pace quickened. She found herself losing control. Her words were no longer intelligible. Only Roman could give her such pleasure. He had taught her the meaning of giving freely and freely receiving in return.

Nor was this just any act of coupling. Their union was the fulfillment of their vows. What God had joined could never be "put asunder."

She was his—heart, body, and soul.

Roman found his release first. He was buried deep within and she suddenly understood what it meant for two to become one.

Leonie met him in his satisfaction, losing herself in the rippling waves of gratification.

When they were done, neither of them could move.

"So precious," he murmured, brushing his lips against her temple.

She caressed his back, his buttock, his hip. He was hers. This was everything their wedding night should be.

Later, curled up under the covers, his arms around her, they talked about their plans for Bonhomie, for themselves, for her roses.

Oh, yes, they had big dreams.

And now, together, they would live them to the fullest.

Dear Readers,

I am not a fan of perfect characters. In Romance, the heroine is often the voice of reason. We can have tortured heroes and villains but the heroine is usually level-headed. Frankly, I believe we are each the heroine of our life and I know I'm not perfect. I suspect you aren't either.

Leonie is definitely flawed. In the craft of writing, one of the many canons is character determines action. I confess that for a long period of my writing this book, Leonie was a flat character. I worried. I understood what had happened to her, I saw her resilience, and yet something was missing. Then she took a nip.

Whoa.

I know it sounds strange to claim I didn't know that was going to happen, but occasionally characters form themselves as an outgrowth of the story.

After a bit of research, I learned that victims who have experienced traumatic incidents often self-medicate with whatever is at hand. It is a survival mechanism when there are experiences too difficult to confront and it is completely in keeping with Leonie. Yes, she is resilient, she is a survivor, and she is filled with conflicting emotions she doesn't understand. Stealing a nip was a reasonable response.

But how does that fit in with Regency England?

Very well.

Drunkenness was a problem on all levels of society. It was also a problem *before* the Regency and the eras *after*. The truth was, ale and wine were probably safer to drink than the water in the cities and many parts of the country—and this wasn't just for England but also for the rest of the world.

The idea of temperance was starting to take hold. For a good seventy years prior and maybe longer, temperance was being batted around in religious institutions, in the government, and with those worried about the country's overconsumption of spirits. Temperance societies didn't fully organize until the 1820s, although during the American Revolution, Connecticut, New York, and a few other states advocated temperance with the banning of whiskey (the American spelling!) distilling.

In my research, I came upon an essay about the famous Georgian writer Dr. Samuel Johnson titled "Samuel Johnson's Alcohol Problem,"[*] by Dr. J. S. Madden, a British expert in alcoholism. Now, over the years, medical researchers have been having a field day with Samuel Johnson. He was a larger than life person during his time and there is a suspicion that he suffered from Tourette syndrome. Dr. Madden offers many quotes of Johnson confessing his troubles with alcohol such as, when offered wine, he replied, "I can't drink a little, child, therefore I

---

[*] Madden, J. S., "Samuel Johnson's Alcohol Problem," *Medical History* 1967 Apr; 11(2): 141–149.

never touch it. Abstinence is as easy to me as temperance would be difficult."

However, what caught my attention in Madden's essay was a reference to Johnson's wife, Elizabeth. She had been a merchant's widow with three almost grown children and was forty-six to Johnson's tender twenty-five when they married. (Yes, fact is always wilder than fiction.)

Of course she died before her husband. From Madden came this description of Elizabeth as documented by one of Samuel Johnson's companions and biographers, Mrs. Thrale: "Mrs. Thrale on this point quoted Levett (a companion of Johnson who practised medicine unofficially but conscientiously) as saying: 'She was always drunk and reading Romances in her Bed, where She killed herself by taking Opium.' "

There it was. Human behavior has not changed that much over the ages. If men are drinking, women are drinking. And, for the record, I, too, like reading romances in bed, though I don't know how good my vision would be on opium.

So, what did a person who suffered from the disease of alcoholism do in those days? Of course, it was considered a character failing and usually they white knuckled it. They abstained, if they could. Samuel Johnson went back and forth over the years. He'd drink wine, switch to port only, then stop altogether for a period of time before wondering if he could enjoy a taste of wine. His wife was not able to control her vices.

Fortunately, Leonie wins over her tendency to drink. Yes, like so many of us, she will carry scars. However, one of the miracles of love is meeting someone who sees beyond our imperfections, who accepts that we have a past, and who is willing to build a future. Love has never required flawlessness.

I pray you have enjoyed Leonie and Roman's story, I hope you are looking forward to Willa and Cassandra finding love, and I wish you many happy hours of reading.

All my best,
Cathy Maxwell
March 17, 2017

Don't miss the next Spinster Heiresses novel

A Match Made in Bed

COMING MAY 2018!